FANTASMAGORIANA DELUXE:

A COMBINED EDITION OF
FANTASMAGORIANA
AND
TALES OF THE DEAD

"The Noblewoman" (from *The Dance of Death*) by Hans Holbein der Jüngere, designed ca. 1526. (Woodblock printing by Hans Lützelburger, 1538.)

FANTASMAGORIANA DELUXE:

A COMBINED EDITION OF
FANTASMAGORIANA
AND
TALES OF THE DEAD

EDITED BY
ERIC J. GUIGNARD AND LESLIE S. KLINGER

DARK MOON BOOKS
Los Angeles, California

FANTASMAGORIANA DELUXE: A COMBINED EDITION OF
FANTASMAGORIANA AND TALES OF THE DEAD

Edited by Eric J. Guignard and Leslie S. Klinger
Copyright © 2023 Eric J. Guignard

Text from *Fantasmagoriana* is that of the 1813 edition, first published in English translation under the title *Tales of the Dead*, by White, Cochrane, and Co. (London, UK)

Text from "The Grey Chamber, a True Story" is by Marjorie Bowen, first published in 1933 in *Great Tales of Horror*, by The Bodley Head (London, UK)

English Translations "The Revenant" and "The Black Chamber" (including second half of "The Grey Chamber") © 2023 by Anna Ziegelhof
www.annaziegelhof.com

Introduction © 2023 by Lisa Morton
www.lisamorton.com/zine

Additional supplemental material © 2023 by Eric J. Guignard and Leslie S. Klinger

Interior layout by Eric J. Guignard
Cover design by Eric J. Guignard
www.ericjguignard.com

Cover art by Hellduriel: *Night of The Cruelty* (2018)
www.deviantart.com/hellduriel

First edition published in November, 2023

Library of Congress Cataloging-in-Publication Data
Fantasmagoriana deluxe: a combined edition of fantasmagoriana and tales of the dead / edited by Eric J. Guignard and Leslie S. Klinger.

Library of Congress Control Number: 2023937421

ISBN-13: 978-1-949491-55-5 (hardback)
ISBN-13: 978-1-949491-53-1 (paperback)
ISBN-13: 978-1-949491-54-8 (e-book)

DARK MOON BOOKS
Los Angeles, California
www.DarkMoonBooks.com

Made in the United States of America
DMB 10 9 8 7 6 5 4 3 2 1

(V081923)

Dedicated to the ghosts
and ghost makers
around the world.

"Necromancy": uncredited interior illustration on the subject of ghosts from *The Astrologer of the Nineteenth Century* by Raphael, pseud. (members of the Mercurii), 1825.

CONTENTS

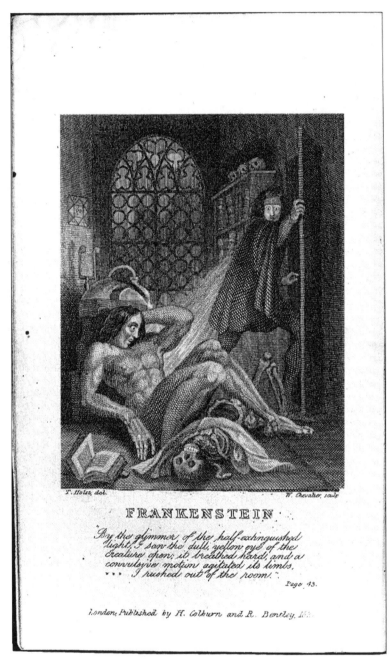

FRANKENSTEIN

"By the glimmer of the half-extinguished
light, I saw the dull, yellow eye of the
creature open; it breathed hard, and a
convulsive motion agitated its limbs.
... I rushed out of the room."
Page 43.

London, Published by H. Colburn and R. Bentley, 1831.

Frontispiece by Theodore Von Holst for the 1831 edition of
Frankenstein; or, The Modern Prometheus.

INTRODUCTION

BY LISA MORTON

"Some volumes of ghost stories, translated from the German into French, fell into our hands. There was the History of the Inconstant Lover, who, when he thought to clasp the bride to whom he had pledged his vows, found himself in the arms of the pale ghost of her whom he had deserted. There was the tale of the sinful founder of his race, whose miserable doom it was to bestow the kiss of death on all the younger sons of his fated house, just when they reached the age of promise. His gigantic, shadowy form, clothed like the ghost in Hamlet, in complete armour, but with the beaver up, was seen at midnight, by the moon's fitful beams, to advance slowly along the gloomy avenue. The shape was lost beneath the shadow of the castle walls; but soon a gate swung back, a step was heard, the door of the chamber opened, and he advanced to the couch of the blooming youths, cradled in healthy sleep. Eternal sorrow sat upon his face as he bent down and kissed the forehead of the boys, who from that hour withered like flowers snapt upon the stalk. I have not seen these stories since then; but their incidents are as fresh in my mind as if I had read them yesterday."

—Mary Shelley, from her 1833 introduction to
FRANKENSTEIN; OR, THE MODERN PROMETHEUS

HOW is it possible that one of the most influential books in the history of horror is known by so few readers?

I've written before[*] about how a French ghost story anthology called *Fantasmagoriana* galvanized eighteen-year-old Mary Godwin (later Shelley) to craft the greatest horror story of all time, but I agreed to write this new foreword not just because this is a subject worth returning to, but primarily because of the extraordinary—dare I say necessary?—literary resurrection Eric J. Guignard and Leslie S. Klinger have performed here.

---

[*] For Firbolg Publishing's 2018 anthology *Birthing Monsters: Frankenstein's Cabinet of Curiosities and Cruelties.*

I don't recall exactly when I first heard about *Fantasmagoriana*, but I remember being astonished that a) I had never heard of it before, and that b) it was impossible to find (at least in English). This was probably back before the days of the internet, because some years later I found Sarah Elizabeth Utterson's (partial) English-language translation, re-titled *Tales of the Dead*, online. I was so taken with the stories that when Leslie S. Klinger and I put together our 2019 anthology *Ghost Stories: Classic Tales of Horror and Suspense*, Utterson's translation of Johann August Apel's "The Family Portraits" was one of the first stories we both wanted to include.

The biggest mystery surrounding *Fantasmagoriana* is why it has remained so obscure for two centuries, a book often referred to but rarely read. More horror fans are familiar with how the Stanley Hotel in Colorado inspired Stephen King to write *The Shining* than know anything whatsoever about *Fantasmagoriana*. Of course age has something to do with it, and even Mary Shelley didn't name the volume when she described it in her introduction to the 1833 edition of *Frankenstein*... but she remembered two of the book's short stories ("The Family Portraits" and "The Death-Bride") so clearly that it wasn't hard for knowledgeable scholars to identify the book in question as Jean-Baptiste Benoît Eyriès' *Fantasmagoriana*.

Fantasmagoriana occupies a curious position in literary history for another reason: although *Frankenstein* (and John Polidori's "The Vampyre," which also resulted from those evenings of reading ghost stories within Lord Byron's rented Villa Diodati beside Lake Geneva) plays with the classic motifs of the Gothic tale, *Fantasmagoriana* is often classified as belonging to the *schauerroman*, a German movement that produced works of horror similar to the Gothic classics but with less romance and more overt horror. While the queen of Gothic literature, Ann Radcliffe, typified that genre's works by producing stories that generate chills but then explain away the ghosts, the *schauerroman* (translating literally to "shudder-novel") remains supernatural throughout, occasionally even becoming occult in nature (Karl Friedrich Kahlert's 1794 *The Necromancer; or, The Tale of the Black Forest*, considered a seminal *schauerroman*, puts its occult creds right in the title). Certainly elements of the *schauerroman* appear in *Frankenstein*; it never shies away from terror or the gruesome.

Then there's *Fantasmagoriana*'s labyrinthine publishing history. Editor Eyriès culled the stories mainly from a German work called *Gespensterbuch* (literally, "Ghost-Book"), but also took one ("Die Graue Stube" or "The Grey Chamber") from a newspaper. When Sarah Utterson translated the book into English, she omitted three of the original stories, slightly added to or changed the remaining five, and included a sixth story ("The Storm") of her own creation (or, as she claims in her preface, a piece based on an incident that had "actually occurred in this country")'. The book appeared in two subsequent English editions (1992 and 2005), but this present volume represents the first attempt to provide a comprehensive English-language edition incorporating both *Fantasmagoriana* and *Tales of the Dead*.

Just how influential was *Fantasmagoriana* on the creation of *Frankenstein*? Although Mary mentioned "The Family Portraits" and "The Death-Bride," one of the stories that may have led most directly to *Frankenstein* is actually "The Grey Chamber," which Utterson chose not to translate for *Tales of the Dead* ... and which is, ironically, easily the most interesting story in *Fantasmagoriana*. Utterson's taste obviously leaned toward the deliberately-paced stories in which fate took a central position; note her own contribution, "The Storm," which spends most of its length describing an isolated chateau and its guests (Utterson herself was critical of the abrupt ending, which provides no satisfactory resolution whatsoever), and hints at a dreadful yearly meeting that is supernatural in some way. Even "The Revenant," the only story in *Tales of the Dead* which is revealed to be non-supernatural, suggests the inevitability of fate.

Heinrich Clauren's "The Grey Chamber," by comparison, is told in the more concise fashion of a newspaper (which it first appeared in), and provides no romantic element or denouement focusing on fate fulfilled. Compare, though, the description of the horrific specter advancing on the paralyzed protagonist in "The Grey Chamber" to *Frankenstein*'s scene of the monster entering its creator's bedroom: "I started from my sleep with horror; a cold dew covered my forehead, my teeth chattered, and every limb became convulsed; when, by the dim and yellow light of the moon, as it forced its way through the window-shutters, I beheld the wretch—the

---

˙ *Tales of the Dead* was the only book produced by Sarah Elizabeth Utterson (1781–1851). She seems to have treasured it, though: the Uttersons' library is now held by the Huntington Library and includes a copy of the book custom-bound in blue leather and with six original watercolor paintings inserted, which are reproduced in this book.

miserable monster whom I had created. He held up the curtain of the bed; and his eyes, if eyes they may be called, were fixed on me."

It's possible, by the way, that "The Grey Chamber" cast an even more entrancing spell on another author, a few years later: Sir Walter Scott's 1828 short story "The Tapestried Chamber" bears an uncanny resemblance to Heinrich Clauren's tale, which was first published in a German newspaper in 1810. Certainly the story of the traveler who spends a terrifying night in a haunted room is one of the oldest in literature; look at the story by Pliny the Younger (dating back to about the first century after Christ) of the philosopher Athenodorus, who rented a house in Athens but found his work interrupted at night by a ghost who showed up rattling chains. Around 1730, the English poet John Gay wrote "The True Story of an Apparition," which tells of a traveler lost on his horse who finds an isolated inn where all the rooms are already taken except "our haunted room"; the weary traveler agrees, but soon finds himself quaking in his bed as he faces "the ghastful Phantom." Clauren's story, though, adds elements of friendship (the traveler is seeking to spend time with an old acquaintance), changes the gender of the ghost to female, and adds a frightful backstory for the apparition . . . as does Scott's story. Although Scott claimed he heard the story from the poet Anna Seward*, who died in 1809—a year before Clauren's "Die Graue Stube" was published—Scott was also a serious student of German literature, so it's certainly possible that he'd read Clauren's tale and incorporated elements of it in setting down Seward's story.† "The Tapestried Chamber" is a seminal ghost story, often considered the progenitor of the nineteenth century short ghost story, so "The Grey Chamber" may genuinely be one of the most important short pieces ever published.

While the stories in *Fantasmagoriana* may have inspired two of the great early works of horror, modern readers may be wondering if these tales can still thrill and delight two centuries later. Certainly the leisurely style of

---

* Scott said of Seward's story, "Miss Seward always affirmed that she had derived her information from an authentic source, although she suppressed the names of the two persons chiefly concerned."

† Marjorie Bowen's 1933 translation of "The Grey Chamber" further complicates the story's history, because Bowen claimed in a letter to a correspondent that she actually wrote the story herself; however, Bowen's version of "The Grey Chamber" is absolutely a translation of Clauren's and closely resembles a translation of the story that appeared in Leonard Wolf's 1993 *The Essential Frankenstein*.

these works was more suitable to a time without television or the internet, when a long evening could happily be given over to a single story. But I challenge any twenty-first-century horror fan not to experience that ancient frisson of fear at scenes of a magician overcome by a talking skull, a traveler forced to endure the services of a ghost barber, a silent masked spirit at a wedding party, a portrait that changes into something far worse, or an unlucky traveler caught in the chilling embrace of an ancient specter. Belief in ghosts is as old and universal as the hope for an afterlife, and ghost stories will doubtless continue to entertain as long as we experience dread at the unknown.

I hope you will enjoy—and possibly be inspired by—*Fantasmagoriana* as much as centuries of readers and writers have before you. Perhaps you'll even feel the need to leave a light on after reading these tales.

Lisa Morton
July 23, 2023
Los Angeles, California

LISA MORTON is a screenwriter, author of non-fiction books, and prose writer whose work was described by the American Library Association's *Readers' Advisory Guide to Horror* as "consistently dark, unsettling, and frightening." She is a six-time winner of the Bram Stoker Award®, the author of four novels and over 150 short stories, and a world-class Halloween and paranormal expert. Her recent releases include the *Calling the Spirits: A History of Seances*; forthcoming in October 2023 from Applause Books is *The Art of the Zombie Movie*. Lisa lives in Los Angeles and online at www.lisamorton.com.
Facebook: www.facebook.com/lisa.morton.165
Instagram: www.instagram.com/lisamortoninla

Memento mori: Der Triumphbogen des Todes,
by Johann Elias Ridinger (ca. 1760).

EDITOR'S NOTE

FANTASMAGORIANA has become one of the most seminal ghost-story anthologies of all time primarily by a singular event of literary history: In June, 1816, five friends rented a mansion in Villa Diodati, Switzerland. Included in this Romantic-era party were: Lord Byron, Mary Shelley, Percy Bysshe Shelley, John William Polidori, and Claire Clairmont. Poor weather ("The Year Without a Summer") kept them indoors, and to entertain themselves at night they read out loud the ghost stories of *Fantasmagoriana*. Afterward, Lord Byron suggested each of them should try their own hand at writing a ghost story.

From Byron's proposition evolved: *Frankenstein; or, The Modern Prometheus*, by Mary Shelley, one of the first and most recognized novels of the horror and science fiction genres; "The Vampyre," by John William Polidori, a short story that became a progenitor to the fantasy vampire genre; "Ernestus Berchtold; or, The Modern Oedipus," a novella also by John William Polidori, inciting scandals based on the rumors of what occurred at the Villa Diodati; "Manfred," a supernatural poem by Lord Byron, later turned into a musical; and more.

The stories in *Fantasmagoriana* were French translations of works originally published in German. *Tales of the Dead* was the (partial) English translation of *Fantasmagoriana*, although each anthology published its stories in a different order.

Therefore some liberty has been taken to arrange this subject book, *Fantasmagoriana Deluxe*, as a sensible combination of both language-versions. As it is the French edition that is most famously recognized for inspiring the minds of those now-famous authors in 1816, we have chosen to follow the order of stories as presented there—with the additional English translator (Sarah Elizabeth Utterson)'s preface "Advertisement" and original-work story "The Storm" added at book's end—in order for this to be an English-reading experience that is as close as possible to the original 1816 occurrence.

An exception is that the literary epigraphs preceding each story have been retained for this work, which are additions by Utterson and were not part of the original French nor German publications.

The artwork, as well, is original to this book and meant merely to enhance the literary and imaginative notion of "phantasmic." In keeping with Utterson's sentiment from her "Advertisement," I employ my own:

The art* was the amusement of an idle hour; and if it afford an equal portion of gratification to the reader, the time has not been altogether misemployed.

---

* Orig. "The translation was the amusement . . ." (—Utterson, 1813)

Available at the same bookstore.

The Caravanserai, or Collection of Oriental Tales, Translated From a Persian Manuscript*, by Adrien de Sarrazin. Paris 1811. 3 vol. in-18[†], 6 fr.[‡], or 7 fr. with shipping.

Alphonse de Lodève, by Madame Countess de Goloffkin. Paris 1809. 2 vol. in-12, 4 fr. 50 c., or 6. fr. 70 c. with shipping. Vellum paper, 8 fr., or 9 fr. 20 c. with shipping.

Eugénie and Mathilde, or Memoirs of the Count de Revel's Family, by the author of *Adèle de Senange*.[§] Paris 1811, 3 vol. in-12, 7 fr. 50 c., or 9 fr. 20 c. with shipping. Vellum paper, 10 fr., or 11 fr. 80 c. with shipping.

Ladislas, or Memoirs of the Count de Revel's Family, by Madame de B... Paris 1811. in-12, 2 fr. 50 c., or 3 fr. with shipping.

Mehaled and Sedli, or History of a Druse Family, by (Monsieur) Baron de Dalberg, brother of S. A. R., the Grand-Duke of Frankfurt. Paris 1812. 2 vol. in-12, 4 fr. 50 c., or 5 fr. 75 c. with shipping. Vellum paper 7 fr. or 8 fr. 25 c. with shipping.

Valérie, or the Letters of Gustave de Linnar to Ernest de G, by Madame Baroness de Krudener. Third edition. Paris 1804. 2 vol. in-12, 3 fr. 75 c., or 5 fr. with shipping. Vellum paper, 7 fr. 50c., or 8 fr. 75 c. with shipping.

Fairy Tales, by Charles Perrault, decorated with illustrations. Paris 1807. 2 vol. in-18, 2 fr. 80 c., or 2 fr. 50 c. with shipping.

---

[*] A roadside inn with a courtyard, where travelers (caravaners) could rest and recover from the day's journey, most common along the historic Silk Road.

[†] A European book-binding measurement indicating how many folds to a full sheet of paper (which will then be cut and bound); i.e. an in-12 would be 1/12th the size of the original sheet of paper (thus larger than an in-18) creating 12 page-fronts and, by also printing on the opposite side, 12 page-backs.

[‡] fr.: Francs; c.: Centimes (French monetary units).

[§] Adélaïde-Emilie Filleul, Marquise de Souza-Botelho.

"Falsis terroribus implet."

—HORAT.[*]

FANTASMAGORIANA,

OU

RECUEIL

D'HISTOIRES D'APPARITIONS DE SPECTRES,

REVENANS, FANTÔMES, etc.;

Traduit de l'allemand, par un Amateur.

Falsis terroribus implet.
HORAT.

TOME SECOND.

PARIS,

Chez F. SCHOELL, rue des Fossés-Montmartre, n°. 14.

1812.

Original title page of *Fantasmagoriana* (second of two volumes), 1812.

PREFACE OF THE
FRENCH TRANSLATOR

IT is generally believed that at this time of day no one puts any faith in ghosts and apparitions. Yet, on reflection, this opinion does not appear to me quite correct: for, without alluding to workmen in mines, and the inhabitants of mountainous countries,—the former of whom believe in spectres and hobgoblins presiding over concealed treasures, and the latter in apparitions and phantoms announcing either agreeable or unfortunate tidings,—may we not ask why amongst ourselves there are certain individuals who have a dread of passing through a church-yard after night-fall? Why others experience an involuntary shuddering at entering a church, or any other large uninhabited edifice, in the dark? And, in fine, why persons who are deservedly considered as possessing courage and good sense, dare not visit at night even places where they are certain of meeting with nothing they need dread from living beings? They are ever repeating, that the living are only to be dreaded; and yet fear night, because they believe, by tradition, that it is the time which phantoms choose for appearing to the inhabitants of the earth.

Admitting, therefore, as an undoubted fact, that, with few exceptions, ghosts are no longer believed in, and that the species of fear we have just mentioned arises from a natural horror of darkness incident to man,—a horror which he cannot account for rationally,—yet it is well known that he listens with much pleasure to stories of ghosts, spectres, and phantoms. The wonderful ever excites a degree of interest, and gains an attentive ear; consequently, all recitals relative to supernatural appearances please us. It was probably from this cause that the study of the sciences which was in former times intermixed with the marvellous, is now reduced to the simple observation of facts. This wise revolution will undoubtedly assist the progress of truth; but it has displeased many men of genius, who maintain that by so doing, the sciences are robbed of their greatest attractions, and that the new mode will tend to weary the mind and disenchant study; and they neglect no means in their power to give back to the supernatural, that empire of which it has been recently deprived: They loudly applaud their efforts, though they cannot pride themselves on their success: for in physic* and natural history prodigies are entirely exploded.

---

* In this context, medicine; the healing arts.

But if in these classes of writing, the marvellous and supernatural would be improper, at least they cannot be considered as misplaced in the work we are now about to publish: and they cannot have any dangerous tendency on the mind; for the title-page announces extraordinary relations, to which more or less faith may be attached, according to the credulity of the person who reads them. Besides which, it is proper that some repertory should exist, in which we may discover the traces of those superstitions to which mankind have so long been subject. We now laugh at, and turn them into ridicule: and yet it is not clear to me, that recitals respecting phantoms have ceased to amuse; or that, so long as human nature exists, there will be wanting those who will attach faith to histories of ghosts and spectres.

I might in this preface have entered into a learned and methodical disquisition respecting apparitions; but should only have repeated what Dom Calmet* and the Abbé Lenglet-Dufresnoy† have already said on the subject, and which they have so thoroughly exhausted, that it would be almost impossible to advance anything new. Persons curious to learn everything relative to apparitions, will be amply recompensed by consulting the two writers above mentioned. They give to the full as strange recitals as any which are to be found in this work. Although the Abbé Lenglet-Dufresnoy says there really are apparitions; yet he does not appear to believe in them himself: but Dom Calmet finishes (as Voltaire observes) as if he believed what he wrote, and especially with respect to the extraordinary histories of Vampires. And we may add, for the benefit of those anxious to make deeper search into the subject in question, that the Abbé Lenglet-Dufresnoy has given a list of the principal authors who have written on spirits, demons, apparitions, dreams, magic, and spectres.

---

* [Author's note:] *Dissertation sur les Apparitions*; par Dom Augustin Calmet: 3me édition. Paris, 1751, 2 tom. 12mo. [In full, *Dissertations sur les apparitions des anges, des démons et des esprits, et sur les revenants et vampires de Hongrie, de Bohême, de Moravie et de Silésie*, translated as *A Study of Angels, Demons, and Spirits, as well as Revenants and Vampires of Hungary, Bohemia, Moravia and Silesia*, regarded as the first serious study of vampires and other supernatural beings.]

† [Author's note:] *Traité Historique et Dogmatique sur les Apparitions, les Visions, et les Révélations particuliers; avec des Remarques sur la Dissertation du R. P. Dom Calmet*: par l'Abbé Lenglet-Dufresnoy. Avignon ou Paris, 1751. 2 tom. 12mo. *Recueil de Dissertations, Anciennes et Nouvelles, sur les Apparitions, les Visions, et les Songes; avec une Preface historique: par l'Abbé L. Dufresnoy.* Avignon ou Paris, 1751. 4 tom. 12mo.

Since this laborious writer has published this list, Swedenborg and St. Martin have rendered themselves notorious by their Works; and there have also appeared in Germany treatises on this question of the appearance of spirits. The two authors who have the most largely entered into the detail are Wagener and Jung. The first, whose book is entitled The Spectres*, endeavours to explain apparitions by attributing them to natural causes. But the second, on the contrary, firmly believes in spirits; and his Theory on Phantasmatology† furnishes us with an undoubted proof of this assertion. This work, the fruit of an ardent and exalted imagination, is in some degree a manual to the doctrines of the modern *Seers*, known in Germany under the denomination of *Stillingianer*. They take their name from *Stilling*, under which head Jung has written memoirs of his life, which forms a series of different works. This sect, which is actually in existence, is grafted on the Swedenborgians and Martinisme, and has a great number of adherents, especially in Switzerland. We also see in the number of the (*English*) Monthly Review for December 1811, that Mrs. Grant has given a pretty circumstantial detail of the apparitions and spirits to which the Scottish mountaineers attach implicit faith.

In making choice of the stories for my translations from the German, which I now offer to the public, I have neglected nothing to merit the approbation of those who take pleasure in this species of reading: and if this selection has the good fortune to meet with any success, it shall be followed by another; in which I shall equally endeavour to excite the curiosity of the lovers of romance; while to those who are difficult to please, and to whom it seems strange that anyone should attach the slightest degree of faith to such relations, I merely say,—Remember the words of Voltaire at the beginning of the article he wrote on "*Apparition*," in his Philosophical Dictionary: "*It is no uncommon thing for a person of lively feelings to fancy he sees what never really existed.*"

—JEAN-BAPTISTE BENOÎT EYRIÈS.
1812.

---

* [Author's note:] *Die Gespenster Kurze Erzæhlungen aus dem Reiche der Wahrheit.* Berlin, 1797, et suiv. in 8vo.
† [Author's note:] *Theorie der Geister-Kunde.* Nuremberg, 1808, in 8vo.—This work has been censured by several Protestant consistories.

"The Spectre-Barber": illustration by Paul Fischer and engraving by Allen Robert Branston, from the anthology *Popular Tales and Romances of the Northern Nations* (1823).

I.

THE SPECTRE-BARBER

(A TALE OF THE SIXTEENTH CENTURY)

BY JOHANN KARL AUGUST MUSÄUS[*]

(TRANSLATED INTO ENGLISH BY
SARAH ELIZABETH UTTERSON)

——"Sir Ryence of North-Gales
greeteth well thee,
And bids thee thy beard anon to him
send,
Or else from thy jaws he will it off
rend."——
—PERCY'S *RELIQUES OF ANC. ENG.
POETRY.*[†]

THERE formerly lived at Bremen a wealthy merchant named Melchior, who, it was remarked, invariably stroked his chin with complacency, whenever the subject of the sermon was the rich man in the Gospel; who, by the bye, in comparison with him, was only a petty retail dealer. This said Melchior possessed such great riches, that he had caused the floor of his dining-room to be paved with crown-pieces. This ridiculous luxury gave great offence to Melchior's fellow-citizens and relations. They attributed it

---

[*] A renowned German folklorist (1735–1787), best remembered for his anthology *Volksmärchen des Deutschen* (1782–1786), a collection of German fairy tales retold as satires.

[†] "King Ryence's Challenge," from the volume titled *Reliques of Ancient English Poetry* (edited by Bishop Thomas Percy and first published in 1765).

to vanity and ostentation, but did not guess its true motive: however, it perfectly answered the end Melchior designed by it; for, by their constantly expressing their disapprobation of this ostentatious species of vanity, they spread abroad the report of their neighbour's immense riches, and thereby augmented his credit in a most astonishing manner.

Melchior died suddenly while at a corporation* dinner, and consequently had not time to make a disposition of his property by will; so that his only son Francis, who was just of age, came into possession of the whole. This young man was particularly favoured by fortune, both with respect to his personal advantages and his goodness of heart; but this immense inheritance caused his ruin. He had no sooner got into the possession of so considerable a fortune, than he squandered it, as if it had been a burthen to him; ran into every possible extravagance, and neglected his concerns. Two or three years passed over without his perceiving, that, owing to his dissipations, his funds were considerably diminished; but at length his coffers were emptied: and one day when Francis had drawn a draft to a very considerable amount on his banker, who had no funds to meet it, it was returned to him protested.† This disappointment greatly vexed our prodigal, but only as it caused a temporary check to his wishes; for he did not even then give himself the trouble to inquire into the reason of it. After swearing and blustering for some time, he gave his steward a positive but laconic order to *get money*.

All the brokers, bankers, money-changers, and usurers, were put in requisition, and the empty coffers were soon filled; for the dining-room floor was in the eyes of the lenders a sufficient security.

This palliative had its effect for a time: but all at once a report was spread abroad in the city that the celebrated silver floor had been taken up; the consequence of which was, that the lenders insisted on examining into and proving the fact, and then became urgent for payment: but as Francis had not the means to meet their demands, they seized on all his goods and chattels; everything was sold by auction, and he had nothing left excepting a few jewels which had formed part of his heritage, and which might for a short time keep him from starving.

He now took up his abode in a small street in one of the most remote quarters of the city, where he lived on his straitened means. He, however,

---

* A company of merchants.

† That is to say, the check was "NSF," in modern bank parlance—non-sufficient funds.

accommodated himself to his situation: but the only resource he found against the *ennui* which overpowered him, was to play on the lute; and when fatigued by this exercise, he used to stand at his window and make observations on the weather; and his intelligent mind was not long in discovering an object which soon entirely engrossed his thoughts.

Opposite his window there lived a respectable woman, who was at her spinning-wheel from morning till night, and by her industry earned a subsistence for herself and her daughter. Meta was a young girl of great beauty and attraction: she had known happier times; for her father had been the proprietor of a vessel freighted by himself, in which he annually made trading voyages to Antwerp: but he, as well as his ship and all its cargo, was lost in a violent storm. His widow supported this double loss with resignation and firmness, and resolved to support herself and her daughter by her own industry. She made over her house and furniture to the creditors of her husband, and took up her abode in the little bye street in which Francis lodged, where by her assiduity she acquired a subsistence without laying herself under an obligation to anyone. She brought up her daughter to spinning and other work, and lived with so much economy, that by her savings she was enabled to set up a little trade in linen.

Mother Bridget, (which was the appellation given to our widow,) did not, however, calculate on terminating her existence in this penurious situation; and the hope of better prospects sustained her courage. The beauty and excellent qualities of her daughter, whom she brought up with every possible care and attention, led her to think that some advantageous offer would one day present itself. Meta lived tranquilly and lonely with her mother, was never seen in any of the public walks, and indeed never went out but to mass once a day.

One day while Francis was making his meteorological observations at the window, he saw the beautiful Meta, who, under her mother's watchful eye, was returning from church. The heart of Francis was as yet quite free; for the boisterous pleasures of his past life did not leave him leisure for a true affection; but at this time, when all his senses were calm, the appearance of one of the most enchanting female forms he had ever seen, ravished him, and he henceforth thought solely of the adorable object which his eyes had thus discovered. He questioned his landlord respecting the two females who lived in the opposite house, and from him learned the particulars we have just related.

He now regretted his want of economy, since his present miserable state prevented him from making an offer to the charming Meta. He was, however, constantly at the window, in hopes of seeing her, and in that consisted his greatest delight. The mother very soon discovered the frequent appearance of her new neighbour at his window, and attributed it to its right cause. In consequence, she rigorously enjoined her daughter not to shew herself at the windows, which were now kept constantly shut.

Francis was not much versed in the arts of finesse, but love awakened all the energies of his soul. He soon discovered that if he appeared much at the window, his views would be suspected, and he resolved therefore studiously to refrain from coming near it. He determined, however, to continue his observation of what occurred in the opposite dwelling without being perceived. He accordingly purchased a large mirror, and fixed it in his chamber in such a position that it distinctly presented to his view what passed in the abode of his opposite neighbour. Francis not being seen at the window, the old lady relaxed in her rigour, and Meta's windows were once more opened. Love more than ever reigned triumphant in the bosom of Francis: but how was he to make known his attachment to its object? he could neither speak nor write to her. Love, however, soon suggested a mode of communication which succeeded. Our prodigal took his lute, and drew from it tones the best adapted to express the subject of his passion; and by perseverance, in less than a month he made a wonderful progress. He soon had the gratification of seeing the fair hand of Meta open the little casement, when he began to tune the instrument. When she made her appearance, he testified his joy by an air lively and gay; but if she did not shew herself, the melancholy softness of his tones discovered the disappointment he experienced.

In the course of a short time he created a great interest in the bosom of his fair neighbour; and various modes which love suggested shortly convinced our prodigal that Meta shared a mutual attachment. She now endeavoured to justify him, when her mother with acrimony spoke of his prodigality and past misconduct, by attributing his ruin to the effect of bad example. But in so doing, she cautiously avoided exciting the suspicions of the old lady; and seemed less anxious to excuse him, than to take a part in the conversation which was going on.

Circumstances which our limits will not allow us to narrate rendered the situation of Francis more and more difficult to be supported: his funds had now nearly failed him; and an offer of marriage from a wealthy brewer, who was called in the neighbourhood the "King of Hops," and which Meta, much to her mother's disappointment, refused, excited still more the apprehensions of poor Francis, lest some more fortunate suitor might yet be received, and blast his hopes forever.

When he received the information that this opulent lover had been rejected for his sake, with what bitterness did he lament his past follies!

"Generous girl!" said he, "you sacrifice yourself for a miserable creature, who has nothing but a heart fondly attached to you, and which is riven with despair that its possessor cannot offer you the happiness you so truly merit."

The King of Hops soon found another female, who listened more kindly to his vows, and whom he wedded with great splendour.

Love, however, did not leave his work incomplete; for its influence created in the mind of Francis a desire of exerting his faculties and actively employing himself, in order, if possible, to emerge from the state of nothingness into which he was at present plunged: and it inspired him also with courage to prosecute his good intentions. Among various projects which he formed, the most rational appeared that of overlooking his father's books, taking an account of the claimable debts, and from that source to get all he possibly could. The produce of this procedure would, he thought, furnish him with the means of beginning in some small way of business; and his imagination led him to extend this to the most remote corners of the earth. In order to equip himself for the prosecution of his plans, he sold all the remainder of his father's effects, and with the money purchased a horse to commence his travels.

The idea of a separation from Meta was almost more than he could endure. "What will she think," said he, "of this sudden disappearance, when she no longer meets me in her way to church? Will she not think me perfidious, and banish me from her heart?" Such ideas as these caused him infinite pain: and for a long while he could not devise any means of acquainting Meta with his plans; but at length the fertile genius of love furnished him with the following idea:—Francis went to the curate of the church which his mistress daily frequented, and requested him before the sermon and during mass to put up prayers for *a happy issue to the affairs of a young traveller;* and these prayers were to be continued till the moment of his return, when they were to be changed into those of thanks.

Everything being arranged for his departure, he mounted his steed, and passed close under Meta's window. He saluted her with a very significant air, and with much less caution than heretofore. The young girl blushed deeply; and mother Bridget took this opportunity of loudly expressing her dislike to this bold adventurer, whose impertinence and foppery induced him to form designs on her daughter.

From this period the eyes of Meta in vain searched for Francis. She constantly heard the prayer which was put up for him; but was so entirely absorbed by grief at no longer perceiving the object of her affection, that she paid no attention to the words of the priest. In no way could she account for his disappearing. Some months afterwards, her grief being somewhat ameliorated, and her mind more tranquillized, when she was one day thinking of the last time she had seen Francis, the prayer arrested her attention; she reflected for an instant, and quickly divined for whom it was said; she naturally joined in it with great fervour, and strongly recommended the young traveller to the protection of her guardian angel.

Meanwhile Francis continued his journey, and had travelled the whole of a very sultry day over one of the desert cantons of Westphalia without meeting with a single house. As night approached, a violent storm came on: the rain fell in torrents; and poor Francis was soaked to the very skin. In this miserable situation he anxiously looked around, and fortunately discovered in the distance a light, towards which he directed his horse's steps; but as he drew near, he beheld a miserable cottage, which did not promise him much succour, for it more resembled a stable than the habitation of a human being. The unfeeling wretch who inhabited it refused him fire or water as if he had been a banished man—he was just about to extend himself on the straw in the midst of the cattle, and his indolence prevented his lighting a fire for the stranger. Francis vainly endeavoured to move the peasant to pity: the latter was inexorable, and blew out his candle with the greatest *nonchalance* possible, without bestowing a thought on Francis. However, as the traveller hindered him from sleeping, by his incessant lamentations and prayers, he was anxious to get rid of him.

"Friend," said he to him, "if you wish to be accommodated, I promise you it will not be here; but ride through the little wood to your left-hand, and you will find the castle belonging to the chevalier Eberhard Bronkhorst, who is very hospitable to travellers; but he has a singular mania, which is, to flagellate all whom he entertains: therefore decide accordingly."

Francis, after considering for some minutes what he had best do, resolved on hazarding the adventure. "In good faith," said he, "there is no great difference between having one's back broken by the miserable accommodation of a peasant, or by the chevalier Bronkhorst: friction disperses fever; possibly its effects may prove beneficial to me, if I am compelled to keep on my wet garments."

Accordingly he put spurs to his horse, and very shortly found himself before a Gothic castle, at the iron gate of which he loudly knocked: and was answered from within by "*Who's there?*" But ere he was allowed time to reply, the gate was opened. However, in the first court he was compelled to wait with patience, till they could learn whether it was the lord of the castle's pleasure to flagellate a traveller, or send him out to pass the night under the canopy of heaven.

This lord of the castle had from his earliest infancy served in the Imperial army, under command of George of Frunsberg,* and had himself led a company of infantry against the Venetians. At length, however, fatigued with warfare, he had retired to his own territory, where, in order to expiate the crimes he had committed during the several campaigns he had been in, he did all the good and charitable acts in his power. But his manner still preserved all the roughness of his former profession. The newly arrived guest, although disposed to submit to the usages of the house for the sake of the good fare, could not help feeling a certain trembling of fear as he heard the bolts grating, ere the doors were opened to him; and the very doors by their groaning noise seemed to presage the catastrophe which awaited him. A cold perspiration came over him as he passed the last door; but finding that he received the utmost attention, his fears a little abated. The servants assisted him in getting off his horse, and unfastened his cloak-bag; some of them led his horse to the stable, while others preceding him with flambeaux conducted Francis to their master, who awaited his arrival in a room magnificently lighted up.

Poor Francis was seized with an universal tremour when he beheld the martial air and athletic form of the lord of the castle, who came up to him and shook him by the hand with so much force that he could scarcely refrain from crying out, and in a thundering voice enough to stun him, told him "he was welcome." Francis shook like an aspen-leaf in every part of his body.

"What ails you, my young comrade?" cried the chevalier Bronkhorst, in his voice of thunder: "What makes you thus tremble, and renders you as pale as if death had actually seized you by the throat?"

Francis recovered himself; and knowing that his shoulders would pay the reckoning, his fears gave place to a species of audacity.

"My lord," answered he with confidence, "you see that I am so soaked with rain that one might suppose I had swam through the Wezer;† order me therefore some dry clothes instead of those I have on, and let us then drink a cup of hot wine, that I may, if possible, prevent the fever which otherwise may probably seize me. It will comfort my heart."

---

* Georg von Frundsberg (1473–1528) was a German military and political leader who served the Holy Roman Empire and the Hapsburgs.
† The Weser is a river in northwest Germany.

"Admirable!" replied the chevalier; "ask for whatever you want, and consider yourself here as at home."

Accordingly Francis gave his orders like a baron of high degree: he sent away the wet clothes, made choice of others, and, in fine, made himself quite at his ease. The chevalier, so far from expressing any dissatisfaction at his free and easy manners, commanded his people to execute whatever he ordered with promptitude, and condemned some of them as blockheads who did not appear to know how to wait on a stranger. As soon as the table was spread, the chevalier seated himself at it with his guest: they drank a cup of hot wine together.

"Do you wish for anything to eat?" demanded the lord of Francis.

The latter desired he would order up what his house afforded, that he might see whether his kitchen was good.

No sooner had he said this, than the steward made his appearance, and soon furnished up a most delicious repast. Francis did not wait for his being requested to partake of it: but after having made a hearty meal, he said to the lord of the castle, "Your kitchen is by no means despicable; if your cellar is correspondent, I cannot but say you treat your guests nobly."

The chevalier made a sign to his butler, who brought up some inferior wine, and filled a large glass of it to his master, who drank to his guest. Francis instantly returned the compliment.

"Well, young man, what say you to my wine?" asked the chevalier.

"'Faith," replied Francis, "I say it is bad, if it is the best you have in your cellar; but if you have none worse, I do not condemn it."

"You are a connoisseur;" answered the chevalier. "Butler, bring us a flask of older wine."

His orders being instantly attended to, Francis tasted it. "This is indeed some good old wine, and we will stick to it if you please."

The servants brought in a great pitcher of it, and the chevalier, being in high good-humour, drank freely with his guest; and then launched out into a long history of his several feats of prowess in the war against the Venetians.* He became so overheated by the recital, that in his enthusiasm he overturned the bottles and glasses, and flourishing his knife as if it were a sword, passed it so near the nose and ears of Francis, that he dreaded he should lose them in the action.

Though the night wore away, the chevalier did not manifest any desire

---

* The Venetian Wars were between the Republic of Venice and the Ottoman Empire and lasted for more than 300 years, from 1396 to 1718.

to sleep; for he was quite in his element, whenever he got on the topic of the Venetian war. Each succeeding glass added to the heat of his imagination as he proceeded in his narration, till at length Francis began to apprehend that it was the prologue to the tragedy in which he was to play the principal part; and feeling anxious to learn whether he was to pass the night in the castle, or to be turned out, he asked for a last glass of wine to enable him to sleep well. He feared that they would commence by filling him with wine, and that if he did not consent to continue drinking, a pretext would be laid hold of for driving him out of the castle with the usual chastisement.

However, contrary to his expectation, the lord of the castle broke the thread of his narration, and said to him: "Good friend, everything in its place: to-morrow we will resume our discourse."

"Excuse me, sir knight," replied Francis; "to-morrow, before sun-rise, I shall be on my road. The distance from hence to Brabant is very considerable, and I cannot tarry here longer, therefore permit me to take leave of you now, that I may not disturb you in the morning."

"Just as you please about that: but you will not leave the castle before I am up; we will breakfast together, and I shall accompany you to the outer gate, and take leave of you according to my usual custom."

Francis needed no comment to render these words intelligible. Most willingly would he have dispensed with the chevalier's company to the gate; but the latter did not appear at all inclined to deviate from his usual custom. He ordered his servants to assist the stranger in undressing, and to take care of him till he was in bed.

Francis found his bed an excellent one; and ere he went to sleep, he owned that so handsome a reception was not dearly bought at the expense of a *trifling* beating. The most delightful dreams (in which Meta bore the sway) occupied him the whole night; and he would have gone on (thus dreaming) till mid-day, if the sonorous voice of the chevalier and the clanking of his spurs had not disturbed him.

It needed all Francis's efforts to quit this delightful bed, in which he was so comfortable, and where he knew himself to be in safety: he turned from side to side; but the chevalier's tremendous voice was like a death-stroke to him, and at length he resolved to get up. Several servants assisted him in dressing, and the chevalier waited for him at a small but well-served table; but Francis, knowing the moment of trial was at hand, had no great inclination to feast. The chevalier tried to persuade him to eat, telling him it was the best thing to keep out the fog and damp air of the morning.

"Sir knight," replied Francis, "my stomach is still loaded from your excellent supper of last evening; but my pockets are empty, and I should much like to fill them, in order to provide against future wants."

The chevalier evinced his pleasure at his frankness by filling his pockets with as much as they could contain. As soon as they brought him his horse, which he discovered had been well groomed and fed, he drank the last glass of wine to say Adieu, expecting that at that signal the chevalier would take him by the collar and make him pay his welcome. But, to his no small surprise, the chevalier contented himself with heartily shaking him by the hand as on his arrival: and as soon as the gate was opened, Francis rode off safe and sound.

In no way could our traveller account for his host permitting him thus to depart without paying the usual score. At length he began to imagine that the peasant had simply told him the story to frighten him; and feeling a curiosity to learn whether or not it had any foundation in fact, he rode back to the castle. The chevalier had not yet quitted the gate, and was conversing with his servants on the pace of Francis's horse, who appeared to trot very roughly: and seeing the traveller return, he supposed that he had forgotten something, and by his looks seemed to accuse his servants of negligence.

"What do you want, young man?" demanded he: "Why do you, who were so much pressed for time, return?"

"Allow me, most noble sir," replied Francis, "to ask you one question, for there are reports abroad which tend to vilify you: It is said, that, after having hospitably received and entertained strangers, you make them at their departure feel the weight of your arm. And although I gave credence to this rumour, I have omitted nothing which might have entitled me to this mark of your favour. But, strange to say, you have permitted me to depart in peace, without even the slightest mark of your strength. You see my surprise; therefore do pray inform me whether there is any foundation for the report, or whether I shall chastise the impudent story-teller who related the false tale to me."

"Young man," replied Bronkhorst, "you have heard nothing but the truth: but it needs some explanations.—I open my door hospitably to every stranger, and in Christian charity I give them a place at my table; but I am a man who hates form or disguise; I say all I think, and only wish in return that my guests openly and undisguisedly ask for all they want. There are unfortunately, however, a tribe of people who fatigue by their mean complaisance and ceremonies without end; who wear me out by their dissimulation, and stun me by propositions devoid of sense, or who do not conduct themselves with decency during the repast. Gracious heavens! I lose all patience when they carry their fooleries to such excesses, and I exert my right as master of the castle, by taking hold of their collars, and giving them tolerably severe chastisement ere I turn them out of my gates.—But a man of your sort, my young friend, will ever be welcome under my roof; for you boldly and openly ask for what you require, and say what you think; and such are the persons I admire. If in your way back you pass through this canton, promise me you will pay me another visit. Good bye! Let me caution you never to place implicit confidence in anything you hear; believe only that there may be a single grain of truth in the whole story: be always frank, and you will succeed through life. Heaven's blessings attend you."

Francis continued his journey towards Anvers most gaily, wishing, as he went, that he might everywhere meet with as good a reception as at the chevalier Bronkhorst's.

Nothing remarkable occurred during the rest of his journey: and he entered the city full of the most sanguine hopes and expectations. In every street his fancied riches stared him in the face. "It appears to me," said he, "that some of my father's debtors must have succeeded in business, and that they will only require my presence to repay their debts with honour."

After having rested from the fatigue of his journey, he made himself acquainted with every particular relative to the debtors, and learnt that the greater part had become rich, and were doing extremely well. This intelligence reanimated his hopes: he arranged his papers, and paid a visit to each of the persons who owed him anything. But his success was by no means what he had expected: some of the debtors pretended that they had paid everything; others, that they had never heard mention of Melchior of Bremen; and the rest produced accounts precisely contradictory to those he had, and which tended to prove they were creditors instead of debtors. In fine, ere three days had elapsed, Francis found himself in the debtors-prison, from whence he stood no chance of being released till he had paid the uttermost farthing of his father's debts.

How pitiable was this poor young man's condition! Even the horrors of the prison were augmented by the remembrance of Meta:—nay, to such a pitch of desperation was he carried, that he resolved to starve himself. Fortunately, however, at twenty-seven years of age such determinations are more easily formed than practised.

The intention of those who put him into confinement was not merely with a view of exacting payment of his pretended debts, but to avoid paying him his due: so, whether the prayers put up for poor Francis at Bremen were effectual, or that the pretended creditors were not disposed to maintain him during his life, I know not; but after a detention of three months they liberated Francis from prison, with a particular injunction to quit the territories of Anvers within four-and-twenty hours, and never to set his foot within that city again:—They gave him at the same time five florins to defray his expenses on the road. As one may well imagine, his horse and baggage had been sold to defray the costs incident to the proceedings.

With a heart overloaded with grief he quitted Anvers, in a very different frame of mind to what he experienced at entering it. Discouraged and irresolute, he mechanically followed the road which chance directed: he paid no attention to the various travellers, or indeed to any object on the road, till hunger or thirst caused him to lift his eyes to discover a steeple or some other token announcing the habitation of human beings. In this state of mind did he continue journeying on for several days incessantly; nevertheless a secret instinct impelled him to take the road leading to his own country.

All on a sudden he roused as if from a profound sleep, and recollected the place in which he was: he stopped an instant to consider whether he should continue the road he was then in, or return; "For," said he, "what a shame to return to my native city a beggar!" How could he thus return to that city in which he formerly felt equal to the richest of its inhabitants? How could he as a beggar present himself before Meta, without causing her to blush for the choice she had made? He did not allow time for his imagination to complete this miserable picture, for he instantly turned back, as if already he had found himself before the gates of Bremen, followed by the shouts of the children. His mind was soon made up as to what he should do: he resolved to go to one of the ports of the Low-Countries, there to engage himself as sailor on board a Spanish vessel, to go to the newly discovered world; and not to return to his native country till he had amassed as much wealth as he had formerly so thoughtlessly squandered. In the whole of this project, Meta was only thought of at an immeasurable distance: but Francis contented himself with connecting her in idea with his future plans, and walked, or rather strode along, as if by hurrying his pace he should sooner gain possession of her.

Having thus attained the frontiers of the Low-Countries, he arrived at sun-set in a village situated near Rheinburg; but since entirely destroyed in the thirty years' war. A caravan of carriers from Liege filled the inn so entirely, that the landlord told Francis he could not give him a lodging; adding, that at the adjoining village he would find accommodations.—Possibly he was actuated to this refusal by Francis's appearance, who certainly in point of garb might well be mistaken for a vagabond.

The landlord took him for a spy to a band of thieves, sent probably to rob the carriers: so that poor Francis, spite of his extreme lassitude, was compelled with his wallet at his back to proceed on his road; and having at his departure muttered through his teeth some bitter maledictions against the cruel and unfeeling landlord, the latter appeared touched with compassion for the poor stranger, and from the door of the inn called after him: "Young man; a word with you! If you resolve on passing the night here, I will procure you a lodging in that castle you now see on the hill; there you will have rooms in abundance, provided you are not afraid of being alone, for it is uninhabited. See, here are the keys belonging to it."

Francis joyfully accepted the landlord's proposition, and thanked him for it as if it had been an act of great charity.

"It is to me a matter of little moment where I pass the night, provided I am at my ease, and have something to eat." But the landlord was an ill-tempered fellow; and wishing to revenge the invectives Francis had poured forth against him, he sent him to the castle in order that he might be tormented by the spirits which were said to frequent it.

This castle was situated on a steep rock, and was only separated from the village by the high-road and a little rivulet. Its delightful prospects caused it to be kept in good repair, and to be well furnished, as its owner made use of it as a hunting-seat: but no sooner did night come on than he quitted it, in order to avoid the apparitions and ghosts which haunted it; but during the day nothing of the sort was visible, and all was tranquil.

When it was quite dark, Francis with a lantern in his hand proceeded towards the castle. The landlord accompanied him, and carried a little basket of provisions, to which he had added a bottle of wine (which he said would stand the test), as well as two candles and two wax-tapers for the night. Francis, not thinking he should require so many things, and being apprehensive he should have to pay for them, asked why they were all brought.

"The light from my lantern," said he, "will suffice me till the time of my getting into bed; and ere I shall get out of it, the sun will have risen, for I am quite worn out with fatigue."

"I will not endeavour to conceal from you," replied the landlord, "that according to the current reports this castle is haunted by evil spirits: but do not let that frighten you; you see I live sufficiently near, that, in case anything extraordinary should happen to you, I can hear you call, and shall be in readiness with my people to render you any assistance. At my house there is somebody stirring all night, and there is also someone constantly on the watch. I have lived on this spot for thirty years, and cannot say that I have ever seen anything to alarm me: indeed, I believe that you may with safety attribute any noises you hear during the night in this castle, to cats and weasels, with which the granaries are overrun. I have only provided you with the means of keeping up a light in case of need, for, at best, night is but a gloomy season; and, in addition, these candles are consecrated, and their light will undoubtedly keep off any evil spirits, should there be such in the castle."

The landlord spoke only the truth, when he said he had not seen any ghosts in the castle; for he never had the courage to set his foot within its doors after dark; and though he now spoke so courageously, the rogue would not have ventured on any account to enter. After having opened the door, he gave the basket into Francis's hand, pointed out the way he was to turn, and wished him good night: while the latter, fully satisfied that the story of the ghosts must be fabulous, gaily entered. He recollected all that had been told him to the prejudice of the chevalier Bronkhorst, but unfortunately forgot what that brave Castellan had recommended to him at parting.

Conformably to the landlord's instructions, he went upstairs and came to a door, which the key in his possession soon unlocked: it opened into a long dark gallery, where his very steps re-echoed; this gallery led to a large hall, from which issued a suite of apartments furnished in a costly manner: he surveyed them all; and made choice of one in which to pass the night, that appeared rather more lively than the rest. The windows looked to the high-road, and everything that passed in front of the inn could be distinctly heard from them. He lighted two candles, spread the cloth, ate very heartily, and felt completely at his ease so long as he was thus employed; for while eating, no thought or apprehension of spirits molested him; but he no sooner arose from table, than he began to feel a sensation strongly resembling fear.

In order to render himself secure, he locked the door, drew the bolts, and looked out from each window; but nothing was to be seen. Everything along the high-road and in front of the inn was tranquil, where, contrary to the landlord's assertions, not a single light was discernible. The sound of the horn belonging to the night-guard was the only thing that interrupted the silence which universally prevailed.

Francis closed the windows, once again looked round the room, and after snuffing the candles that they might burn the better, he threw himself on the bed, which he found good and comfortable: but although greatly fatigued, he could not get to sleep so soon as he had hoped. A slight palpitation of the heart, which he attributed to the agitation produced by the heat of his journey, kept him awake for a considerable time, till at length sleep came to his aid. After having as he imagined been asleep somewhat about an hour, he awoke and started up in a state of horror possibly not unusual to a person whose blood is overheated: this idea in some degree allayed his apprehensions; and he listened attentively, but could hear nothing excepting the clock, which struck the hour of midnight. Again he listened for an instant; and turning on his side, he was just going off to sleep again, when he fancied he heard a distant door grinding on its hinges, and then shut with a heavy noise. In an instant the idea of the ghost approaching caused him no little fear: but he speedily got the better of his alarm, by fancying it was only the wind; however, he could not comfort himself long with this idea, for the sound approached nearer and nearer, and resembled the noise made by the clanking of chains, or the rattling of a large bunch of keys.

The terror which Francis experienced was beyond all description, and he put his head under the clothes. The doors continued to open with a frightful noise, and at last he heard someone trying different keys at the door of his room; one of them seemed perfectly to fit the lock, but the bolts kept the door fast; however, a violent shock like a clap of thunder caused them to give way, and in stalked a tall thin figure with a black beard, whose appearance was indicative of chagrin and melancholy. He was habited in the antique style, and on his left shoulder wore a red cloak or mantle, while his head was covered with a high-crowned hat. Three times with slow and measured steps he walked round the room, examined the consecrated candles, and snuffed them: he then threw off his cloak, unfolded a shaving apparatus, and took from it the razors, which he sharpened on a large leather strop hanging to his belt.

No powers are adequate to describe the agonies Francis endured: he recommended himself to the Virgin Mary, and endeavoured, as well as his fears would permit, to form an idea of the spectre's designs on him. Whether he purposed to cut his throat, or only take off his beard, he was at a loss to determine. The poor traveller, however, was a little more composed, when he saw the spectre take out a silver shaving-pot, and in a basin of the same metal put some water; after which he made a lather, and then placed a chair. But a cold perspiration came over Francis, when the spectre with a grave air, made signs for him to sit in that chair.

He knew it was useless to resist this mandate, which was but too plainly given: and thinking it most prudent to make a virtue of necessity, and to put a good face on the matter, Francis obeyed the order, jumped nimbly out of bed, and seated himself as directed.

The spirit placed the shaving-bib round his neck: then taking a comb and scissors, cut off his hair and whiskers; after which he lathered, according to rule, his beard, his eye-brows and head, and shaved them all off completely from his chin to the nape of his neck. This operation ended, he washed his head, wiped and dried it very nicely, made him a low bow, folded up his case, put his cloak on his shoulder, and made towards the door to go away.

The consecrated candles had burnt most brilliantly during the whole of this operation; and by their clear light Francis discovered, on looking into the glass, that he had not a single hair remaining on his head. Most bitterly did he deplore the loss of his beautiful brown hair: but he regained courage on remarking, that, however great the sacrifice, all was now over, and that the spirit had no more power over him.

In effect, the ghost walked towards the door with as grave an air as he had entered: but after going a few steps, he stopped, looked at Francis with a mournful air, and stroked his beard. He three times repeated this action; and was on the point of quitting the room, when Francis began to fancy he wanted something. With great quickness of thought he imagined it might be, that he wished him to perform a like service for him to that which he had just been executing on himself.

As the spectre, spite of his woe-begone aspect, appeared more inclined to raillery than gravity, and as his proceedings towards Francis appeared more a species of frolic than absolute ill treatment, the latter no longer appeared to entertain any apprehension of him; and in consequence determined to hazard the adventure. He therefore beckoned the phantom to seat himself in the chair. It instantly returned, and obeyed: taking off its cloak, and unfolding the case, it placed it on the table, and seated itself in the chair, in the attitude of one about to be shaved. Francis imitated precisely all he had seen it do: he cut off its hair and whiskers, and then lathered its head. The spirit did not move an inch. Our barber's apprentice did not handle the razor very dexterously; so that having taken hold of the ghost's beard against the grain, the latter made a horrible grimace. Francis did not feel much assured by this action: however, he got through the job as well as he could, and rendered the ghost's head as completely bald as his own.

Hitherto the scene between the two performers had passed in profound silence; but on a sudden the silence was interrupted by the ghost exclaiming with a smiling countenance:—"Stranger, I heartily thank you for the eminent service you have rendered me; for to you am I indebted for deliverance from my long captivity. During the space of three hundred years I have been immersed within these walls, and my soul has been condemned to submit to this chastisement as a punishment for my crimes, until some living being had the courage to exercise retaliation on me, by doing to me what I have done by others during my life.

"Count Hartmann formerly resided in this castle: he was a man who recognized no law nor superior; was of an arrogant and overbearing disposition; committed every species of wickedness, and violated the most sacred rights of hospitality: he played all sorts of malicious tricks to strangers who sought refuge under his roof, and to the poor who solicited his charity. I was his barber, and did everything to please him. No sooner did I perceive a pious pilgrim, than in an endearing tone I urged him to come into the castle, and prepared a bath for him; and while he was enjoying the idea of being taken care of, I shaved his beard and head quite close, and then turned him out of the bye door, with raillery and ridicule. All this was seen by count Hartmann from his window with a sort of devilish pleasure, while the children would assemble round the abused stranger, and pursue him with cries of derision.

"One day there came a holy man from a far distant country; he wore a penitentiary cross at his back, and his devotion had imprinted scars on his feet, hands, and sides; his head was shaved, excepting a circle of hair left to resemble the crown of thorns worn by our Saviour. He asked some water to wash his feet as he passed by, and some bread to eat. I instantly put him into the bath; but did not respect even *his* venerable head. Upon which the pilgrim pronounced this terrible curse on me: 'Depraved wretch,' said he, 'know that at your death, the formidable gates of heaven, of hell, and of purgatory will alike be closed against your sinful soul, which shall wander through this castle, in the form of a ghost, until some man, without being invited or constrained, shall do to you, what you have so long done to others.'

"From that moment the marrow in my bones dried up, and I became a perfect shadow; my soul quitted my emaciated body, and remained wandering within these walls, according to the prediction of the holy man. In vain did I look and hope for release from the painful ties which held me to earth; for know, that no sooner is the soul separated from the body, than it aspires to the blissful regions of peace, and the ardour of its wishes causes years to appear as long as centuries, while it languishes in a strange element. As a punishment, I am compelled to continue the trade that I had exercised during my life; but, alas! my nocturnal appearance soon rendered this castle deserted. Now and then a poor pilgrim entered to pass the night here: when they did, however, I treated them all as I have done you; but not one has understood me, or rendered me the only service which could deliver my soul from this sad servitude. Henceforth no spirit will haunt this castle; for I shall now enjoy that repose of which I have been so long in search. Once again let me thank you, gallant youth; and believe, that had I power over the hidden treasures of the globe, I would give them all to you; but, unfortunately, during my life riches did not fall to my lot, and this castle contains no store: however, listen to the advice I am now about to give you.

"Remain here till your hair has grown again; then return to your own country; and at that period of the year when the days and nights are of equal length, go on the bridge which crosses the Weser, and there remain till a friend, whom you will there meet, shall tell you what you ought to do to get possession of terrestrial wealth. When you are rolling in riches and prosperity, remember me; and on every anniversary of the day on which you released me from the heavy maledictions which overwhelmed me, cause a mass to be said for the repose of my soul. Adieu! I must now leave you."

Thus saying, the phantom vanished, and left his liberator perfectly astonished at the strange history he had just related. For a considerable time Francis remained immoveable, and reasoned with himself as to the reality of what he had seen; for he could not help fancying still that it was only a dream: but his closely shaved head soon convinced him that the event had actually taken place. He got into bed again, and slept soundly till mid-day.

The malicious inn-keeper had been on the watch from dawn of day for the appearance of the traveller, in order that he might enjoy a laugh at his expense, and express his surprise at the night's adventure. But after waiting till his patience was nearly exhausted, and finding it approached to noon, he began to apprehend that the spirit had either strangled the stranger, or that he had died of fright. He therefore called his servants together, and ran with them to the castle, passing through every room till he reached the one in which he had observed the light over-night: there he found a strange key in the door, which was still bolted; for Francis had drawn the bolts again after the ghost had vanished. The landlord, who was all anxiety, knocked loudly; and Francis on awaking, at first thought it was the phantom come to pay him a second visit; but at length recognising the landlord's voice, he got up and opened the door.

The landlord, affecting the utmost possible astonishment, clasped his hands together, and exclaimed, "Great God and all the saints! then the *red cloak* has actually been here and shaved you completely? I now see that the story was but too well founded. But pray relate to me all the particulars: tell me what the spirit was like; how he came thus to shave you; and what he said to you?"

Francis, having sense enough to discover his roguery, answered him by saying: "The spirit resembled a man wearing a red cloak; you know full well how he performed the operation: and his conversation I perfectly remember;—listen attentively:—'Stranger,' said he to me, 'do not trust to a certain inn-keeper who has a figure of malice for his sign; the rogue knew well what would happen to you. Adieu! I now quit this abode, as my time is come; and in future no spirit will make its appearance here. I am now about to be transformed into a night-mare, and shall constantly torment and haunt this said inn-keeper, unless he does penance for his villainy, by lodging, feeding, and furnishing you with everything needful, till your hair shall grow again and fall in ringlets over your shoulders.'"

At these words the landlord was seized with a violent trembling: he crossed himself, and vowed to the Virgin Mary that he would take care of the young stranger, lodge him, and give him everything he required free of cost. He then conducted him to his house, and faithfully fulfilled what he promised.

The spirit being no longer heard or seen, Francis was naturally looked on as a conjuror. He several times passed a night in the castle; and one evening a courageous villager accompanied him, and returned without having lost his hair. The lord of the castle, hearing that the formidable *red cloak* was no longer to be seen, was quite delighted, and gave orders that the stranger who had delivered him from this spirit should be well taken care of.

Early in the month of September, Francis's hair began to form into ringlets, and he prepared to depart; for all his thoughts were directed towards the bridge over the Weser, where he hoped, according to the barber's predictions, to find the friend who would point out to him the way to make his fortune.

When Francis took leave of the landlord, the latter presented him with a handsome horse well appointed, and loaded with a large cloak-bag on the back of the saddle, and gave him at the same time a sufficient sum of money to complete his journey. This was a present from the lord of the castle, expressive of his thanks for having delivered him from the spirit, and rendered his castle again habitable.

Francis arrived at his native place in high spirits. He returned to his lodging in the little street, where he lived very retired, contenting himself for the present with secret information respecting Meta. All the tidings he thus gained were of a satisfactory nature; but he would neither visit her, nor make her acquainted with his return, till his fate was decided.

He waited with the utmost impatience for the equinox; till which, time seemed immeasurably long. The night preceding the eventful day, he could not close his eyes to sleep; and that he might be sure of not missing the friend with whom as yet he was unacquainted, he took his station ere sun-rise on the bridge, where no human being but himself was to be discovered. Replete with hopes of future good fortune, he formed a thousand projects in what way to spend his money.

Already had he, during the space of nearly an hour, traversed the bridge alone, giving full scope to his imagination; when on a sudden the bridge presented a moving scene, and amongst others, many beggars took their several stations on it, to levy contributions on the passengers. The first of this tribe who asked charity of Francis was a poor devil with a wooden leg, who, being a pretty good physiognomist, judged from the gay and contented air of the young man that his request would be crowned with success; and his conjecture was not erroneous, for he threw a demi-florin into his hat.

Francis, meanwhile, feeling persuaded that the friend he expected must belong to the highest class of society, was not surprised at not seeing him at so early an hour, and waited therefore with patience. But as the hour for visiting the Exchange and the Courts of Justice drew near, his eyes were in constant motion. He discovered at an immense distance every well-dressed person who came on the bridge, and his blood was in a perfect ferment as each approached him, for in some one of them did he hope to discover the author of his good fortune; but it was in vain his looking the people in the face, no one paid attention to him. The beggars, who at noon were seated on the ground eating their dinner, remarking that the young man they had seen from the first of the morning was the only person remaining with them on the bridge, and that he had not spoken to anyone, or appeared to have any employment, took him for a lazy vagabond; and although they had received marks of his beneficence, they began to make game of him, and in derision called him the *provost* of the bridge. The physiognomist with the wooden leg remarked that his air was no longer so gay as in the morning, and that having drawn his hat over his face he appeared entirely lost in thought, for he walked slowly along, nibbling an apple with an abstracted air. The observer, resolving to benefit by what he had remarked, went to the further extremity of the bridge, and after well examining the visionary, came up to him as a stranger, asked his charity, and succeeded to his utmost wish; for Francis, without turning round his head, gave him another demi-florin.

In the afternoon a crowd of new faces presented themselves to Francis's observation, while he became quite weary at his friend's tardiness; but hope still kept up his attention. However, the fast declining sun gave notice of the approach of night, and yet scarcely any of the many passers-by had noticed Francis. Some few, perhaps, had returned his salutation, but not one had, as he expected and hoped, embraced him. At length, the day so visibly declined that the bridge became nearly deserted; for even the beggars went away. A profound melancholy seized the heart of poor Francis, when he found his hopes thus deceived; and giving way to despair, he would have precipitated himself into the Weser, had not the recollection of Meta deterred him. He felt anxious, ere he terminated his days in so tragical a manner, to see her once again as she went to mass, and feast on the contemplation of her features.

He was preparing to quit the bridge, when the beggar with the wooden leg accosted him, for he had in vain puzzled his brains to discover what could possibly have caused the young man to remain on the bridge from morning till night. The poor cripple had waited longer than usual on account of Francis, in order to see when he went; but as he remained longer than he wished, curiosity at length induced him openly to address him, in order to learn what he so ardently desired to know.

"Pray excuse me, worthy sir," said he; "and permit me to ask you a question."

Francis, who was by no means in a mood to talk, and who now heard from the mouth of a beggar the words which he had so anxiously expected from a friend, answered him in rather an angry tone: "Well then! what is it you want to know, old man?"

"Sir, you and I were the two first persons on this bridge to-day; and here we are still the only remaining two. As for me and my companions, it is pretty clear that we only come to ask alms: but it is equally evident you do not belong to our profession; and yet you have not quitted the bridge the whole day. My dear sir, for the love of God, if it is no secret, tell me I entreat you for what purpose you came, and what is the grief that rends your heart?"

"What can it concern you, old dotard, to know where the shoe pinches me, or what afflictions I am labouring under?"

"My good sir, I wish you well; you have twice bestowed your charity on me, which I hope the Almighty will return to you with interest. I could not but observe, however, that this evening your countenance no longer looked gay and happy as in the morning; and, believe me, I was sorry to see the change."

The unaffected interest evinced by the old man pleased Francis. "Well," replied he, "since you attach so much importance to the knowledge of the reason I have for remaining the whole day here plaguing myself, I will inform you that I came in search of a friend who appointed to meet me on this bridge, but whom I have expected in vain."

"With your permission I should say your friend is a rogue, to play the fool with you in this manner. If he had so served *me*, I should make him feel the weight of my crutch whenever I met him: for if he has been prevented from keeping his word by any unforeseen obstacle, he ought at least to have sent to you, and not have kept you here on your feet a whole day."

"And yet I have no reason to complain of his not coming, for he promised me nothing. In fact, it was only in a dream that I was told I should meet a friend here."

Francis spoke of it as a dream, because the history of the ghost was too long to relate.

"That alters the case," replied the old man. "Since you rest your hopes on dreams, I am not astonished at your being deceived. I have also had many dreams in my life; but I was never fool enough to pay attention to them. If I had all the treasures that have been promised me in dreams, I could purchase the whole city of Bremen: but I have never put faith in dreams, and have not taken a single step to prove whether they were true or false; for I know full well, it would be useless trouble: and I am astonished that you should have lost so fine a day, which you might have employed so much more usefully, merely on the strength of a dream which appears to me so wholly devoid of sense or meaning."

"The event proves the justness of your remark, old father; and that dreams generally are deceitful. But it is rather more than three months since I had a very circumstantial dream relative to my meeting a friend on this particular day, here on this bridge; and it was so clearly indicated that he should communicate things of the utmost importance, that I thought it worthwhile to ascertain whether this dream had any foundation in truth."

"Ah! sir, no one has had clearer dreams than myself; and one of them I shall never forget. I dreamt, several years since, that my good angel stood at the foot of my bed, in the form of a young man, and addressed me as follows:—'Berthold, listen attentively to my words, and do not lose any part of what I am about to say. A treasure is allotted you; go and secure it, that you may be enabled to live happily the rest of your days. To-morrow evening, when the sun is setting, take a pick-axe and spade over your shoulder, and go out of the city by the gate leading to Hamburgh: when you arrive facing the convent of Saint Nicholas, you will see a garden, the entrance to which is ornamented by two pillars; conceal yourself behind one of these until the moon rises: then push the door hard, and it will yield to your efforts; go without fear into the garden, follow a walk covered by a treillage of vines, and to the left you will see a great apple-tree: place yourself at the foot of this tree, with your face turned towards the moon, and you will perceive, at fifteen feet distance, two bushy rose-trees: search between these two shrubs, and at the depth of about six feet you will discover a great flag-stone, which covers the treasure enclosed within an iron chest; and although it is heavy and difficult to handle, do not regret the labour it will occasion you to move it from the hole where it now is. You will be well rewarded for your pains and trouble, if you look for the key which is hid under the box.'"

Francis remained like one stupefied at this recital; and certainly would have been unable to conceal his astonishment, if the darkness of the night had not favoured him. The various particulars pointed out by the beggar brought to his recollection a little garden which he had inherited from his father, and which garden was the favourite spot of that good man; but possibly for that very reason it was not held in estimation by the son. Melchior had caused it to be laid out according to his own taste, and his son in the height of his extravagance had sold it at a very low price.

The beggar with his wooden leg was now become a very interesting personage to Francis, who perceived that he was the friend alluded to by the ghost in the castle of Rummelsbourg. The first impulse of joy would have led him to embrace the mendicant; but he restrained his feelings, thinking it best not to communicate the result of his intelligence to him.

"Well, my good man," said he, "what did you when you awoke? did you not attend to the advice given by your good angel?"

"Why should I undertake a hopeless labour? It was only a vague dream; and if my good angel was anxious to appear to me, he might choose a night when I am not sleeping, which occurs but too frequently: but he has not troubled his head much about me; for if he had, I should not have been reduced, as I now am, to his shame, to beg my bread."

Francis took from his pocket another piece of money, and gave it to the old man, saying: "Take this to procure half a pint of wine, and drink it ere you retire to rest. Your conversation has dispelled my sorrowful thoughts; do not fail to come regularly to this bridge, where I hope we shall meet again."

The old lame man, not having for a long while made so good a day's work, overwhelmed Francis with his grateful benedictions. They separated, and each went their way. Francis, whose joy was at its height from the near prospect of his hopes being realised, very speedily reached his lodging in the bye street.

The following day he ran to the purchaser of the little garden, and proposed to re-purchase it. The latter, to whom this property was of no particular value, and indeed who began to be tired of it, willingly consented to part with it. They very soon agreed as to the conditions of the purchase, and went immediately to sign the contract: with the money he had found in his bag, as a gift from the lord of Rummelsbourg, Francis paid down half the price: he then procured the necessary tools for digging a hole in the earth, conveyed them to the garden, waited till the moon was up, strictly adhered to the instructions given him by the old beggar, set to work, and without any unlucky adventure he obtained the hidden treasure.

His father, as a precaution against necessity, had buried this money, without any intention to deprive his son of this considerable portion of his inheritance; but dying suddenly, he had carried the secret to his grave, and nothing but a happy combination of circumstances could have restored this lost treasure to its rightful owner.

The chest filled with gold pieces was too heavy for Francis to remove to his lodging without employing some person to assist him: and feeling unwilling to become a topic of general conversation, he preferred concealing it in the summer-house belonging to the garden, and fetching it at several times. On the third day the whole was safely conveyed to his lodging in the little back street.

Francis dressed himself in the best possible style, and went to the church to request that the priest would substitute for the prayers which had been previously offered up, a thanksgiving *for the safe return of a traveller to his native country, after having happily terminated his business.* He concealed himself in a corner, where, unseen, he could observe Meta. The sight of her gave him inexpressible delight, especially when he saw the beautiful blush which overspread her cheeks, and the brilliancy of her eyes, when the priest offered up the thanksgiving. A secret meeting took place as had been formerly arranged; and so much was Meta affected by it, that any indifferent person might have divined the cause.

Francis repaired to the Exchange, set up again in business, and in a very short time had enough to do; his fortune each succeeding day becoming better known, his neighbours judged that he had had greater luck than sense in his journey to collect his father's debts. He hired a large house in the best part of the town, engaged clerks, and continued his business with laudable and indefatigable assiduity; he conducted himself with the utmost propriety and sagacity, and abstained from the foolish extravagancies which had formerly been his ruin.

The re-establishment of Francis's fortune formed the general topic of conversation. Everyone was astonished at the success of his foreign voyage: but in proportion to the spreading fame of his riches, did Meta's tranquility and happiness diminish; for it appeared that her silent lover was now in a condition to declare himself openly, and yet he remained dumb, and only manifested his love by the usual rencontre on coming out of church; and even this species of rendezvous became less frequent, which appeared to evince a diminution of his affection.

Poor Meta's heart was now torn by jealousy; for she imagined that the inconstant Francis was offering up his vows to some other beauty. She had experienced secret transports of delight on learning the change of fortune of the man she loved, not from interested motives and the wish to participate in his bettered fortune herself, but from affection to her mother, who, since the failure of the match with the rich brewer, absolutely seemed to despair of ever enjoying happiness or comfort in this world. When she thought Francis faithless, she wished that the prayers put up for him in the church had not been heard, and that his journey had not been attended with such entire success; for had he been reduced to means merely sufficient to procure the necessaries of life, in all probability he would have shared them with her.

Mother Bridget failed not to perceive her daughter's uneasiness, and easily guessed the cause; for she had heard of her old neighbour's surprising return, and she knew he was now considered an industrious intelligent merchant; therefore she thought if his love for her daughter was what it ought to be, he would not be thus tardy in declaring it; for she well knew Meta's sentiments towards him. However, feeling anxious to avoid the probability of wounding her daughter's feelings, she avoided mentioning the subject to her: but the latter, no longer able to confine her grief to her own bosom, disclosed it to her mother, and confided the whole to her.

Mother Bridget did not reproach her daughter for her past conduct, but employed all her eloquence to console her, and entreated her to bear up with courage under the loss of all her hopes:

"You must resign him," said she: "you scorned at the happiness which presented itself to your acceptance, therefore you must now endeavour to be resigned at its departure. Experience has taught me that those hopes which appear the best founded are frequently the most delusive; follow my example, and never again deliver up your heart. Do not reckon on any amelioration of your condition, and you will be contented with your lot. Honour this spinning-wheel which produces the means of your subsistence, and then fortune and riches will be immaterial to you: you may do without them."

Thus saying, mother Bridget turned her wheel round with redoubled velocity, in order to make up for the time lost in conversation. She spoke nothing but the truth to her daughter: for since the opportunity was gone by when she hoped it was possible to have regained her lost comforts, she had in such a manner simplified her present wants and projects of future life, that it was not in the power of destiny to produce any considerable derangement in them. But as yet Meta was not so great a philosopher; so that her mother's exhortations, consolations, and doctrines, produced a precisely different effect on her from what they were intended. Meta looked on herself as the destroyer of the flattering hopes her mother had entertained. Although she did not formerly accept the offer of marriage proposed to her, and even then could not have reckoned on possessing beyond the common necessaries of life; yet, since she had heard the tidings of the great fortune obtained by the man of her heart, her views had become enlarged, and she anticipated with pleasure that by her choice she might realize her mother's wishes.

Now, however, this golden dream had vanished: Francis would not come again; and indeed they even began to talk in the city of an alliance about to take place between him and a very rich young lady of Anvers. This news was a death-blow to poor Meta: she vowed she would banish him from her thoughts; but still moistened her work with her tears.

Contrary, however, to her vow, she was one day thinking of the faithless one: for whenever she filled her spinning-wheel, she thought of the following distich,* which her mother had frequently repeated to her to encourage her in her work:

> "Spin the thread well; spin, spin it more,
> For see your intended is now at the door."

Someone did in reality knock gently at the door; and mother Bridget went to see who it was. Francis entered, attired as for the celebration of a

---

* A couplet or a few lines of verse.

wedding. Surprise for a while suspended mother Bridget's faculties of speech. Meta, blushing deeply and trembling, arose from her seat, but was equally unable with her mother to say a word. Francis was the only one of the three who could speak; and he candidly declared his love, and demanded of Bridget the hand of her daughter. The good mother, ever attentive to forms, asked eight days to consider the matter, although the tears of joy which she shed, plainly evinced her ready and prompt acquiescence: but Francis, all impatience, would not hear of delay: finding which, she, conformable to her duty as a mother, and willing to satisfy Francis's ardour, adopted a mid-way, and left the decision to her daughter. The latter, obeying the dictates of her heart, placed herself by the side of the object of her tenderest affection; and Francis, transported with joy, thanked her by a kiss.

The two lovers then entertained themselves with talking over the delights of the time when they so well communicated their sentiments by signs. Francis had great difficulty in tearing himself away from Meta and such 'converse sweet,' but he had an important duty to fulfil.

He directed his steps towards the bridge over the Weser, where he hoped to find his old friend with the wooden leg, whom he had by no means forgotten, although he had delayed making the promised visit. The latter instantly recognised Francis; and no sooner saw him at the foot of the bridge, than he came to meet him, and shewed evident marks of pleasure at sight of him.

"Can you, my friend," said Francis to him, after returning his salutation, "come with me into the new town and execute a commission? You will be well rewarded for your trouble."

"Why not?—with my wooden leg I walk about just as well as other people; and indeed have an advantage over them, for it is never fatigued. I beg you, however, my good sir, to have the kindness to wait till the man with the grey great-coat arrives."

"What has this man in the grey great-coat to do with you?"

"He every day comes as evening approaches and gives me a demi-florin; I know not from whom. It is not indeed always proper to learn all things; so I do not breathe a word. I am sometimes tempted to believe, that it is the devil who is anxious to buy my soul; but it matters little, I have not consented to the bargain, therefore it cannot be valid."

"I verily believe that grey surtout has some malice in his head; so follow me, and you shall have a quarter-florin over and above the bargain."

Francis conducted the old man to a distant corner, near the ramparts of the city, stopped before a newly built house, and knocked at the door. As soon as the door was opened, he thus addressed the old beggar: "You have procured a very agreeable evening for me in the course of my life; it is but just, therefore, that I should shed some comforts over your declining days. This house and everything appertaining thereto belongs to you. The kitchen and cellar are both well stocked; there is a person to take care of you, and every day at dinner you will find a quarter-florin under your plate. It is now time for you to know that the man in the grey surtout is my servant, whom I every day sent with my alms till this house was ready to receive you. You may, if you please, consider me as your guardian angel, since your good angel did not acquit himself uprightly in return for your gratitude."

Saying this, he made the old man go into his house; where the latter found everything he could possibly desire or want. The table was spread; and the old man was so much astonished at this unexpected good fortune, that he thought it must be a dream; for he could in no way imagine why a rich man should feel so much interest for a miserable beggar. Francis having again assured him that everything he saw was his own, a torrent of tears expressed his thanks; and before he could sufficiently recover from his astonishment to express his gratitude by words, Francis had vanished.

The following day, mother Bridget's house was filled with merchants and shopkeepers of all descriptions, whom Francis had sent to Meta, in order that she might purchase and get ready everything she required for her appearance in the world with suitable *éclat*. Three weeks afterwards he conducted her to the altar. The splendour of the wedding far exceeded that of the *King of Hops*. Mother Bridget enjoyed the satisfaction of adorning her daughter's forehead with the nuptial crown, and thereby obtained the accomplishment of all her desires, and was recompensed for her virtuous and active life. She witnessed her daughter's happiness with delight, and proved the very best of grand-mothers to her daughter's children.

The Spectre-Barber, by Edward Vernon Utterson.* (Watercolor illustration painted in homage to the story in *Tales of the Dead*, 1813.)

---

* Husband of author and translator Sarah Elizabeth Utterson.

"Double Portrait" (from Basel's *Dance of Death*) by Matthäus Merian, 1538.

II.

THE FAMILY PORTRAITS

BY JOHANN AUGUST APEL*

(TRANSLATED INTO ENGLISH BY
SARAH ELIZABETH UTTERSON)

"No longer shall you gaze on't;
lest your fancy
May think anon, it moves.——
The fixure of her eye has motion in't."
—WINTER'S TALE.†

NIGHT had insensibly superseded day, when Ferdinand's carriage continued its slow course through the forest; the postilion uttering a thousand complaints on the badness of the roads, and Ferdinand employing the leisure which the tedious progress of his carriage allowed, with reflections to which the purpose of his journey gave rise.

As was usual with young men of rank, he had visited several universities; and after having travelled over the principal parts of Europe, he was now returning to his native country to take possession of the property of his father, who had died in his absence.

Ferdinand was an only son, and the last branch of the ancient family of Meltheim: it was on this account that his mother was the more anxious that he should form a brilliant alliance, to which both his birth and fortune entitled him; she frequently repeated that Clotilde of Hainthal was of all

---

* Apel (1771–1816) was a German jurist and writer. He co-edited (with Friedrich Laun) an anthology titled *Gespensterbuch* ("gespenster" means "ghostly" or "haunted") in 1811 and wrote the story "Der Freischutz" ("The Sharpshooter") for it. The story was the basis for an eponymous 1821 opera by Friedrich Kind and Carl Maria von Weber.

† Shakespeare's *The Winter's Tale* (1623), Act V, Scene 3.

others the person she should be most rejoiced to have as a daughter-in-law, and who should give to the world an heir to the name and estates of Meltheim. In the first instance, she merely named her amongst other distinguished females whom she recommended to her son's attention: but after a short period she spoke of none but her: and at length declared, rather positively, that all her happiness depended on the completion of this alliance, and hoped her son would approve her choice.

Ferdinand, however, never thought of this union but with regret; and the urgent remonstrances which his mother ceased not to make on the subject, only contributed to render Clotilde, who was an entire stranger to him, less amiable in his eyes: he determined at last to take a journey to the capital, whither Mr. Hainthal and his daughter were attracted by the carnival. He wished at least to know the lady, ere he consented to listen to his mother's entreaties; and secretly flattered himself that he should find some more cogent reasons for opposing this union than mere caprice, which was the appellation the old lady gave to his repugnance.

Whilst travelling alone in his carriage, as night approached, the solitary forest, his imagination drew a picture of his early life, which happy recollections rendered still happier. It seemed, that the future presented no charms for him to equal the past; and the greater pleasure he took in retracing what no longer existed, the less wish he felt to bestow a thought on that futurity to which, contrary to his inclinations, he seemed destined. Thus, notwithstanding the slowness with which his carriage proceeded over the rugged ground, he found that he was too rapidly approaching the termination of his journey.

The postilion at length began to console himself; for one half of the journey was accomplished, and the remainder presented only good roads: Ferdinand, however, gave orders to his groom to stop at the approaching village, determining to pass the night there.

The road through the village which led to the inn was bordered by gardens, and the sound of different musical instruments led Ferdinand to suppose that the villagers were celebrating some rural *fête*. He already anticipated the pleasure of joining them, and hoped that this recreation would dissipate his melancholy thoughts. But on listening more attentively, he remarked that the music did not resemble that usually heard at inns; and the great light he perceived at the window of a pretty house from whence came the sounds that had arrested his attention, did not permit him to doubt that a more select party than are accustomed to reside in the country at that unfavourable season, were amusing themselves in performing a concert.

The carriage now stopped at the door of a small inn of mean appearance. Ferdinand, who counted on much inconvenience and few comforts, asked who was the lord of the village. They informed him that he occupied a *château* situated in an adjoining hamlet. Our traveller said no more, but was obliged to content himself with the best apartment the landlord could give him. To divert his thoughts, he determined to walk in the village, and directed his steps towards the spot where he had heard the music; to this the harmonious sounds readily guided him: he approached softly, and found himself close to the house where the concert was performing. A young girl, sitting at the door, was playing with a little dog, who began to bark. Ferdinand, drawn from his reverie by this singular accompaniment, begged the little girl to inform him who lived in that house. "It is my father," she replied, smiling; "come in, sir." And saying this, she slowly went up the steps.

Ferdinand hesitated for an instant whether to accept this unceremonious invitation. But the master of the house came down, saying to him in a friendly tone: "Our music, sir, has probably been the only attraction to this spot; no matter, it is the pastor's abode, and to it you are heartily welcome. My neighbours and I," continued he, whilst leading Ferdinand in, "meet alternately at each other's houses once a week, to form a little concert; and to-day it is my turn. Will you take a part in the performance, or only listen to it? Sit down in this apartment. Are you accustomed to hear better music than that performed simply by amateurs? or do you prefer an assemblage where they pass their time in conversation? If you like the latter, go into the adjoining room, where you will find my wife surrounded by a young circle: here is our musical party, there is their *conversazióni*."* Saying this, he opened the door, made a gentle inclination of the head to Ferdinand, and seated himself before his desk. Our traveller would fain have made apologies; but the performers in an instant resumed the piece he had interrupted. At the same time the pastor's wife, a young and pretty woman, entreated Ferdinand, in the most gracious manner possible, entirely to follow his own inclinations, whether they led him to remain with the musicians, or to join the circle assembled in the other apartment. Ferdinand, after uttering some common-place terms of politeness, followed her into the adjoining room.

The chairs formed a semicircle round the sofa, and were occupied by several women and by some men. They all rose on Ferdinand's entering, and appeared a little disconcerted at the interruption. In the middle of the circle

---

* A scholarly social gathering held for the discussion of literature and art.

was a low chair, on which sat, with her back to the door, a young and sprightly female, who, seeing everyone rise, changed her position, and at sight of a stranger blushed and appeared embarrassed. Ferdinand entreated the company not to interrupt the conversation. They accordingly reseated themselves, and the mistress of the house invited the new guest to take a seat on the sofa by two elderly ladies, and drew her chair near him. "The music," she said to him, "drew you amongst us, and yet in this apartment we have none; I hear it nevertheless with pleasure myself: but I cannot participate in my husband's enthusiasm for simple quartetts and symphonies; several of my friends are of the same way of thinking with me, which is the reason that, while our husbands are occupied with their favourite science, we here enjoy social converse, which sometimes, however, becomes too loud for our *virtuoso* neighbours. To-day, I give a long-promised tea-drinking. Everyone is to relate a story of ghosts, or something of a similar nature. You see that my auditors are more numerous than the band of musicians."

"Permit me, madam," replied Ferdinand, "to add to the number of your auditors; although I have not much talent in explaining the marvellous."

"That will not be any hinderance to you here," answered a very pretty brunette; "for it is agreed amongst us that no one shall search for any explanation, even though it bears the stamp of truth, as explanations would take away all pleasure from ghost stories."

"I shall benefit by your instructions," answered Ferdinand: "but without doubt I interrupt a very interesting recital;—dare I entreat—?"

The young lady with flaxen hair, who rose from the little seat, blushed anew; but the mistress of the house drew her by the arm, and laughing, conducted her to the middle of the circle. "Come, child," said she, "don't make any grimace; reseat yourself, and relate your story. This gentleman will also give us his."

"Do you promise to give us one, sir?" said the young lady to Ferdinand. He replied by a low bow. She then reseated herself in the place destined for the narrator, and thus began:

"One of my youthful friends, named Juliana, passed every summer with her family at her father's estate. The *château* was situated in a romantic country; high mountains formed a circle in the distance; forests of oaks and fine groves surrounded it. It was an ancient edifice, and had descended through a long line of ancestry to Juliana's father; for which reason, instead of making any alterations, he was only anxious to preserve it in the same state they had left it to him.

"Among the number of antiquities most prized by him was the family picture gallery; a vaulted room, dark, high, and of Gothic architecture, where hung the portraits of his forefathers, as large as the natural size, covering the walls, which were blackened by age. Conformable to an immemorial custom, they ate in this room: and Juliana has often told me, that she could not overcome, especially at supper-time, a degree of fear and repugnance; and that she had frequently feigned indisposition, to avoid entering this formidable apartment. Among the portraits there was one of a female, who, it would seem, did not belong to the family; for Juliana's father could neither tell whom it represented, nor how it had become ranged amongst his ancestry: but as to all appearance it had retained its station for ages, my friend's father was unwilling to remove it.

"Juliana never looked at this portrait without an involuntary shuddering: and she has told me, that from her earliest infancy she has felt this secret terror, without being able to define the cause. Her father treated this sentiment as puerile, and compelled her sometimes to remain alone in that room. But as Juliana grew up, the terror this singular portrait occasioned, increased; and she frequently supplicated her father, with tears in her eyes, not to leave her alone in that apartment—'That portrait,' she would say, 'regards me not gloomily or terribly, but with looks full of a mild melancholy. It appears anxious to draw me to it, and as if the lips were about to open and speak to me.—That picture will certainly cause my death.'

"Juliana's father at length relinquished all hope of conquering his daughter's fears. One night at supper, the terror she felt had thrown her into convulsions, for she fancied she saw the picture move its lips; and the physician enjoined her father in future to remove from her view all similar causes of fear. In consequence, the terrifying portrait was removed from the gallery, and it was placed over the door of an uninhabited room in the attic story.

"Juliana, after this removal, passed two years without experiencing any alarms. Her complexion resumed its brilliancy, which surprised everyone; for her continual fears had rendered her pale and wan: but the portrait and the fears it produced had alike disappeared, and Juliana—"

"Well," cried the mistress of the house, smiling, when she perceived that the narrator appeared to hesitate, "confess it, my dear child; Juliana found an admirer of her beauty;—was it not so?"

"'Tis even so," resumed the young lady, blushing deeply; "she was affianced: and her intended husband coming to see her the day previous to that fixed on for her marriage, she conducted him over the *château*, and from the attic rooms was shewing him the beautiful prospect which extended to the distant mountains. On a sudden she found herself, without being aware of it, in the room where the unfortunate portrait was placed. And it was natural that a stranger, surprised at seeing it there alone, should ask who it represented. To look at it, recognise it, utter a piercing shriek, and run towards the door, were but the work of an instant with poor Juliana. But whether in effect owing to the violence with which she opened the door the picture was shaken, or whether the moment was arrived in which its baneful influence was to be exercised over Juliana, I know not; but at the moment this unfortunate girl was striving to get out of the room and avoid her destiny, the portrait fell; and Juliana, thrown down by her fears, and overpowered by the heavy weight of the picture, never rose more."——

A long silence followed this recital, which was only interrupted by the exclamations of surprise and interest excited for the unfortunate Juliana. Ferdinand alone appeared untouched by the general emotions. At length, one of the ladies sitting near him broke the silence by saying, "This story is literally true; I knew the family where the fatal portrait caused the death of a charming young girl: I have also seen the picture; it has, as the young lady truly observed, an indescribable air of goodness which penetrates the heart, so that I could not bear to look on it long; and yet, as you say, its look is so full of tender melancholy, and has such infinite attractions, that it appears that the eyes move and have life."

"In general," resumed the mistress of the house, at the same time shuddering, "I don't like portraits, and I would not have any in the rooms I occupy. They say that they become pale when the original expires; and the more faithful the likeness, the more they remind me of those waxen figures I cannot look at without aversion."

"That is the reason," replied the young person who had related the history, "that I prefer those portraits where the individual is represented occupied in some employment, as then the figure is entirely independent of those who look at it; whereas in a simple portrait the eyes are inanimately fixed on everything that passes. Such portraits appear to me as contrary to the laws of illusion as painted statues."

"I participate in your opinion," replied Ferdinand; "for the remembrance of a terrible impression produced on my mind when young, by a portrait of that sort, will never be effaced."

"O! pray relate it to us," said the young lady with flaxen hair, who had not as yet quitted the low chair; "you are obliged according to promise to take my place." She instantly arose, and jokingly forced Ferdinand to change seats with her.

"This history," said he, "will resemble a little too much the one you have just related; permit me therefore—"

"That does not signify," resumed the mistress of the house, "one is never weary with recitals of this kind; and the greater repugnance I feel in looking at these horrible portraits, the greater is the pleasure I take in listening to histories of their eyes or feet being seen to move."

"But seriously," replied Ferdinand, who would fain have retracted his promise, "my history is too horrible for so fine an evening. I confess to you that I cannot think of it without shuddering, although several years have elapsed since it happened."

"So much the better, so much the better!" cried nearly all present; "how you excite our curiosity! and its having happened to yourself will afford double pleasure, as we cannot entertain any doubt of the fact."

"It did not happen personally to me," answered Ferdinand, who reflected that he had gone too far, "but to one of my friends, on whose word I have as firm a reliance as if I had been myself a witness to it."

They reiterated their entreaties; and Ferdinand began in these words:—
"One day, when I was arguing with the friend of whom I am about to make mention, on apparitions and omens, he told me the following story:—

"I had been invited,' said he, 'by one of my college companions, to pass my vacations with him at an estate of his father's. The spring was that year unusually late, owing to a long and severe winter, and appeared in consequence more gay and agreeable, which gave additional charms to our projected pleasures. We arrived at his father's in the pleasant month of April, animated by all the gaiety the season inspired.

"As my companion and I were accustomed to live together at the university, he had recommended to his family, in his letters, so to arrange matters that we might live together at his father's also: we in consequence occupied two adjoining rooms, from whence we enjoyed a view of the garden and a fine country, bounded in the distance by forests and vineyards. In a few days I found myself so completely at home in the house, and so familiarised with its inhabitants, that nobody, whether of the family or among the domesticks, made any difference between my friend and myself. His younger brothers, who were absent from me in the day, often passed the night in my room, or in that of their elder brother. Their sister, a charming girl about twelve years of age, lovely and blooming as a newly blown rose, gave me the appellation of brother, and fancied that under this title she was privileged to shew me all her favourite haunts in the garden, to gratify my wishes at table, and to furnish my apartment with all that was requisite. Her cares and attention will never be effaced from my recollection; they will long outlive the scenes of horror that *château* never ceases to recall to my recollection. From the first of my arrival, I had remarked a huge portrait affixed to the wall of an antechamber through which I was obliged to pass to go to my room; but, too much occupied by the new objects which on all sides attracted my attention, I had not particularly examined it. Meanwhile I could not avoid observing that, though the two younger brothers of my friend were so much attached to me, that they would never permit me to go at night into my room without them, yet they always evinced an unaccountable dread in crossing the hall where this picture hung. They clung to me, and embraced me that I might take them in my arms; and whichever I was compelled to take by the hand, invariably covered his face, in order that he might not see the least trace of the portrait.

"Being aware that the generality of children are afraid of colossal figures, or even of those of a natural height, I endeavoured to give my two young friends courage. However, on more attentively considering the portrait which caused them so much dread, I could not avoid feeling a degree of fear myself. The picture represented a knight in the costume of a very remote period; a full grey mantle descended from his shoulders to his knees; one of his feet placed in the foreground, appeared as if it was starting from the canvass; his countenance had an expression which petrified me with fear. I had never before seen anything at all like it in nature. It was a frightful mixture of the stillness of death, with the remains of a violent and baneful passion, which not even death itself was able to overcome. One would have thought the artist had copied the terrible features of one risen from the grave, in order to paint this terrific portrait. I was seized with a terror little less than the children, whenever I wished to contemplate this picture. Its aspect was disagreeable to my friend, but did not cause him any terror: his sister was the only one who could look at this hideous figure with a smiling countenance; and said to me with a compassionate air, when I discovered my aversion to it, 'That man is not wicked, but he is certainly very unhappy.' My friend told me that the picture represented the founder of his race, and that his father attached uncommon value to it; it had, in all probability, hung there from time immemorial, and it would not be possible to remove it from this chamber without destroying the regularity of its appearance.

"Meanwhile, the term of our vacation was speedily drawing to its close, and time insensibly wore away in the pleasures of the country. The old count, who remarked our reluctance to quit him, his amiable family, his *château*, and the fine country that surrounded it, applied himself with kind and unremitting care, to make the day preceding our departure a continual succession of rustic diversions: each succeeded the other without the slightest appearance of art; they seemed of necessity to follow each other. The delight that illumined the eyes of my friend's sister when she perceived her father's satisfaction; the joy that was painted in Emily's countenance (which was the name of this charming girl) when she surprised even her father by her arrangements, which outstripped his projects, led me to discover the entire confidence that existed between the father and daughter, and the active part Emily had taken in directing the order which reigned in that day's festivities.

"Night arrived; the company in the gardens dispersed; but my amiable companions never quitted my side. The two young boys skipped gaily before us, chasing the may-bug, and shaking the shrubs to make them come out. The dew arose, and aided by the light of the moon formed silver spangles on the flowers and grass. Emily hung on my arm; and an affectionate sister conducted me, as if to take leave, to all the groves and places I had been accustomed to visit with her, or with the family. On arriving at the door of the *château*, I was obliged to repeat the promise I had made to her father, of passing some weeks in the autumn with him. 'That season,' said she, 'is equally beautiful with the spring!' With what pleasure did I promise to decline all other engagements for this. Emily retired to her apartment, and, according to custom, I went up to mine, accompanied by my two little boys: they ran gaily up the stairs; and in crossing the range of apartments but faintly lighted, to my no small surprise their boisterous mirth was not interrupted by the terrible portrait.

"For my own part, my head and heart were full of the intended journey, and of the agreeable manner in which my time had passed at the count's *château*. The images of those happy days crowded on my recollection; my imagination, at that time possessing all the vivacity of youth, was so much agitated, that I could not enjoy the sleep which already overpowered my friend. Emily's image, so interesting by her sprightly grace, by her pure affection for me, was present to my mind like an amiable phantom shining in beauty. I placed myself at the window, to take another look at the country I had so frequently ranged with her, and traced our steps again probably for the last time. I remembered each spot illumined by the pale light the moon afforded. The nightingale was singing in the groves where we had delighted to repose; the little river on which while gaily singing we often sailed, rolled murmuringly her silver waves.

"Absorbed in a profound reverie, I mentally exclaimed: With the flowers of spring, this soft pure peaceful affection will probably fade; and as frequently the after seasons blight the blossoms and destroy the promised fruit, so possibly may the approaching autumn envelop in cold reserve that heart which, at the present moment, appears only to expand with mine!

"Saddened by these reflections, I withdrew from the window, and overcome by a painful agitation I traversed the adjoining rooms; and on a sudden found myself before the portrait of my friend's ancestor. The moon's beams darted on it in the most singular manner possible, insomuch as to give the appearance of a horrible moving spectre; and the reflexion of the light gave to it the appearance of a real substance about to quit the darkness by which it was surrounded. The inanimation of its features appeared to give place to the most profound melancholy; the sad and glazed look of the eyes appeared the only hinderance to its uttering its grief.

"My knees tremblingly knocked against each other, and with an unsteady step I regained my chamber: the window still remained open; I reseated myself at it, in order that the freshness of the night air, and the aspect of the beautiful surrounding country, might dissipate the terror I had experienced. My wandering eyes fixed on a long vista of ancient linden trees, which extended from my window to the ruins of an old tower, which had often been the scene of our pleasures and rural *fêtes*. The remembrance of the hideous portrait had vanished; when on a sudden there appeared to me a thick fog issuing from the ruined tower, which advancing through the vista of lindens came towards me.

"I regarded this cloud with an anxious curiosity: it approached; but again it was concealed by the thickly-spreading branches of the trees.

"On a sudden I perceived, in a spot of the avenue less dark than the rest, the same figure represented in the formidable picture, enveloped in the grey mantle I so well knew. It advanced towards the *château*, as if hesitating: no noise was heard of its footsteps on the pavement; it passed before my window without looking up, and gained a back door which led to the apartments in the colonnade of the *château*.

"Seized with trembling apprehension, I darted towards my bed, and saw with pleasure that the two children were fast asleep on either side. The noise I made awoke them; they started, but in an instant were asleep again. The agitation I had endured took from me the power of sleep, and I turned to awake one of the children to talk with me: but no powers can depict the horrors I endured when I saw the frightful figure at the side of the child's bed.

"I was petrified with horror, and dared neither move nor shut my eyes. I beheld the spectre stoop towards the child and softly kiss his forehead: he then went round the bed, and kissed the forehead of the other boy.

"I lost all recollection at that moment; and the following morning, when the children awoke me with their caresses, I was willing to consider the whole as a dream.

"Meanwhile, the moment for our departure was at hand. We once again breakfasted all together in a grove of lilacs and flowers. 'I advise you to take a little more care of yourself,' said the old count in the midst of other conversation; 'for I last night saw you walking rather late in the garden, in a dress ill suited to the damp air; and I was fearful such imprudence would expose you to cold and fever. Young people are apt to fancy they are invulnerable; but I repeat to you, Take advice from a friend.'

"'In truth,' I answered, 'I believe readily that I have been attacked by a violent fever, for never before was I so harassed by terrifying visions: I can now conceive how dreams afford to a heated imagination subjects for the most extraordinary stories of apparitions.'

"'What would you tell me?' demanded the count in a manner not wholly devoid of agitation. I related to him all that I had seen the preceding night; and to my great surprise he appeared to me in no way astonished, but extremely affected.

"'You say,' added he in a trembling voice, 'that the phantom kissed the two children's foreheads?' I answered him, that it was even so. He then exclaimed, in accents of the deepest despair, 'Oh heavens! they must then both die!'"—

Till now the company had listened without the slightest noise or interruption to Ferdinand: but as he pronounced the last words, the greater part of his audience trembled; and the young lady who had previously occupied the chair on which he sat, uttered a piercing shriek.

"Imagine," continued Ferdinand, "how astonished my friend must have been at this unexpected exclamation. The vision of the night had caused him excess of agitation; but the melancholy voice of the count pierced his heart, and seemed to annihilate his being, by the terrifying conviction of the existence of the spiritual world, and the secret horrors with which this idea was accompanied. It was not then a dream, a chimera, the fruit of an over-heated imagination! but a mysterious and infallible messenger, which, dispatched from the world of spirits, had passed close to him, had placed itself by his couch, and by its fatal kiss had dropt the germ of death in the bosom of the two children.

"He vainly entreated the count to explain this extraordinary event. Equally fruitless were his son's endeavours to obtain from the count the developement of this mystery, which apparently concerned the whole family. 'You are as yet too young,' replied the count: 'too soon, alas! for your peace of mind, will you be informed of these terrible circumstances which you now think mysterious.'

"Just as they came to announce to my friend that all was ready, he recollected that during the recital the count had sent away Emily and her two younger brothers. Deeply agitated, he took leave of the count and the two young children who came towards him, and who would scarcely permit themselves to be separated from him. Emily, who had placed herself at a window, made a sign of adieu. Three days afterwards the young count received news of the death of his two younger brothers. They were both taken off in the same night.

"You see," continued Ferdinand, in a gayer tone, in order to counteract the impression of sadness and melancholy his story had produced on the company; "You see my history is very far from affording any natural explication of the wonders it contains; explanations which only tend to shock one's reason: it does not even make you entirely acquainted with the mysterious person, which one has a right to expect in all marvellous recitals. But I could learn nothing more; and the old count dying without revealing the mystery to his son, I see no other means of terminating the history of the portrait, which is undoubtedly by no means devoid of interest, than by inventing according to one's fancy a *dénouement* which shall explain all."

"That does not appear at all necessary to me," said a young man: "this history, like the one that preceded it, is in reality finished, and gives all the satisfaction one has any right to expect from recitals of this species."

"I should not agree with you," replied Ferdinand, "if I was capable of explaining the mysterious connection between the portrait and the death of the two children in the same night, or the terror of Juliana at sight of the other portrait, and her death, consequently caused by it. I am, however, not the less obliged to you for the entire satisfaction you evince."

"But," resumed the young man, "what benefit would your imagination receive, if the connections of which you speak were known to you?"

"Very great benefit, without doubt," replied Ferdinand; "for imagination requires the completion of the objects it represents, as much as the judgment requires correctness and accuracy in its ideas."

The mistress of the house, not being partial to these metaphysical disputes, took part with Ferdinand: "We ladies," said she, "are always curious; therefore don't wonder that we complain when a story has no termination. It appears to me like seeing the last scene of Mozart's *Don Juan*[*] without having witnessed the preceding ones; and I am sure no one would be the better satisfied, although the last scene should possess infinite merit."

The young man remained silent, perhaps less through conviction than politeness. Several persons were preparing to retire; and Ferdinand, who had vainly searched with all his eyes for the young lady with flaxen hair, was already at the door, when an elderly gentleman, whom he remembered to have seen in the music-room, asked him whether the friend concerning whom he had related the story was not called Count Meltheim?

"That is his name," answered Ferdinand a little drily; "how did you guess it?—are you acquainted with his family?"

"You have advanced nothing but the simple truth," resumed the unknown. "Where is the count at this moment?"

"He is on his travels," replied Ferdinand. "But I am astonished—"

"Do you correspond with him?" demanded the unknown.

"I do," answered Ferdinand. "But I don't understand—"

"Well then," continued the old man, "tell him that Emily still continues to think of him, and that he must return as speedily as possible, if he takes any interest in a secret that very particularly concerns her family."

On this the old man stepped into his carriage, and had vanished from Ferdinand's sight ere he had recovered from his surprise. He looked around him in vain for someone who might inform him of the name of the unknown: everyone was gone; and he was on the point of risking being considered indiscreet, by asking for information of the pastor who had so courteously treated him, when they fastened the door of the house, and he was compelled to return in sadness to his inn, and leave his researches till the morning.

The frightful scenes of the night preceding Ferdinand's departure from the *château* of his friend's father, had tended to weaken the remembrance of Emily; and the distraction which his journey so immediately after had produced, had not contributed to recall it with any force: but all at once the recollection of Emily darted across his mind with fresh vigour, aided by the recital of the previous evening and the old man's conversation: it presented itself even with greater vivacity and strength than at the period of its birth. Ferdinand now fancied that he could trace Emily in the pretty girl with flaxen hair. The more he reflected on her figure, her eyes, the sound of her

---

[*] Usually titled *Don Giovanni*, this classic opera was first performed in 1787.

voice, the grace with which she moved; the more striking the resemblance appeared to him. The piercing shriek that had escaped her, when he mentioned the old count's explication of the phantom's appearance; her sudden disappearance at the termination of the recital; her connection with Ferdinand's family, (for the young lady, in her history of Juliana, had recounted the fatal accident which actually befell Ferdinand's sister,) all gave a degree of certainty to his suppositions.

He passed the night in forming projects and plans, in resolving doubts and difficulties; and Ferdinand impatiently waited for the day which was to enlighten him. He went to the pastor's, whom he found in the midst of his quires of music; and by giving a natural turn to the conversation, he seized the opportunity of enquiring concerning the persons with whom he had passed the preceding evening.

He unfortunately, however, could not get satisfactory answers to his questions concerning the young lady with flaxen hair, and the mysterious old gentleman; for the pastor had been so absorbed in his music, that he had not paid attention to many persons who had visited him: and though Ferdinand in the most minute manner possible described their dress and other particulars, it was impossible to make the pastor comprehend the individuals whose names he was so anxious to learn. "It is unfortunate," said the pastor, "that my wife should be out; she would have given you all the information you desire. But according to your description, it strikes me the young person with flaxen hair must be Mademoiselle de Hainthal;—but—"

"Mademoiselle de Hainthal!" reiterated Ferdinand, somewhat abruptly.

"I think so," replied the clergyman. "Are you acquainted with the young lady?"

"I know her family," answered Ferdinand; "but from her features bearing so strong a resemblance to the family, I thought it might have been the young countess of Wartbourg, who was so much like her brother."

"That is very possible," said the pastor. "You knew then the unfortunate count Wartbourg?"

"Unfortunate!" exclaimed Ferdinand, greatly surprised.

"You don't then know anything," continued the pastor, "of the deplorable event that has recently taken place at the *château* of Wartbourg? The young count, who had probably in his travels seen some beautifully laid-out gardens, was anxious to embellish the lovely country which surrounds his *château*; and as the ruins of an old tower seemed to be an obstacle to his plans, he ordered them to be pulled down. His gardener in vain represented to him, that seen from one of the wings of the *château* they presented, at the termination of a majestic and ancient avenue of linden trees, a magnificent *coup d'œil*, and that they would also give a more romantic appearance to the new parts they were about to form. An old servant, grown grey in the service of his forefathers, supplicated him with tears in his eyes to spare the venerable remains of past ages. They even told him of an ancient tradition, preserved in the neighbourhood, which declared, that the existence of the house of Wartbourg was by supernatural means linked with the preservation of that tower.

"The count, who was a well-informed man, paid no attention to these sayings; indeed they possibly made him the more firmly adhere to his resolution. The workmen were put to their task: the walls, which were constructed of huge masses of rock, for a long while resisted the united efforts of tools and gunpowder; the architect of this place appeared to have built it for eternity.

"At length perseverance and labour brought it down. A piece of the rock separating from the rest, precipitated itself into an opening which had been concealed for ages by rubbish and loose sticks, and fell into a deep cavern. An immense subterranean vault was discovered by the rays of the setting sun, supported by enormous pillars:—but ere they proceeded in their researches, they went to inform the young count of the discovery they had made.

"He came; and being curious to see this dark abode, descended into it with two servants. The first thing they discovered were chains covered with rust, which being fixed in the rock, plainly shewed the use formerly made of the cavern. On another side was a corpse, dressed in female attire of centuries past, which had surprisingly resisted the ravages of time: close to it was extended a human skeleton almost destroyed.

"The two servants related that the young count, on seeing the body, cried in an accent of extreme horror, 'Great God! it is she then whose portrait killed my intended wife.' Saying which, he fell senseless by the body. The shake which his fall occasioned reduced the skeleton to dust.

"They bore the count to his *château*, where the care of the physicians restored him to life; but he did not recover his senses. It is probable that this tragical event was caused by the confined and unwholesome air of the cavern. A very few days after, the count died in a state of total derangement.

"It is singular enough, that the termination of his life should coincide with the destruction of the ruined tower, and there no longer exists any male branch of that family. The deeds relative to the succession, ratified and sealed by the emperor Otho,˙ are still amongst the archives of his house. Their contents have as yet only been transmitted verbally from father to son, as an hereditary secret, which will now, however, be made known. It is also true, that the affianced bride of the count was killed by the portrait's falling on her."

"I yesterday heard that fatal history recited by the lady with flaxen hair," replied Ferdinand.

"It is very possible that young person is the countess Emily," replied the pastor; "for she was the bosom-friend of the unfortunate bride."

"Does not then the countess Emily live at the castle of Wartbourg?" asked Ferdinand.

"Since her brother's death," answered the clergyman, "she has lived with a relation of her mother's at the *château* of Libinfelt, a short distance from hence. For as they yet know not with certainty to whom the castle of Wartbourg will belong, she prudently lives retired."

Ferdinand had learnt sufficient to make him abandon the projected journey to the capital. He thanked the pastor for the instructions he had given him, and was conducted to the *château* where Emily now resided.

It was still broad day when he arrived. The whole journey he was thinking of the amiable figure which he had recognised too late the preceding evening. He recalled to his idea her every word, the sound of her voice, her actions; and what his memory failed to represent, his imagination depicted with all the vivacity of youth, and all the fire of rekindled affection. He already addressed secret reproaches to Emily for not recognising him; as if he had himself remembered her; and in order to ascertain whether his features were entirely effaced from the recollection of her whom he adored, he caused himself to be announced as a stranger, who was anxious to see her on family matters.

While waiting impatiently in the room into which they had conducted him, he discovered among the portraits with which it was decorated, that of the young lady whose features had the over-night charmed him anew: he was contemplating it with rapture when the door opened and Emily entered. She instantly recognised Ferdinand; and in the sweetest accents accosted him as the friend of her youth.

Surprise rendered Ferdinand incapable of answering suitably to so gracious a reception: it was not the charming person with flaxen hair; it was

---

˙ Otho was a Roman emperor who ruled for four months in the late first century C.E.

not a figure corresponding with his imagination, which at this moment presented itself to his view. But it was Emily, shining in every possible beauty, far beyond what Ferdinand had expected: he recollected notwithstanding each feature which had already charmed him, but now clothed in every perfection which nature bestows on her most favoured objects. Ferdinand was lost in thought for some moments: he dared not make mention of his love, and still less did he dare speak of the portrait, and the other wonders of the castle of Wartbourg. Emily spoke only of the happiness she had experienced in her earlier days, and slightly mentioned her brother's death.

As the evening advanced, the young female with flaxen hair came in with the old stranger. Emily presented them both to Ferdinand, as the baron of Hainthal and his daughter Clotilde. They remembered instantly the stranger whom they had seen the preceding evening. Clotilde rallied him on his wish to be *incognito*; and he found himself on a sudden, by a short train of natural events, in the company of the person whom his mother intended for his wife; the object of his affection whom he had just discovered; and the interesting stranger who had promised him an explanation relative to the mysterious portraits.

Their society was soon augmented by the mistress of the *château*, in whom Ferdinand recognised one of those who sat by his side the preceding evening. In consideration for Emily, they omitted all the subjects most interesting to Ferdinand; but after supper the baron drew nearer to him.

"I doubt not," said he to him, "that you are anxious to have some light thrown on events, of which, according to your recital last night, you were a spectator. I knew you from the first; and I knew also, that the story you related as of a friend, was your own history. I cannot, however, inform you of more than I know: but that will perhaps be sufficient to save Emily, for whom I feel the affection of a daughter, from chagrin and uneasiness; and from your recital of last evening, I perceive you take a lively interest concerning her."

"Preserve Emily from uneasiness," replied Ferdinand with warmth; "explain yourself: what is there I ought to do?"

"We cannot," answered the baron, "converse here with propriety; to-morrow morning I will come and see you in your apartment."

Ferdinand asked him for an audience that night; but the baron was inflexible. "It is not my wish," said he, "to work upon your imagination by any marvellous recital, but to converse with you on the very important concerns of two distinguished families. For which reason, I think the freshness of morning will be better suited to lessen the horror that my recital must cause you: therefore, if not inconvenient to you, I wish you to attend me at an early hour in the morning: I am fond of rising with the sun; and yet I have never found the time till mid-day too long for arranging my affairs," added he, smiling, and turning half round towards the rest of the party, as if speaking on indifferent topics.

Ferdinand passed a night of agitation, thinking of the conference he was to have with the baron; who was at his window at dawn of day. "You know," said the baron, "that I married the old count of Wartbourg's sister; which alliance was less the cause, than the consequence, of our intimate friendship. We reciprocally communicated our most secret thoughts, and the one never undertook anything, without the other taking an equal interest with himself in his projects. The count had, however, one secret from me, of which I should never have come at the knowledge but for an accident.

"On a sudden, a report was spread abroad, that the phantom of the Nun's rock had been seen, which was the name given by the peasantry to the old ruined tower which you knew. Persons of sense only laughed at the report: I was anxious the following night to unmask this spectre, and I already anticipated my triumph: but to my no small surprise, the count endeavoured to dissuade me from the attempt; and the more I persisted, the more serious his arguments became; and at length he conjured me in the name of friendship to relinquish the design.

"His gravity of manner excited my attention; I asked him several questions; I even regarded his fears in the light of disease, and urged him to take suitable remedies: but he answered me with an air of chagrin, 'Brother, you know my sincerity towards you; but this is a secret sacred to my family. My son can alone be informed of it, and that only on my death-bed. Therefore ask me no more questions.'

"I held my peace; but I secretly collected all the traditions known amongst the peasantry. The most generally believed one was that the phantom of the Nun's rock was seen when any one of the count's family were about to die; and in effect, in a few days after the count's youngest son expired. The count seemed to apprehend it: he gave the strictest possible charge to the nurse to take care of him; and under pretext of feeling indisposed himself, sent for two physicians to the castle: but these extreme precautions were precisely the cause of the child's death; for the nurse passing over the stones near the ruins, in her extreme care took the child in her arms to carry him, and her foot slipping, she fell, and in her fall wounded the child so much, that he expired on the spot. She said she fancied that she saw the child extended, bleeding in the midst of the stones; that her fright had made her fall with her face on the earth; and that when she came to herself, the child was absolutely lying weltering in his blood, precisely on the same spot where she had seen his ghost.

"I will not tire you with a relation of all the sayings uttered by an illiterate woman to explain the cause of the vision, for under similar accidents invention far outstrips reality. I could not expect to gain much more satisfactory information from the family records; for the principal documents were preserved in an iron chest, the key of which was never out of the possession of the owner of the castle. I however discovered, by the genealogical register and other similar papers, that this family had never had collateral male branches; but further than this, my researches could not discover.

"At length, on my friend's death-bed I obtained some information, which, however, was far from being satisfactory. You remember, that while the son was on his travels, the father was attacked by the complaint which carried him off so suddenly. The evening previous to his decease, he sent for me express, dismissed all those who were with him, and turning towards me, said: 'I am aware that my end is fast approaching, and am the first of my family that has been carried off without communicating to his son the secret on which the safety of our house depends. Swear to me to reveal it only to my son, and I shall die contented.'

"In the names of friendship and honour, I promised what he exacted of me, and he thus began:

"'The origin of my race, as you know, is not to be traced. Ditmar, the first of my ancestry mentioned in the written records, accompanied the emperor Otho to Italy. His history is also very obscure. He had an enemy called count Bruno, whose only son he killed in revenge, according to ancient tradition, and then kept the father confined till his death in that tower, whose ruins, situated in the Nun's rock, still defy the hand of time. That portrait which hangs alone in the state-chamber, is Ditmar's; and if the traditions of the family are to be believed, it was painted by the Dead. In fact, it is almost impossible to believe that any human being could have contemplated sufficiently long to paint the portrait, the outline of features so hideous. My forefathers have frequently tried to plaster over this redoubtable figure; but in the night, the colours came through the plaster, and re-appeared as distinctly as before; and often in the night, this Ditmar has been seen wandering abroad dressed in the garb represented in the picture; and by kissing the descendants of the family, has doomed them to death. Three of my children have received this fatal kiss. It is said, a monk imposed on him this penance in expiation of his crimes. But he cannot destroy all the children of his race: for so long as the ruins of the old tower shall remain, and whilst one stone shall remain on another, so long shall the count de Wartbourg's family exist; and so long shall the spirit of Ditmar wander on earth, and devote to death the branches of his house, without being able to annihilate the trunk. His race will never be extinct; and his punishment will only cease when the ruins of the tower are entirely dispersed. He brought up, with a truly paternal care, the daughter of his enemy, and wedded her to a rich and powerful knight; but notwithstanding this, the monk never remitted his penance. Ditmar, however, foreseeing that one day or other his race would perish, was certainly anxious ere then, to prepare for an event on which his deliverance depended; and accordingly made a relative disposition of his hereditary property, in case of his family becoming extinct. The act which contained his will, was ratified by the emperor Otho: as yet it has not been opened, and nobody knows its contents. It is kept in the secret archives of our house.'

"The speaking thus much was a great effort to my friend. He required a little rest, but was shortly after incapable of articulating a single word. I performed the commission with which he charged me to his son."

"And he did, notwithstanding—" replied Ferdinand.

"Even so," answered the baron: "but judge more favourably of your excellent friend. I have often seen him alone in the great state-chamber, with his eyes fixed on this horrible portrait: he would then go into the other rooms, where the portraits of his ancestors were ranged for several successive generations; and after contemplating them with visible internal emotion, would return to that of the founder of his house. Broken sentences, and frequent soliloquies, which I overheard by accident, did not leave me a shadow of doubt, but that he was the first of his race who had magnanimity of soul sufficient to resolve on liberating the spirit of Ditmar from its penance, and of sacrificing himself to release his house from the malediction that hung over it. Possibly he was strengthened in his resolutions by the grief he experienced for the death of his dearly beloved."

"Oh!" cried Ferdinand deeply affected, "how like my friend!"

"He had, however, in the ardour of his enthusiasm, forgotten to guard his sister's sensibility," said the baron.

"How so?" demanded Ferdinand.

"It is in consequence of this," answered the baron, "that I now address myself to you, and reveal to you the secret. I have told you that Ditmar demonstrated a paternal affection to the daughter of his enemy, had given her a handsome portion, and had married her to a valiant knight. Learn then, that this knight was Adelbert de Meltheim, from whom the counts of this name descended in a direct line."

"Is it possible?" exclaimed Ferdinand, "the author of my race!"

"The same," answered the baron; "and according to appearances, Ditmar designed that the family of Meltheim should succeed him on the extinction of his own. Haste, then, in order to establish your probable right to the—"

"Never—" said Ferdinand "—so long as Emily—"

"This is no more than I expected from you," replied the baron; "but remember, that in Ditmar's time the girls were not thought of in deeds of this kind. Your inconsiderate generosity would be prejudicial to Emily. For the next of kin who lay claim to the fief, do not probably possess very gallant ideas."

"As a relation, though only on the female side, I have taken the necessary measures; and I think it right you should be present at the castle of Wartbourg when the seals are broken, that you may be immediately recognised as the only immediate descendant of Adelbert, and that you may take instant possession of the inheritance."

"And Emily?" demanded Ferdinand.

"As for what is to be done for her," replied the baron, "I leave to you; and feel certain of her being provided for suitably, since her destiny will be in the hands of a man whose birth equals her own, who knows how to appreciate the rank in which she is placed, and who will evince his claims to merit and esteem."

"Have I a right, then," said Ferdinand, "to flatter myself with the hope that Emily will permit me to surrender her the property to which she is actually entitled?"

"Consult Emily on the subject," said the baron.—And here finished the conference.

Ferdinand, delighted, ran to Emily. She answered with the same frankness he had manifested; and they were neither of them slow to confess their mutual passion.

Several days passed in this amiable delirium. The inhabitants of the *château* participated in the joy of the young lovers; and Ferdinand at length wrote to his mother, to announce the choice he had made.

They were occupied in preparations for removing to the castle of Wartbourg, when a letter arrived, which at once destroyed Ferdinand's happiness. His mother refused to consent to his marriage with Emily: her husband having, she said, on his death-bed, insisted on his wedding the baron of Hainthal's daughter, and that she should refuse her consent to any other marriage. He had discovered a family secret, which forced him peremptorily to press this point, on which depended his son's welfare, and the happiness of his family; she had given her promise, and was obliged to maintain it, although much afflicted at being compelled to act contrary to her son's inclinations.

In vain did Ferdinand conjure his mother to change her determination; he declared to her that he would be the last of his race, rather than renounce Emily. She was not displeased with his entreaties, but remained inflexible.

The baron plainly perceived, from Ferdinand's uneasiness and agitation, that his happiness had fled; and as he possessed his entire confidence, he soon became acquainted with the cause of his grief. He wrote in consequence to the countess Meltheim, and expressed his astonishment at the singular disposition the count had made on his death-bed: but all he could obtain from her, was a promise to come to the castle of Wartbourg, to see the female whom she destined for her son, and the one whom he had himself chosen; and probably to elucidate by her arrival so singular and complicated an affair.

Spring was beginning to enliven all nature, when Ferdinand, accompanied by Emily, the baron, and his daughter, arrived at the castle of Wartbourg. The preparations which the principal cause of their journey required, occupied some days. Ferdinand and Emily consoled themselves in the hope that the countess of Meltheim's presence would remove every obstacle which opposed their love, and that at sight of the two lovers she would overcome her scruples.

A few days afterwards she arrived, embraced Emily in the most affectionate manner, and called her, her dear daughter, at the same time expressing her great regret that she could not really consider her such, being obliged to fulfil a promise made to her dying husband.

The baron at length persuaded her to reveal the motive for this singular determination: and after deliberating a short time, she thus expressed herself:—

"The secret you are anxious I should reveal to you, concerns your family, Monsieur le Baron: consequently, if you release me from the necessity of longer silence, I am very willing to abandon my scruples. A fatal picture has, you know, robbed me of my daughter; and my husband, after this melancholy accident, determined on entirely removing this unfortunate portrait: he accordingly gave orders for it to be put in a heap of old furniture, where no one would think of looking for it; and in order to discover the best place to conceal it, he was present when it was taken there. In the removal, he perceived a piece of parchment behind the canvass which the fall had a little damaged: having removed it, he discovered it to be an old document, of a singular nature. The original of this portrait, (said the deed,) was called Bertha de Hainthal; she fixes her looks on her female descendants, in order that if any one of them should receive its death by this portrait, it may prove an expiatory sacrifice which will reconcile her to God. She will then see the families of Hainthal and Meltheim united by the bonds of love; and finding herself released, she will have cause to rejoice in the birth of her after-born descendants.

"This then is the motive which made my husband anxious to fulfil, by the projected marriage, the vows of Bertha; for the death of his daughter, caused by Bertha, had rendered her very name formidable to him. You see, therefore, I have the same reasons for adhering to the promise made my dying husband."

"Did not the count," demanded the baron, "allege any more positive reason for this command?"

"Nothing more, most assuredly," replied the countess.

"Well then," answered the baron, "in case the writing of which you speak should admit of an explanation wholly differing from, but equally clear with, the one attached thereto by the deceased, would you sooner follow the sense than the letter of the writing?"

"There is no doubt on that subject," answered the countess; "for no one is more anxious than myself to see that unfortunate promise set aside."

"Know then," said the baron, "that the corpse of that Bertha, who occasioned the death of your daughter, reposes here at Wartbourg; and that, on this subject, as well as all the other mysteries of the castle, we shall have our doubts satisfied."

The baron would not at this time explain himself further; but said to the countess, that the documents contained in the archives of the castle would afford the necessary information; and recommended that Ferdinand should, with all possible dispatch, hasten everything relative to the succession. Conformable to the baron's wish, it was requisite that, previous to any other research, the secret deeds contained in the archives should be opened. The law commissioners, and the next of kin who were present, who, most likely, promised themselves an ample compensation for their curiosity in the contents of the other parts of the records, were anxious to raise objections; but the baron represented to them, that the secrets of the family appertained to the unknown heir alone, and that consequently no one had a right to become acquainted with them, unless permitted by him.

These reasons produced the proper effect. They followed the baron into the immense vault in which were deposited the family records. They therein discovered an iron chest, which had not been opened for nearly a thousand years. A massive chain, which several times wound round it, was strongly fixed to the floor and to the wall; but the emperor's grand seal was a greater security for this sacred deposit, than all the chains and bolts which guarded it. It was instantly recognised and removed: the strong bolts yielded; and from the chest was taken the old parchment which had resisted the effects of time. This piece contained, as the baron expected, the disposition which confirmed the right of inheritance to the house of Meltheim, in case of the extinction of the house of Wartbourg: and Ferdinand, according to the baron's advice, having in readiness the deeds justifying and acknowledging him as the lawful heir to the house of Meltheim, the next of kin with regret permitted what they could not oppose; and he took possession of the inheritance. The baron having made him a signal, he immediately sealed the chest with his seal. He afterwards entertained the strangers in a splendid manner; and at night found himself in possession of his castle, with only his mother, Emily, the baron, and his daughter.

"It will be but just," said the baron, "to devote this night, which introduces a new name into this castle, to the memory of those who have hitherto possessed it. And we shall acquit ourselves most suitably in this duty, by reading in the council-chamber the documents which, without doubt, are destined to explain, as supplementary deeds, the will of Ditmar."

This arrangement was instantly adopted. The hearts of Emily and Ferdinand were divided between hope and fear; for they impatiently, yet doubtingly, awaited the denouement of Bertha's history, which, after so many successive generations, had in so incomprehensible a manner interfered with their attachment.

The chamber was lighted: Ferdinand opened the iron case; and the baron examined the old parchments.

"This," cried he, after having searched some short time, "will inform us." So saying, he drew from the chest some sheets of parchment. On the one which enveloped the rest was the portrait of a knight of an agreeable figure, and habited in the costume of the tenth century: and the inscription at the bottom called him Ditmar; but they could scarcely discover the slightest resemblance in it to the frightful portrait in the state-chamber.

The baron offered to translate, in reading to them the document written in Latin, provided they would make allowances for the errors which were likely to arise from so hasty a translation. The curiosity of his auditors was so greatly excited, that they readily consented; and he then read as follows:

"I the undersigned Tutilon, monk of St. Gall, have, with the lord Ditmar's consent, written the following narrative: I have omitted nothing, nor written aught of my own accord.

"Being sent for to Metz, to carve in stone the image of the Virgin Mary; and that mother of our blessed Saviour having opened my eyes and directed my hands, so that I could contemplate her celestial countenance, and represent it on stone to be worshipped by true believers, the lord Ditmar discovered me, and engaged me to follow him to his castle, in order that I might execute his portrait for his descendants. I began painting it in the state-chamber of his castle; and on returning the following day to resume my task, I found that a strange hand had been at work, and had given to the portrait quite a different countenance, which was horrible to look at, for it resembled one who had risen from the dead. I trembled with terror: however, I effaced these hideous features, and I painted anew the count Ditmar's figure, according to my recollection; but the following day I again discovered the nocturnal labour of the stranger hand. I was seized with still greater fear, but resolved to watch during the night; and I recommenced painting the knight's figure, such as it really was. At midnight I took a torch, and advancing softly into the chamber to examine the portrait, I perceived a spectre resembling the skeleton of a child; it held a pencil, and was endeavouring to give Ditmar's image the hideous features of death.

"On my entering, the spectre slowly turned its head towards me, that I might see its frightful visage. My terror became extreme: I advanced no further, but retired to my room, where I remained in prayer till morning; for I was unwilling to interrupt the work executed in the dead of night. In the morning, discovering the same strange features in Ditmar's portrait as that of the two preceding mornings, I did not again risk effacing the work of the nightly painter; but went in search of the knight, and related to him what I had seen. I shewed him the picture. He trembled with horror, and confessed his crimes to me, for which he required absolution. Having for three successive days invoked all the saints to my assistance, I imposed on him as a penance for the murder of his enemy, which he had avowed to me, to submit to the most rigid mortifications in a dungeon during the rest of his life. But I told him, that as he had murdered an innocent child, his spirit would never be at rest till it had witnessed the extermination of his race; for the Almighty would punish the death of that child by the death of the children of Ditmar, who, with the exception of one in each generation, would all be carried off in early life; and as for him, his spirit would wander during the night, resembling the portrait painted by the hand of the skeleton child; and that he would condemn to death, by a kiss, the children who were the sacrifices to his crimes, in the same manner as he had given one to his enemy's child before he killed it: and that, in fine, his race should not become extinct, so long as stone remained on stone in the tower where he had permitted his enemy to die of hunger. I then gave him absolution. He immediately made over his seigniory to his son; and married the daughter of his enemy, who had been brought up by him, to the brave knight Sir Adalbert. He bequeathed all his property, in case of his race becoming extinct, to this knight's descendants, and caused this will to be ratified by the emperor Otho. After having done so, he retired to a cave near the tower, where his corpse is interred; for he died like a pious recluse, and expiated his crimes by extreme penance. As soon as he was laid in his coffin, he resembled the portrait in the state-chamber; but during his life he was like the portrait depicted on this parchment, which I was able to paint without interruption, after having given him absolution: and by his command I have written and signed this document since his death; and I deposit it, with the emperor's letters patent, in an iron chest, which I have caused to be sealed. I pray God speedily to deliver his soul, and to cause his body to rise from the dead to everlasting felicity!"

"He is delivered," cried Emily, greatly affected; "and his image will no longer spread terror around. But I confess that the sight of that figure, and even that of the frightful portrait itself, would never have led me to dream of such horrible crimes as the monk Tutilon relates. Certain I am, his enemy must have mortally wounded his happiness, or he undoubtedly would have been incapable of committing such frightful crimes."

"Possibly," said the baron, continuing his researches, "we shall discover some explanation on that point."

"We must also find some respecting Bertha," replied Ferdinand in a low tone, and casting a timid look on Emily and his mother.

"This night," answered the baron, "is consecrated to the memory of the dead; let us therefore forget our own concerns, since those of the past call our attention."

"Assuredly," exclaimed Emily, "the unfortunate person who secured these sheets in the chest, ardently looked forward to the hope of their coming to light; let us therefore delay it no longer."

The baron, after having examined several, read aloud these words:

"The confession of Ditmar." And he continued thus:—"Peace and health. When this sheet is drawn from the obscurity in which it is now buried, my soul will, I hope firmly in God and the saints, be at eternal rest and peace. But for your good I have ordered to be committed to paper the cause of my chastisement, in order that you may learn that vengeance belongs to God alone, and not to men; for the most just amongst them knows not how to judge: and again, that you may not in your heart condemn me, but rather that you may pity me; for my misery has nearly equaled my crimes; and my spirit would never have dreamt of evil, if man had not rent my heart."

"How justly," exclaimed Ferdinand, "has Emily's good sense divined thus much!"

The baron continued: "My name is Ditmar; they surnamed me The Rich, though I was then only a poor knight, and my only possession was a very small castle. When the emperor Otho departed for Italy, whither he was called by the beautiful Adelaide to receive her hand, I followed him; and I gained the affection of the most charming woman in Pavia, whom I conducted as my intended spouse to the castle of my forefathers. Already the day appointed for the celebration of my nuptials was at hand: the emperor sent for me. His favourite, the count Bruno de Hainthal had seen Bertha—"

"Bertha!" exclaimed everyone present. But the baron, without permitting them to interrupt him, continued his translation.

"One day, when the emperor had promised to grant him any recompence that he thought his services merited, he asked of him my intended bride. Otho was mute with astonishment;—but his imperial word was given. I presented myself before the emperor, who offered me riches, lands, honours, if I would but consent to yield Bertha to the count: but she was dearer to me than every worldly good. The emperor yielded to a torrent of anger: he carried off my intended bride by force, ordered my castle to be pulled down, and caused me to be thrown into prison.

"I cursed his power and my destiny. The amiable figure of Bertha, however, appeared to me in a dream; and I consoled myself during the day by the sweet illusions of the night. At length my keeper said to me: 'I pity you, Ditmar; you suffer in a prison for your fidelity, while Bertha abandons you. To-morrow she weds the count: accede then to the emperor's wish, ere it be too late; and ask of him what you think fit, as a recompence for the loss of the faithless fair.' These words froze my heart. The following night, instead of the gracious image of Bertha, the frightful spirit of vengeance presented itself to me. The following morning I said to my keeper: Go and tell the emperor, I yield Bertha to his Bruno; but as a recompence, I demand this tower, and as much land as will be requisite to build me a new castle.' The emperor was satisfied; for he frequently repented his violent passions, but he could not alter what he had already decided. He therefore gave me the tower in which I had been confined, and all the lands around it for the space of four leagues. He also gave me more gold and silver than was sufficient to build a castle much more magnificent than the one he had caused to be pulled down. I took unto myself a wife, in order to perpetuate my race; but Bertha still reigned sole mistress of my heart. I also built myself a castle, from which I made a communication, by subterranean and secret passages, with my former prison the tower, and with the castle of Bruno, the residence of my mortal enemy. As soon as the edifice was completed, I entered the fortress by the secret passage, and appeared as the spirit of one of his ancestors before the bed of his son, the heir with which Bertha had presented him. The women who lay beside him were seized with fear: I leaned over the child, who was the precise image of its mother, and kissed its forehead; but—it was the kiss of death; it carried with it a secret poison.

"Bruno and Bertha acknowledged the vengeance of Heaven: they received it as a punishment for the wrongs they had occasioned me; and they devoted their first child to the service of God. As it was a girl, I spared it: but Bertha had no more children; and Bruno, irritated to find his race so nearly annihilated, repudiated his wife, as if he repented the injustice of which he had been guilty in taking her, and married another. The unfortunate Bertha took refuge in a monastery, and consecrated herself to Heaven: but her reason fled; and one night she quitted her retreat, came to the tower in which I had been confined in consequence of her perfidy, there bewailed her crime, and there grief terminated her existence; which circumstance gave rise to that tower being called the Nun's Rock. I heard, during the night, her sobs; and ongoing to the tower found Bertha extended motionless; the dews of night had seized her:—she was dead. I then resolved to avenge her loss. I placed her corpse in a deep vault beneath the tower; and having by means of my subterranean passage discovered all the count's movements, I attacked him when unguarded; and dragging him to the vault which contained his wife's corpse, I there abandoned him. The emperor, irritated against him for having divorced Bertha, gave me all his possessions, as a remuneration for the injustice I had heretofore experienced.

"I caused all the subterranean passages to be closed. I took under my care his daughter Hildegarde, and brought her up as my child: she loved the count Adalbert de Meltheim. But one night her mother's ghost appeared to her, and reminded her that she was consecrated to the Almighty: this vision, however, could not deter her from marrying Adalbert. The night of her marriage the phantom appeared again before her bed, and thus addressed her:

"'Since you have infringed the vow I made, my spirit can never be at rest, till one of your female descendants receives its death from me.'

"This discourse occasioned me to send for the venerable Tutilon, monk of St. Gall, who was very celebrated, in order that he might paint a portrait of Bertha, as she had painted herself in the monastery during her insanity; and I gave it to her daughter.

"Tutilon concealed behind that portrait a writing on parchment, the contents of which were as follows:

"'I am Bertha; and I look at my daughters, to see whether one of them will not die for me, in expiation of my crimes, and thus reconcile me to God. Then shall I see the two families of Meltheim and Hainthal reunited by love, and in the birth of their descendants I shall enjoy happiness.'"

"This then," exclaimed Ferdinand, "is the fatal writing that is to separate me from Emily; but which, in fact, only unites me to her more firmly! and Bertha, delivered from her penance, blesses the alliance; for by my marriage with Emily, the descendants of Bertha and Ditmar will be reunited."

"Do you think," demanded the baron of the countess, "that this explanation can admit of the slightest doubt?"

The only answer the countess made, was by embracing Emily, and placing her hand in that of her son.

The joy was universal. Clotilde in particular had an air of extreme delight; and her father several times, in a jocular manner, scolded her for expressing her joy so vehemently. The following morning they removed the seals from the state-chamber, in order to contemplate the horrible portrait with somewhat less of sadness than heretofore: but they found that it had faded in a singular manner, and the colours, which formerly appeared so harsh, had blended and become softened.

Shortly after arrived the young man who was anxious to enter into an argument with Ferdinand on the explication of the mysteries relative to the portraits. Clotilde did not conceal that he was far from indifferent to her; and they discovered the joy she had evinced, in discovering the favourable turn Emily's attachment had taken, was not altogether disinterested, but occasioned by the prospect it afforded of happiness to herself. Her father, in fact, would never have approved her choice, had not the countess Meltheim removed all pretensions to Clotilde.

"But," asked Ferdinand of Clotilde's intended, "do you not forgive our having searched into certain mysteries which concerned us?"

"Completely," he answered; "but not less disinterestedly than formerly, when I maintained a contrary opinion. I ought now to confess to you, that I was present at the fatal accident which caused your sister's death, and that I then discovered the writing concealed behind the portrait. I naturally explained it as your father did afterwards; but I held my peace; for the consequences have brought to light what the discovery of that writing had caused me to apprehend for my love."

"Unsatisfactory explanations are bad," replied Ferdinand, laughing.

The happy issue of these discoveries spread universal joy amongst the inhabitants of the castle, which was in some degree heightened by the beauty of the season. The lovers were anxious to celebrate their marriage ere the fall of the leaf. And when next the primrose's return announced the approach of spring, Emily gave birth to a charming boy.

Ferdinand's mother, Clotilde and her husband, and all the friends of the family, among whom were the pastor who was so fond of music, and his pretty little wife, assembled at the *fête* given in honour of the christening. When the priest who was performing the ceremony asked what name he was to give the child, that of Ditmar was uttered by every mouth, as if they had previously agreed on it. The christening over, Ferdinand, elate with joy, accompanied by his relations and guests, carried his son to the state-chamber, before his forefather's portrait; but it was no longer perceptible; the colours, figure,—all had disappeared; not the slightest trace remained.

The Family Portraits, by Edward Vernon Utterson. (Watercolor illustration painted in homage to the story in *Tales of the Dead,* 1813.)

Memento Mori, by Hendrik Hondius (1626).

III.

THE DEATH'S HEAD

BY FRIEDRICH LAUN[*]

(TRANSLATED INTO ENGLISH BY
SARAH ELIZABETH UTTERSON)

——"What guilt
Can equal violations of the dead?
The dead how sacred!"——
—YOUNG'S NIGHT THOUGHTS.[†]

THE beauty of the evening which succeeded to a very sultry day tempted colonel Kielholm to sit, surrounded by his little family, on the stone bench placed before the door of the noble mansion he had recently purchased. In order to become acquainted by degrees with his new tenants, he took pleasure in questioning on their occupations and conditions the greater part of those who passed by; he alleviated their little sufferings by his advice as well as by his bounty. His family enjoyed particular pleasure in seeing the little inn situated in front of the *château*, which, instead of presenting a disgusting object, as when the late owner lived there, became each succeeding day better and more orderly. Their pleasure was heightened from the circumstance that the new landlord, who had been many years a servant in the family, was loud in praises of its amended condition, and delighted himself in his new calling, with the idea of the happy prospects it held forth to himself, his wife, and children.

---

[*] Friedrich August Schulze (1770–1849) was a prolific and popular German novelist who wrote under the penname "Friedrich Laun." He co-edited an anthology of ghost stories with Johann August Apel.
[†] From poem "The Complaint: or, Night-Thoughts on Life, Death, & Immortality," better known simply as "Night-Thoughts," by Edward Young, written between 1742–1745.

Formerly, though the road was greatly frequented, nobody ventured to pass a night at this inn; but now each day there was a succession of travellers; carriages were constantly seen at the door or in the court-yard; and the air of general satisfaction of each party as they proceeded on their route, incontestably proved to the landlord, (who always, hat in hand, was at the door of their carriages as they drove off,) that his efforts to give the various travellers satisfaction were completely successful.

A moving scene of this nature had just disappeared, which furnished conversation for the moment, when a whimsical equipage, which arrived from another quarter, attracted the attention of the colonel and his family. A long carriage, loaded with trunks and all sorts of luggage, and drawn by two horses, whose form and colour presented the most grotesque contrast imaginable, but which in point of meagreness were an excellent match, was succeeded by a second long and large vehicle, which they had, most probably at the expense of the adjacent forest, converted into a travelling thicket. The four steeds which drew it, did not in any respect make a better appearance than the two preceding. But the colonel and his family were still more struck by the individuals who filled this second carriage: it was a strange medley of children and grown persons, closely wedged together; but not one of their countenances bore the slightest mark of similarity of ideas. Discontent, aversion, and hatred, were legible in the face of each of these sun-burnt strangers. It was not a family, but a collection of individuals which fear or necessity kept together without uniting.

The colonel's penetrating eye led him to discover thus much, though the distance was considerable. He at length saw descend from the back part of the carriage a man of better appearance than the others. At something which he said, the whole troop turned their eyes towards the inn; they assumed an air of greater content, and appeared a little better satisfied.

The first carriage had already stopped at the door of the inn, while the second was passing the *château*; and the extremely humble salutations from the passengers in the latter, seemed to claim the good-will of the colonel and his family.

The second carriage had scarcely stopped, ere the troop were out of it, each appearing anxious to quit those next to whom they had been sitting with all possible speed. The spruce and agile manner in which they leapt out of the vehicle, left no doubt on the mind what their profession was,—they could be none other than rope-dancers.[*]

---

[*] This likely means high-wire walkers, either on a tightrope or slack rope—in other words, a small circus, possibly a band of gypsies.

The colonel remarked, that "notwithstanding the humble salutations they had made, he did not think they would exhibit in these parts; but according to appearances they would proceed to the capital with all possible dispatch; as it was hardly to be expected that they would be delayed a single day, by the very trivial profit to be expected from exhibiting in a mere country village."

"We have," said he, "seen the worst side of these gentry, without the probability of ascertaining whether they have anything to recommend them to our notice."

His wife was on the point of expressing her dislike to all those tricks which endanger the neck, when the person whom they had observed as being superior to the rest, advanced towards them, and after making a low bow, asked permission to remain there a few days. The colonel was unable to refuse this request, as he shewed him a passport properly signed.

"I beg you," replied the colonel, "to declare most positively to your company, that every equivocal action is punished in my villages; as I am anxious to avoid all possibility of quarrels."

"Do not in the least alarm yourself, Monsieur; an extremely severe discipline is kept up in my troop, which has in some respects the effect of a secret police among ourselves: all can answer for one, and one can answer for all. Each is bound to communicate any misconduct on the part of another to me, and is always rewarded for such communication; but, on the contrary, if he omits so to do, he is severely punished."

The colonel's lady could not conceal her aversion to such a barbarous regulation; which the stranger perceiving, shrugged his shoulders.

"We must all accommodate our ideas to our condition. I have found, that if persons of this stamp are not so treated, there is no possibility of governing them. And you may the more confidently rely on my vigilance, as I had the happiness of being born in this place, and in consequence feel a double obligation: first, to the place of my birth; secondly, to his worship."

"Were you born here?" demanded the colonel's wife with surprise.

"Yes, my lady; my father was Schurster the schoolmaster, who died lately. But I call myself Calzolaro, finding that my profession succeeds better under an Italian than a German name."

This explanation redoubled the interest the colonel and his lady already felt for this man, who appeared to have received a tolerable education. They knew that the schoolmaster, whose profession had been pretty lucrative, owing to the numerous population of the village, had died worth some considerable property; but that he had named a distant female relation as his sole heiress, leaving his only son an extremely scanty pittance.

"My father," continued Calzolaro, "did not behave to me as he ought: and I cannot but think I should be justified in availing myself of some important informalities in his will, and endeavouring to set it aside, which is my present intention. But excuse, I pray you, my having tired your patience with relations to which the conversation has involuntarily given rise. I have still one more request to make: Permit me to return you my best thanks for your gracious condescension, and to shew you some of the exercises for which my troop is famous."

The colonel acceded to Calzolaro's request, and a day was fixed for the performance.

Calzolaro went that very evening to the village pastor, and communicated to him his intentions relative to his father's will. The worthy minister condemned such procedure, and endeavoured to convince Calzolaro that his father's anger was just. "Picture to yourself, young man," said he, "a father who has grown old in an honest profession, and who rejoices in having a son to whom he can leave it: added to which, this son has great talents, a good understanding, and is well-disposed. It was natural that the father should use every possible exertion to obtain for this son his own situation at his death. The son is in truth nominated to succeed him. The father, thinking himself secure from misfortune, feels quite happy. It was at this period that the son, enticed by hair-brained companions, gave up a certain and respectable, though not very brilliant provision. My dear Schurster, if, when shaking off the salutary yoke, and quitting your venerable father, to ramble over the world, you could lightly forget the misery it would occasion him, you ought at least in the present instance to behave differently; or, in plain terms, I shall say you are a good-for-nothing fellow. Did not your father, even after this, do all he could to reclaim you? but you were deaf to his remonstrances."

"Because the connection which I had formed imposed obligations on me, from which I could not free myself, as from a garment of which one is tired. For had I then been my own master, as I now am—"

"Here let us stop, if you please: I have only one request to make of you. You ought, from respect to your father's memory, not to dispute his will."

This conversation and the venerable air of the pastor had somewhat shaken Calzolaro's resolutions: but the next day they returned with double force; for he heard several persons say, that shortly before his death, his father was heard to speak of him with great bitterness.

This discourse rendered him so indignant, that he would not even accede to a proposal of accommodation with the heiress, made to him by the pastor.

The colonel tried equally, but without success, to become a mediator, and at length determined to let the matter take its course.

He however assisted at the rehearsals made by the troop; and took so much pleasure in the performances prepared for the amusement of him and his family by Calzolaro, that he engaged him to act again, and invited several of his neighbours to witness them.

Calzolaro said to him on this occasion: "You have as yet seen very trifling proofs of our abilities. But do not fancy that I am an idle spectator, and merely stand by to criticize: I, as well as each individual of my troop, have a sphere of action; and I reserve myself to give you, before we take our leave, some entertaining experiments in electricity and magnetism."

The colonel then told him, that he had recently seen in the capital a man who exhibited experiments of that sort, which had greatly delighted him; and above all, he had been singularly astonished by his powers of ventriloquism.

"It is precisely in that particular point," replied Calzolaro, "that I think myself equal to anyone, be they whom they may."

"I am very glad of it," answered the colonel. "But what would produce the most astonishing effect on those who have never heard a ventriloquist, would be a dialogue between the actor and a death's head:—the man of whom I made mention gave us one."

"If you command it, I can undertake it."

"Delightful!" exclaimed the colonel. And Calzolaro having given some unequivocal proofs of his powers as a ventriloquist, the colonel added: "The horror of the scene must be augmented by every possible means: for instance, we must hang the room with black; the lights must be extinguished; we must fix on midnight. It will be a species of phantasmagoria dessert after supper; an unexpected spectacle. We must contrive to throw the audience into a cold perspiration, in order that when the explanation takes place they may have ample reason to laugh at their fears. For if all succeeds, no one will be exempt from a certain degree of terror."

Calzolaro entered into the project, and promised that nothing should be neglected to make it successful. They unfurnished a closet, and hung it with black.

The colonel's wife was the only one admitted to their confidence, as they could rely on her discretion. Her husband had even a little altercation on the subject with her. She wished, that for the ventriloquist scene they should use the model of a head in plaster, which her son used to draw from; whereas the colonel maintained that they must have a real skull: "Otherwise," said he, "the spectators' illusion will speedily be at an end; but after they have heard the death's head speak, we will cause it to be handed round, in order to convince them that it is in truth but a skull."

"And where can we procure this skull?" asked the colonel's wife.

"The sexton will undertake to provide us with it."

"And whose corpse will you thus disturb, for a frivolous amusement?"

"How sentimental you are!" replied Kielholm, who did not consider the subject in so serious a light: "We may easily see you are not accustomed to the field of battle, where no further respect is paid to the repose of the dead, than suits the convenience of the labourer in the fields where they are buried."

"God preserve me from such a spectacle!" exclaimed the colonel's lady in quitting them, when she perceived her husband was insensible to her representations.

According to the orders which he received, the sexton one night brought a skull in good preservation.

The morning of the day destined for the representation, Calzolaro went into the adjacent forest to rehearse the dialogue which he was to have with the death's head. He considered in what way to place the head, so as to avoid all suspicion of the answers given by it being uttered by a person concealed. In the meanwhile the pastor arrived at the spot from a neighbouring hamlet, where he had been called to attend a dying person: and believing that the interposition of Providence was visible in this accidental meeting, the good man stopped, in order once again to exhort Calzolaro to agree to an accommodation with the heiress.

"I yesterday," said he, "received a letter from her, in which she declares that, rather than any disrespect should be paid to your father's last will and testament, she will give up to you half the inheritance to which she is thereby entitled. Ought you not to prefer this to a process at law, the issue of which is doubtful, and which at all events will never do you credit?"

Calzolaro persisted in declaring that the law should decide between him and the testator.—The poor young man was not in a state to see in a proper point of view his father's conduct towards him.—The pastor, finding all his representations and entreaties fruitless, left him. Calzolaro proceeded slowly to the inn, to assign to each of his band their particular part. He told them that he should not be with them; but notwithstanding he should have an eye over their conduct. He was not willing to appear as the manager of these mountebanks, to the party assembled at the colonel's, thinking that if he appeared for the first time in the midnight scene, as an entire stranger, it would add still more to the marvellous.

The tumblers' tricks and rope-dancing were performed to admiration. And those of the spectators whose constant residence in the country prevented their having witnessed similar feats, were the most inclined to admire and praise the agility of the troop. The little children in particular were applauded. The compassion excited by their unhappy destiny, mingled with the approbation bestowed on them; and the ladies were subjects of envy, in giving birth to the satisfaction depicted in the countenances of these little wretches by their liberal donations.

The agility of the troop formed the subject of general conversation the whole afternoon. They were even speaking in their praise after supper, when the master of the house said to the company assembled:

"I am rejoiced, my dear friends, to see the pleasure you have received from the little spectacle that I have been enabled to give you. My joy is so much the greater, since I find you doubting the possibility of things which are very natural; for I have it in my power to submit for your examination something of a very incomprehensible nature. At this very moment I have in my house a person who entertains a most singular intercourse with the world of spirits, and who can compel the dead to answer his questions."

"O!" exclaimed a lady smiling, "don't terrify us."

"You jest *now*," replied the colonel; "but I venture to affirm your mirth will be a little changed when the scene takes place."

"I accept the challenge," answered the incredulous fair one. All the party was of her opinion, and declared themselves so openly and so loudly against the truth of these terrific scenes, that the colonel began to be really apprehensive for the effects likely to be produced by those he had prepared. He would have even relinquished his project, if his guests, one and all, had not intreated him to the contrary. They even went further: they besought him not long to delay the wonderful things he promised. But the colonel, keeping his own counsel, feigned ignorance that they were laughing at him; and with a grave air declared that the experiment could not take place till midnight.

The clock at length struck twelve. The colonel gave his servants orders to place chairs facing the door of a closet which had been hitherto kept shut: he invited the company to sit down, and gave orders for all the lights to be put out. While these preparations were making, he thus addressed the company:

"I entreat you, my friends, to abstain from all idle curiosity." The grave and solemn tone in which he uttered these words made a deep impression on the party, whose incredulity was not a little lessened by the striking of the clock, and the putting out the lights one after the other. Presently they heard from the closet facing them the hoarse and singular sounds by which it is pretended spirits are conjured up; and which were interrupted at intervals by loud strokes of a hammer. All on a sudden the door of the closet opened: and as by slow degrees the cloud of incense which filled it evaporated, they gradually discovered the black trappings with which it was hung, and an altar in the middle also hung with black drapery. On this altar was placed a skull, which cast its terrifying regards on all the company present.

Meanwhile the spectators' breathing became more audible and difficult, and their embarrassment increased in proportion as the vapour gave place to a brilliant light issuing from an alabaster lamp suspended from the ceiling. Many of them indeed turned their heads away in alarm on hearing a noise behind them; which, however, they discovered simply proceeded from some of the servants, whom the colonel had given permission to be present during the exhibition, at a respectful distance.

After a moment of profound silence, Calzolaro entered. A long beard had so effectually altered his youthful appearance, that though several of the spectators had previously seen him, they could not possibly recognize him under this disguise. And his Oriental costume added so much to the deceit, that his entrance had an excellent effect.

In order that his art should impose the more, the colonel recommended to him a degree of haughtiness in addressing the company; and that he should not salute them according to any prescribed forms of politeness, but to announce himself in terms foreign from all ordinary modes of conversation. They both agreed that a mysterious jargon would best answer their purpose.

In consequence of such determination, Calzolaro, assuming a deep sepulchral tone, thus began: "After our present state of existence, we are swallowed up in the obscure abyss which we call death, in order that we may become incorporated in an entirely new and peaceful state. It is in order to emancipate the soul from this state, that the sublime arts are exercised; and to create among fools and weak persons the idea of its being impossible! The wise and learned pity them for their ignorance, in not knowing what is possible and impossible, true or false, light or dark; because they do not know and cannot comprehend the exalted spirits, who, from the silence of the vault and the grave, from the mouldering bones of the dead, speak to the living in a voice no less formidable than true. As to you, who are now here assembled, listen to a word of advice: Avoid provoking by any indiscreet question the vengeance of the spirit, who at my command will be invisibly stationed beneath this human skull. Endeavour to moderate your fear: listen to everything with calmness and submission; for I take under my especial care all those who are obedient, and only leave the guilty as a prey to the destruction they merit."

The colonel remarked with secret satisfaction the impression produced on the company, hitherto so incredulous, by this pompous harangue.

"Everything succeeds better than I could have hoped," said he, in an undertone to his wife, who was not at all amused by the performance, and who was only present to please her husband.

Meanwhile Calzolaro continued: "Look on this pitiful and neglected head: my magic art has removed the bolts of the tomb to which it was consigned, and in which reposes a long line of princes. The owner of it is now actually there, rendering up to the spirits an exact account of the life he had led. Don't be alarmed, even though it should burst forth in terrible menaces against you: and against me his impotency will be manifest, as, spite of his former grandeur, he cannot resist the power I have over him, provided no culpable precipitation on your part interrupt the solemnity of my questions."

He then opened a door of the closet hitherto concealed from the company, brought a chafing-dish filled with red-hot coals, threw thereon some incense, and walked three times round the altar, pronouncing at each circle a spell. He then drew from its scabbard a sword which hung in his girdle, plunged it in the smoke issuing from the incense, and making frightful contortions of his face and limbs, pretended to endeavour to cleave the head, which, however, he did not touch. At last he took the head up on the point of his sword, held it up in the air before him, and advanced towards the spectators a little moved.

"Who art thou, miserable dust, that I hold at the point of my sword?" demanded Calzolaro with a confident air and a firm voice.—But scarcely had he uttered this question, when he turned pale; his arm trembled; his knees shook; his haggard eyes, which were fixed on the head, were horror-struck: he had hardly strength sufficient to place the head and the sword on the altar, ere he suddenly fell on the floor with every symptom of extreme terror.

The spectators, frightened out of their wits, looked at the master of the house, who in his turn looked at them. No one seemed to know whether this was to be considered part of the scene, nor whether it was possible to explain it. The curiosity of the audience was raised to its utmost pitch: they waited still a considerable time, but no explanation took place. At length Calzolaro, half-raising himself, asked if his father's shadow had disappeared.

Stupefaction succeeded astonishment. The colonel was anxious to know whether he was still attempting to impose on the company by a pretended dialogue with the death's head?

Calzolaro answered that he would do anything, and that he would willingly submit to any punishment they chose to inflict on him for his frightful crime: but he entreated they would instantly carry back the head to its place of repose.

His countenance had undergone a complete change, and only resumed its wonted appearance on the colonel's wife acquiescing in his wish: she ordered the head to be instantly conveyed to the church-yard, and to be replaced in the grave.

During this unexpected denouement, every eye was turned on Calzolaro; he, who not long ago was talking with so much emphasis and in such a lofty strain, could now scarcely draw his breath; and from time to time threw supplicating looks on the spectators, as if entreating them to wait patiently till he had recovered strength sufficient to continue his performance.

The colonel informed them in the meanwhile of the species of jest that he had projected to play on them, and for the failure of which he could not at that moment account. At last Calzolaro, with an abashed air, spoke as follows:—

"The spectacle which I designed to have given, has terminated in a terrible manner for me. But, happily for the honourable company present, I perceive they did not see the frightful apparition which caused me a temporary privation of my reason. Scarcely had I raised the death's head on the point of my sword, and had begun to address it, than it appeared to me in my father's features: and whether my ears deceived me or not, I am ignorant; neither do I know how I was restored to my senses; but I heard it say, 'Tremble, parricide, whom nothing can convert, and who wilt not turn to the path thou hast abandoned!'"

The very recollection produced such horror on Calzolaro's mind as to stop his respiration and prevent his proceeding. The colonel briefly explained to the spectators what appeared to them mysterious in his words, and then said to the penitent juggler:

"Since your imagination has played you so strange a trick, I exhort you in future to avoid all similar accidents, and to accept the arrangement proposed to you by the person whom your father has named as his heir."

"No, monsieur," answered he, "no agreement, no bargain; else I shall only half fulfil my duty. Everything shall belong to this heiress, and the lawsuit shall be abandoned."

He at the same time declared that he was weary of the mode of life he had adopted, and that every wish of his father's should be fulfilled.

The colonel told him that such a resolution compensated for what had failed in the evening's amusement.

The company, however, did not cease making numberless inquiries of Calzolaro, many of which were very ludicrous. They were anxious to know, among other things, whether the head which had appeared to him, resembled that of a corpse or a living being.

"It most probably belongs to a corpse," he replied. "I was so thunderstruck with the horrible effect of it, that I cannot remember minutiæ. Imagine an only son, with the point of a sword which he holds in his hand, piercing his father's skull! The bare idea is sufficient to deprive one of one's senses."

"I did not believe," answered the colonel, after having for some time considered Calzolaro, "that the conscience of a man, who like you has rambled the world over, could still be so much overcome by the powers of imagination."

"What! monsieur, do you still doubt the reality of the apparition, though I am ready to attest it by the most sacred oaths?"

"Your assertion contradicts itself. We have also our eyes to see what really exists; and nobody, excepting yourself, saw any other than a simple skull."

"That is what I cannot explain: but this I can add, that I am firmly persuaded, although even now I cannot account for my so thinking, that as sure as I exist, that head is actually and truly the head of my father: I am ready to attest it by my most solemn oath."

"To prevent your perjuring yourself, they shall instantly go to the sexton, and learn the truth."

Saying this, the colonel went out to give the necessary orders. He returned an instant afterwards, saying:—

"Here is another strange phænomenon. The sexton is in this house, but is not able to answer my questions. Anxious to enjoy the spectacle I was giving my friends, he mixed with some of my servants, who, possessing the same degree of curiosity, had softly opened the door through which the chaffing-dish was conveyed. But at the moment of the conjurer falling on the floor, the same insensibility overcame the sexton; who even now has not recovered his reason, although they have used every possible method to restore him."

One of the party said, that, being subject to fainting himself, he constantly carried about him a liquor, the effect of which was wonderful in such cases, and that he would go and try it now on the sexton. They all followed him: but this did not succeed better than the methods previously resorted to.

"This man must indeed be dead," said the person who had used the liquor without effect on him.

The clock in the tower had just struck one, and every person thought of retiring; but slight symptoms of returning life being perceptible in the sexton, they still remained.

"God be praised!" exclaimed the sexton awaking; "he is at length restored to rest!"

"Who, old dad?" said the colonel.

"Our late schoolmaster."

"What then, that head was actually his?"

"Alas! if you will only promise not to be angry with me, I will confess— It was his."

The colonel then asked him how the idea of disturbing the schoolmaster's corpse in particular came into his head.

"Owing to a diabolical boldness. It is commonly believed, that when a child speaks to the head of its deceased parent at the midnight hour, the head comes to life again. I was anxious to prove the fact, but shall never recover from its effects: happily, however, the head is actually restored to rest."

They asked him how he knew it. He answered, that he had seen it all the while he was in a state of lethargy; that as the clock struck one, his wife had finished re-interring the head in its grave. And he described in the most minute manner how she held it.

The curiosity of the company assembled was so much excited by witnessing these inexplicable events, that they awaited the return of the servant whom the colonel had dispatched to the sexton's wife. Everything had happened precisely as he described;—the clock struck one at the very moment the head was laid in the grave.

These events had produced to the spectators a night of much greater terrors than the colonel had prepared for them. Nay, even *his* imagination was raised to such a pitch, that the least breath of wind, or the slightest noise, appeared to him as a forerunner to some disagreeable visitor from the world of spirits.

He was out of his bed at dawn of day, to look out of his window and see the occasion of the noise which at that hour was heard at the inn-door. He saw the rope-dancers seated in the carriage, about to take their departure. Calzolaro was not with them; but presently afterwards came to the side of the vehicle, where he took leave of them: the children seemed to leave him behind with regret.

The carriage drove off; and the colonel made a signal to Calzolaro to come and speak to him.

"I apprehend," said he to him, when he came in, "that you have taken entire leave of your troop."

"Well, monsieur, ought I not so to do?"

"It appears to me a procedure in which you have acted with as little reflection as the one which tempted you first to join them. You ought rather to have availed yourself of some favourable occasion for withdrawing the little capital that you have in their funds."

"Do you then, monsieur colonel, forget what has happened to me; and that I could not have enjoyed another moment of repose in the society of persons who are only externally men? Every time I recall the scene of last night to my recollection, my very blood freezes in my veins. From this moment I must do all in my power to appease my father's shade, which is now so justly incensed against me. Without much effort I have withdrawn myself from a profession which never had any great charms for me. Reflect only on the misery of being the chief of a troop, who, to earn a scanty morsel of bread, are compelled every moment to risk their lives!—and even this morsel of bread not always attainable. Moreover, I know that the clown belonging to the troop, who is a man devoid of all sentiment, has for a long while aspired to become the chief: and I know that he has for some time been devising various means to remove me from this world; therefore it appears to me that I have not been precipitate in relinquishing my rights to him for a trifling sum of money. I only feel for the poor children; and would willingly have purchased them, to save them from so unhappy a career; but he would not take any price for them. I have only one consolation, which is, the hope that the inhuman treatment they will experience at his hands will induce them to make their escape, and follow a better course of life."

"And what do you purpose doing yourself?"

"I have told you, that I shall retire to some obscure corner of Germany, and follow the profession to which my father destined me."

The colonel made him promise to wait a little; and, if possible, he would do something for him.

In the interim, the heiress to his father's property arrived, to have a conference on the subject with him. As soon as he had made known his intentions to her, she entreated him no longer to refuse half the inheritance, or at least to receive it as a voluntary gift on her part. The goodness, the sweetness of this young person, (who was pretty also,) so pleased Calzolaro, that a short time afterwards he asked her hand in marriage. She consented to give it to him. And the colonel then exerted himself more readily in behalf of this man, who had already gained his favour. He fulfilled his wishes, by sending him to a little property belonging to his wife, to follow the profession his father had fixed on for him.

Ere he set off, Calzolaro resumed his German name of Schurster. The good pastor, who had so recently felt indignant at his obstinacy, gave the nuptial benediction to the happy couple in presence of the colonel and his family, who on this occasion gave an elegant entertainment at the *château*.

In the evening, a little after sun-set, the bride and bridegroom were walking in the garden, at some little distance from the rest of the company, and appeared plunged in a deep reverie. All on a sudden they looked at each other; for it seemed to them, that someone took a hand of each and united them. They declared, at least, that the idea of this action having taken place came to them both so instantaneously and so involuntarily, that they were astonished at it themselves.

An instant afterwards, they distinctly heard these words:—

"May God bless your union!" pronounced by the voice of Calzolaro's father.

The bridegroom told the colonel, sometime afterwards, that without these consolatory words, the terrible apparition which he saw on the memorable night, would assuredly have haunted him all his life, and have impoisoned his happiest moments.

The Death's Head, by Edward Vernon Utterson. (Watercolor illustration painted in homage to the story in *Tales of the Dead*, 1813.)

"The King" (from *The Dance of Death*) by Hans Holbein der Jüngere, designed ca. 1526. (Woodblock printing by Hans Lützelburger, 1538.)

IV.

THE DEATH-BRIDE

BY FRIEDRICH LAUN

(TRANSLATED INTO ENGLISH BY
SARAH ELIZABETH UTTERSON)

——"She shall be such
As walk'd your first queen's ghost!——"
—SHAKSPEARE.*

THE summer had been uncommonly fine, and the baths crowded with company beyond all comparison: but still the public rooms were scarce ever filled, and never gay. The nobility and military associated only with those of their own rank, and the citizens contented themselves by slandering both parties. So many partial divisions necessarily proved an obstacle to a general and united assembly.

Even the public balls did not draw the *beau-monde* together, because the proprietor of the baths appeared there bedizened with insignia of knighthood; and this glitter, added to the stiff manners of this great man's family, and the tribe of lackeys in splendid liveries who constantly attended him, compelled the greater part of the company assembled, silently to observe the rules prescribed to them according to their different ranks.

For these reasons the balls became gradually less numerously attended. Private parties were formed, in which it was endeavoured to preserve the charms that were daily diminishing in the public assemblies.

One of these societies met generally twice a week in a room which at that time was usually unoccupied. There they supped, and afterwards enjoyed, either in a walk abroad, or remaining in the room, the charms of unrestrained conversation.

The members of this society were already acquainted, at least by name;

---

* *The Winter's Tale*, Act V, Scene 1.

but an Italian marquis, who had lately joined their party, was unknown to them, and indeed to everyone assembled at the baths.

The title of *Italian* marquis appeared the more singular, as his name, according to the entry of it in the general list, seemed to denote him of Northern extraction, and was composed of so great a number of consonants, that no one could pronounce it without difficulty.

His physiognomy and manners likewise presented many singularities. His long and wan visage, his black eyes, his imperious look, had so little of attraction in them, that everyone would certainly have avoided him, had he not possessed a fund of entertaining stories, the relation of which proved an excellent antidote to *ennui:* the only drawback against them was, that in general they required rather too great a share of credulity on the part of his auditors.

The party had one day just risen from table, and found themselves but ill inclined for gaiety. They were still too much fatigued from the ball of the preceding evening to enjoy the recreation of walking, although invited so to do by the bright light of the moon. They were even unable to keep up any conversation; therefore it is not to be wondered at, that they were more than usually anxious for the marquis to arrive.

"Where can he be?" exclaimed the countess in an impatient tone.

"Doubtless still at the faro-table, to the no small grief of the bankers," replied Florentine. "This very morning he has occasioned the sudden departure of two of these gentlemen."

"No great loss," answered another.

"To us—," replied Florentine; "but it is to the proprietor of the baths, who only prohibited gambling, that it might be pursued with greater avidity."

"The marquis ought to abstain from such achievements," said the chevalier with an air of mystery. "Gamblers are revengeful, and have generally advantageous connections. If what is whispered be correct, that the marquis is unfortunately implicated in political affairs—."

"But," demanded the countess, "what then has the marquis done to the bankers of the gaming-table?"

"Nothing; except that he betted on cards which almost invariably won. And what renders it rather singular, he scarcely derived any advantage from it himself, for he always adhered to the weakest party. But the other punters were not so scrupulous; for they charged their cards in such a manner that the bank broke before the deal had gone round."

The countess was on the point of asking other questions, when the marquis coming in changed the conversation.

"Here you are at last!" exclaimed several persons at the same moment.

"We have," said the countess, "been most anxious for your society; and just on this day you have been longer than usual absent."

"I have projected an important expedition; and it has succeeded to my wishes. I hope by to-morrow there will not be a single gaming-table left here. I have been from one gambling-room to another; and there are not sufficient post-horses to carry off the ruined bankers."

"And cannot you," asked the countess, "teach us your wonderful art of always winning?"

"It would be a difficult task, my fair lady; and in order to do it, one must ensure a fortunate hand, for without that nothing could be done."

"Nay," replied the chevalier, laughing, "never did I see so fortunate an one as yours."

"As you are still very young, my dear chevalier, you have many novelties to witness."

Saying these words, the marquis threw on the chevalier so piercing a look that the latter cried:

"Will you then cast my nativity?"

"Provided that it is not done to-day," said the countess; "for who knows whether your future destiny will afford us so amusing a history as that which the marquis two days since promised we should enjoy?"

"I did not exactly say *amusing*."

"But at least full of extraordinary events: and we require some such, to draw us from the lethargy which has overwhelmed us all day."

"Most willingly: but first I am anxious to learn whether any of you know aught of the surprising things related of the *Death-Bride*."

No one remembered to have heard speak of her.

The marquis appeared anxious to add something more by way of preface; but the countess and the rest of the party so openly manifested their impatience, that the marquis began his narration as follows:—

"I had for a long time projected a visit to the count Lieppa, at his estates in Bohemia. We had met each other in almost every country in Europe: attracted *hither* by the frivolity of youth to partake of every pleasure which presented itself, but led *thither* when years of discretion had rendered us more sedate and steady.—At length, in our more advanced age, we ardently desired, ere the close of life, once again to enjoy, by the charms of recollection, the moments of delight which we had passed together. For my part, I was anxious to see the castle of my friend, which was, according to his description, in an extremely romantic district. It was built some hundred years back by his ancestors; and their successors had preserved it with so much care, that it still maintained its imposing appearance, at the same time it afforded a comfortable abode. The count generally passed the greater part of the year at it with his family, and only returned to the capital at the approach of winter. Being well acquainted with his movements, I did not think it needful to announce my visit; and I arrived at the castle one evening precisely at the time when I knew he would be there; and as I approached it, could not but admire the variety and beauty of the scenery which surrounded it.

"The hearty welcome which I received could not, however, entirely conceal from my observation the secret grief depicted on the countenances of the count, his wife, and their daughter, the lovely Ida. In a short time I discovered that they still mourned the loss of Ida's twin-sister, who had died about a year before. Ida and Hildegarde resembled each other so much, that they were only to be distinguished from each other by a slight mark of a strawberry visible on Hildegarde's neck. Her room, and everything in it, was left precisely in the same state as when she was alive, and the family were in the habit of visiting it whenever they wished to indulge the sad satisfaction of meditating on the loss of this beloved child. The two sisters had but one heart, one mind: and the parents could not but apprehend that their separation would be but of short duration; they dreaded lest Ida should also be taken from them.

"I did everything in my power to amuse this excellent family, by entertaining them with laughable anecdotes of my younger days, and by directing their thoughts to less melancholy subjects than that which now wholly occupied them. I had the satisfaction of discovering that my efforts were not ineffectual. Sometimes we walked in the canton round the castle, which was decked with all the beauties of summer; at other times we took a survey of the different apartments of the castle, and were astonished at their wonderful state of preservation, whilst we amused ourselves by talking over the actions of the past generation, whose portraits hung in a long gallery.

"One evening the count had been speaking to me in confidence, on the subject of his future plans: among other subjects he expressed his anxiety, that Ida (who had already, though only in her sixteenth year, refused several offers) should be happily married; when suddenly the gardener, quite out of breath, came to tell us he had seen the ghost (as he believed, the old chaplain belonging to the castle), who had appeared a century back. Several of the servants followed the gardener, and their pallid countenances confirmed the alarming tidings he had brought.

"'I believe you will shortly be afraid of your own shadow,' said the count to them. He then sent them off, desiring them not again to trouble him with the like fooleries.

"'It is really terrible,' said he to me, 'to see to what lengths superstition will carry persons of that rank of life; and it is impossible wholly to undeceive them. From one generation to another an absurd report has from time to time been spread abroad, of an old chaplain's ghost wandering in the environs of the castle; and that he says mass in the chapel, with other idle stories of a similar nature. This report has greatly died away since I came into possession of the castle; but it now appears to me, it will never be altogether forgotten.'

"At this moment the duke de Marino was announced. The count did not recollect ever having heard of him.

"I told him that I was tolerably well acquainted with his family; and that I had lately been present, in Venice, at the betrothing of a young man of that name.

"The very same young man came in while I was speaking. I should have felt very glad at seeing him, had I not perceived that my presence caused him evident uneasiness.

"'Ah,' said he in a tolerably gay tone, after the customary forms of politeness had passed between us; 'the finding you here, my dear marquis, explains to me an occurrence, which with shame I own caused me a sensation of fear. To my no small surprise, they knew my name in the adjacent district; and as I came up the hill which leads to the castle, I heard it pronounced three times in a voice wholly unknown to me: and in a still more audible tone this strange voice bade me welcome. I now, however, conclude it was yours.'

"I assured him, (and with truth,) that till his name was announced the minute before, I was ignorant of his arrival, and that none of my servants knew him; for that the valet who accompanied me into Italy was not now with me.

"'And above all,' added I, 'it would be impossible to discover any equipage, however well known to one, in so dark an evening.'

"'That is what astonishes me,' exclaimed the duke, a little amazed.

"The incredulous count very politely added, 'that the voice which had told the duke he was welcome, had at least expressed the sentiments of all the family.'

"Marino, ere he said a word relative to the motive of his visit, asked a private audience of me; and confided in me, by telling me that he was come with the intention of obtaining the lovely Ida's hand; and that if he was able to procure her consent, he should demand her of her father.

"'The countess Apollonia, your bride elect, is then no longer living?' asked I.

"'We will talk on that subject hereafter,' answered he.

"The deep sigh which accompanied these words led me to conclude that Apollonia had been guilty of infidelity or some other crime towards the duke; and consequently I thought that I ought to abstain from any further questions, which appeared to rend his heart, already so sensibly wounded.

"Yet, as he begged me to become his mediator with the count, in order to obtain from him his consent to the match, I painted in glowing colours the danger of an alliance, which he had no other motive for contracting, than the wish to obliterate the remembrance of a dearly, and without doubt, still more tenderly, beloved object. But he assured me that he was far from thinking of the lovely Ida from so blameable a motive, and that he should be the happiest of men if she but proved propitious to his wishes.

"His expressive and penetrating tone of voice, while he said this, lulled the uneasiness that I was beginning to feel; and I promised him I would prepare the count Lieppa to listen to his entreaties, and would give him the necessary information relative to the fortune and family of Marino. But I declared to him at the same time, that I should by no means hurry the conclusion of the affair by my advice, as I was not in the habit of taking upon myself so great a charge as the uncertain issue of a marriage.

"The duke signified his satisfaction at what I said, and made me give (what then appeared to me of no consequence) a promise, that I would not make mention of the former marriage he was on the point of contracting, as it would necessarily bring on a train of unpleasant explanations.

"The duke's views succeeded with a promptitude beyond his most sanguine hopes. His well-proportioned form and sparkling eyes smoothed the paths of love, and introduced him to the heart of Ida. His agreeable conversation promised to the mother an amiable son-in-law; and the knowledge in rural economy, which he evinced as occasions offered, made the count hope for an useful helpmate in his usual occupations; for since the first day of the duke's arrival he had been prevented from pursuing them.

"Marino followed up these advantages with great ardour; and I was one evening much surprised by the intelligence of his being betrothed, as I did not dream of matters drawing so near a conclusion. They spoke at table of some bridal preparations of which I had made mention just before the duke's arrival at the castle; and the countess asked me whether that young Marino was a near relation of the one who was that very day betrothed to her daughter.'

"'Near enough,' I answered, recollecting my promise.—Marino looked at me with an air of embarrassment.

"'But, my dear duke,' continued I, 'tell me who mentioned the amiable Ida to you; or was it a portrait, or what else, which caused you to think of looking for a beauty, the selection of whom does so much honour to your taste, in this remote corner; for, if I am not mistaken, you said but yesterday that you had purposed travelling about for another six months; when all at once (I believe while in Paris) you changed your plan, and projected a journey wholly and solely to see the charming Ida?'

"'Yes, it was at Paris,' replied the duke; 'you are very rightly informed. I went there to see and admire the superb gallery of pictures at the Museum; but I had scarcely entered it, when my eyes turned from the inanimate beauties, and were riveted on a lady whose incomparable features were heightened by an air of melancholy. With fear and trembling I approached her, and only ventured to follow without speaking to her. I still followed her after she quitted the gallery; and I drew her servant aside to learn the name of his mistress. He told it me: but when I expressed a wish to become acquainted with the father of this beauty, he said that was next to impossible while at Paris, as the family were on the point of quitting that city; nay, of quitting France altogether.

"'Possibly, however,' said I, 'some opportunity may present itself.' And I looked everywhere for the lady: but she, probably imagining that her servant was following her closely, had continued to walk on, and was entirely out of sight. While I was looking around for her, the servant had likewise vanished from my view.'

"'Who was this beautiful lady?' asked Ida, in a tone of astonishment.

"'What! you really did not then perceive me in the gallery?'

"'Me!'—'My daughter—!' exclaimed at the same moment Ida and her parents.

"'Yes, you yourself, mademoiselle. The servant, whom fortunately for me you left at Paris, and whom I met the same evening unexpectedly, as my guardian angel, informed me of all; so that after a short rest at home, I was able to come straight hither.'

"'What a fable!' said the count to his daughter, who was mute with astonishment.

"'Ida,' he added, turning to me, 'has never yet been out of her native country; and for myself, I have not been in Paris these seventeen years.'

"The duke looked at the count and his daughter with similar marks of astonishment visible in their countenances; and conversation would have been entirely at an end, if I had not taken care to introduce other topics: but I had it nearly all to myself.

"The repast was no sooner over, than the count took the duke into the recess of a window; and although I was at a considerable distance, and appeared wholly to fix my attention on a new chandelier, I overheard all their conversation.

"'What motive,' demanded the count with a serious and dissatisfied air, 'could have induced you to invent that singular scene in the gallery of the Museum at Paris? for according to my judgment, it could in no way benefit you. Since you are anxious to conceal the cause which brought you to ask my daughter in marriage, at least you might have plainly said as much; and though possibly you might have felt repugnance at making such a declaration, there were a thousand ways of framing your answer, without its being needful thus to offend probability.'

"'Monsieur le comte,' replied the duke much piqued; 'I held my peace at table, thinking that possibly you had reasons for wishing to keep secret your and your daughter's journey to Paris. I was silent merely from motives of discretion; but the singularity of your reproaches compels me to maintain what I have said; and, notwithstanding your reluctance to believe the truth, to declare before all the world, that the capital of France was the spot where I first saw your daughter Ida.'

"'But what if I prove to you, not only by the witness of my servants, but also by that of all my tenants, that my daughter has never quitted her native place?'—

"'I shall still believe the evidence of my own eyes and ears, which have as great authority over me.'

"'What you say is really enigmatical,' answered the count in a graver tone: 'your serious manner convinces me you have been the dupe of some illusion; and that you have seen some other person, whom you have taken for my daughter. Excuse me, therefore, for having taken up the thing so warmly.'

"'Another person! What then, I not only mistook another person for your daughter; but the very servant of whom I made mention, and who gave me so exact a description of this castle, was, according to what you say, some other person!'

"'My dear Marino, that servant was some cheat who knew this castle, and who, God only knows for what motive, spoke to you of my daughter as resembling the lady.'

"'Tis certainly no wish of mine to contradict you; but Ida's features are precisely the same as those which made so deep an impression on me at Paris, and which my imagination has preserved with such scrupulous fidelity.'

"The count shook his head; and Marino continued:—

"'What is still more—(but pray pardon me for mentioning a little particularity, which nothing short of necessity would have drawn from me)—while in the gallery, I was standing behind the lady, and the handkerchief that covered her neck was a little disarranged, which occasioned me distinctly to perceive the mark of a small strawberry.'

"'Another strange mystery!' exclaimed the count, turning pale: 'it appears you are determined to make me believe wonderful stories.'

"'I have only one question to ask:—Has Ida such a mark on her neck?'

"'No, monsieur,' replied the count, looking steadfastly at Marino.

"'No!' exclaimed the latter, in the utmost astonishment.

"'No, I tell you: but Ida's twin-sister, who resembled her in the most surprising manner, had the mark you mention on her neck, and a year since carried it with her into the grave.'

"'And yet 'tis only within the last few months that I saw this person in Paris!'

"At this moment the countess and Ida, who had kept aside, a prey to uneasiness, not knowing what to think of the conversation, which appeared of so very important a nature, approached; but the count in a commanding tone ordered them to retire immediately. He then led the duke entirely away into a retired corner of the window, and continued the conversation in so low a voice that I could hear nothing further.

"My astonishment was extreme when, that very same evening, the count gave orders to have Hildegarde's tomb opened in his presence: but he beforehand related briefly what I have just told you, and proposed my assisting the duke and him in opening the grave. The duke excused himself, by saying that the very idea made him tremble with horror; for he could not overcome, especially at night, his fear of a corpse.

"The count begged he would not mention the gallery scene to anyone; and above all, to spare the extreme sensibility of the affianced bride from a recital of the conversation they had just had, even if she should request to be informed of it.

"In the meantime the sexton arrived with his lantern. The count and I followed him.

"'It is morally impossible,' said the count to me, as we walked together, 'that any trick can have been played respecting my daughter's death: the circumstances attendant thereon are but too well known to me. You may readily believe also, that the affection we bore our poor girl would prevent our running any risk of burying her too soon: but suppose even the possibility of that, and that the tomb had been opened by some avaricious persons, who found, on opening the coffin, that the body became re-animated; no one can believe for a moment that my daughter would not have instantly returned to her parents, who doted on her, rather than have fled to a distant country. This last circumstance puts the matter beyond doubt: for even should it be admitted as a truth, that she was carried by force to some distant part of the world, she would have found a thousand ways of returning. My eyes are, however, about to be convinced, that the sacred remains of my Hildegarde really repose in the grave.

"'To convince myself!' cried he again, in a tone of voice so melancholy yet loud that the sexton turned his head.

"This movement rendered the count more circumspect; and he continued in a lower tone of voice:

"'How should I for a moment believe it possible that the slightest trace of my daughter's features should be still in existence, or that the destructive hand of time should have spared her beauty? Let us return, marquis; for who could tell, even were I to see the skeleton, that I should know it from that of an entire stranger, whom they may have placed in the tomb to fill her place?'

"He was even about to give orders not to open the door of the chapel, (at which we were just arrived,) when I represented to him, that were I in his place I should have found it extremely difficult to determine on such a measure; but that having gone thus far, it was requisite to complete the task, by examining whether some of the jewels buried with Hildegarde's corpse were not wanting. I added, that judging by a number of well-known facts, all bodies were not destroyed equally soon.

"My representations had the desired effect: the count squeezed my hand; and we followed the sexton, who, by his pallid countenance and trembling limbs, evidently shewed that he was unaccustomed to nocturnal employments of this nature.

"I know not whether any of this present company were ever in a chapel at midnight, before the iron doors of a vault, about to examine the succession of leaden coffins enclosing the remains of an illustrious family. Certain it is, that at such a moment the noise of bolts and bars produces such a remarkable sensation, that one is led to dread the sound of the door grating on its hinges; and when the vault is opened, one cannot help hesitating for an instant to enter it.

"The count was evidently seized with these sensations of terror, which I discovered by a stifled sigh; but he concealed his feelings: notwithstanding, I remarked that he dared not trust himself to look on any other coffin than the one containing his daughter's remains. He opened it himself.

"'Did I not say so?' cried he, seeing that the features of the corpse bore a perfect resemblance to those of Ida. I was obliged to prevent the count, who was seized with astonishment, from kissing the forehead of the inanimate body.

"'Do not,' I added, 'disturb the peace of those who repose in death.' And I used my utmost efforts to withdraw the count immediately from this dismal abode.

"On our return to the castle, we found those persons whom we had left there, in an anxious state of suspense. The two ladies had closely questioned the duke on what had passed; and would not admit as a valid excuse, the promise he had made of secrecy. They entreated us also, but in vain, to satisfy their curiosity.

"They succeeded better the following day with the sexton, whom they sent for privately, and who told them all he knew: but it only tended to excite their anxious wish to learn the subject of the conversation which had occasioned this nocturnal visit to the sepulchral vault.

"As for myself, I dreamt the whole of the following night of the apparition Marino had seen at Paris; I conjectured many things which I did not think fit to communicate to the count, because he absolutely questioned the connection of a superior world with ours. At this juncture of affairs, I with pleasure saw that this singular circumstance, if not entirely forgotten, was at least but rarely and slightly mentioned.

"But I now began to find another cause for anxious solicitude. The duke constantly persisted in refusing to explain himself on the subject of his previous engagement, even when we were alone: and the embarrassment he could not conceal, whenever I made mention of the good qualities that I believed his intended to have possessed, as well as several other little singularities, led me to conclude that Marino's attachment for Apollonia had been first shaken at the picture gallery, at sight of the lovely incognita; and that Apollonia had been forsaken, owing to his yielding to temptations; and that doubtless she could never have been guilty of breaking off an alliance so solemnly contracted.

Foreseeing from this that the charming Ida could never hope to find much happiness in an union with Marino, and knowing that the wedding-day was nigh at hand, I resolved to unmask the perfidious deceiver as quickly as possible, and to make him repent his infidelity. An excellent occasion presented itself one day for me to accomplish my designs. Having finished supper, we were still sitting at table; and someone said that iniquity is frequently punished in this world: upon which I observed, that I myself had witnessed striking proofs of the truth of this remark;—when Ida and her mother entreated me to name one of these examples.

"'Under these circumstances, ladies,' answered I, 'permit me to relate a history to you, which, according to my opinion, will particularly interest you.'

"'Us!' they both exclaimed. At the same time I fixed my eyes on the duke, who for several days past had evidently distrusted me; and I saw that his conscience had rendered him pale.

"'That at least is *my* opinion,' replied I: 'But, my dear count, will you pardon me, if the supernatural is sometimes interwoven with my narration?'

"'Very willingly,' answered he smiling: 'and I will content myself with expressing my surprise at so many things of this sort having happened to you, as I have never experienced any of them myself.'

"I plainly perceived that the duke made signs of approval at what he said: but I took no notice of it, and answered the count by saying, 'That all the world have not probably the use of their eyes.'

"'That may be,' replied he, still smiling.

"'But,' said I to him in a low and expressive voice, 'think you an uncorrupted body in the vault is a *common* phænomenon?'

"He appeared staggered: and I thus continued in an undertone of voice:—

"'For that matter, 'tis very possible to account for it naturally, and therefore it would be useless to contest the subject with you.'

"'We are wandering from the point,' said the countess a little angrily; and she made me a sign to begin, which I accordingly did, in the following words:—

"'The scene of my anecdote lies in Venice.'

"'I possibly then may know something of it,' cried the duke, who entertained some suspicions.

"'Possibly so,' replied I; 'but there were reasons for keeping the event secret: it happened somewhere about eighteen months since, at the period you first set out on your travels.

"The son of an extremely wealthy nobleman, whom I shall designate by the name of Filippo, being attracted to Leghorn by the affairs consequent on his succession to an inheritance, had won the heart of an amiable and lovely girl, called Clara. He promised her, as well as her parents, that ere his return to Venice he would come back and marry her. The moment for his departure was preceded by certain ceremonies, which in their termination were terrible: for after the two lovers had exhausted every protestation of reciprocal affection, Filippo invoked the aid of the spirit of vengeance, in case of infidelity: they prayed even that whichever of the lovers should prove faithful might not be permitted to repose quietly in the grave, but should haunt the perjured one, and force the inconstant party to come amongst the dead, and to share in the grave those sentiments which on earth had been forgotten.

"The parents, who were seated by them at table, remembered their youthful days, and permitted the overheated and romantic imagination of the young people to take its free course. The lovers finished by making punctures in their arms, and letting their blood run into a glass filled with white champaigne.

"'Our souls shall be inseparable as our blood!' exclaimed Filippo; and drinking half the contents of the glass, he gave the rest to Clara."

At this moment the duke experienced a violent degree of agitation, and from time to time darted such menacing looks at me, that I was led to conclude, that in *his* adventure some scene of a similar nature had taken place. I can however affirm, that I related the details respecting Filippo's departure, as they were represented in a letter written by the mother of Clara.

"Who," continued I, "after so many demonstrations of such a violent passion, could have expected the denouement? Filippo's return to Venice happened precisely at the period at which a young beauty, hitherto educated in a distant convent, made her first appearance in the great world: she on a sudden exhibited herself as an angel whom a cloud had till then concealed, and excited universal admiration. Filippo's parents had heard frequent mention of Clara, and of the projected alliance between her and their son; but they thought that this alliance was like many others, contracted one day without the parties knowing why, and broken off the next with equal want of thought; and influenced by this idea, they presented their son to the parents of Camilla, (which was the name of the young beauty,) whose family were of the highest rank.

"They represented to Filippo the great advantages he would obtain by an alliance with her. The Carnival happening just at this period completed the business, by affording him so many favourable opportunities of being with Camilla; and in the end, the remembrance of Leghorn held but very little place in his mind. His letters became colder and colder each succeeding day; and on Clara expressing how sensibly she felt the change, he ceased writing to her altogether, and did everything in his power to hasten his union with Camilla, who was, without compare, much the handsomer and more wealthy. The agonies poor Clara endured were manifest in her illegible writing, and by the tears which were but too evidently shed over her letters: but neither the one nor the other had any more influence over the fickle heart of Filippo, than the prayers of the unfortunate girl. Even the menace of coming, according to their solemn agreement, from the tomb to haunt him, and carry him with her to that grave which threatened so soon to enclose her, had but little effect on his mind, which was entirely engrossed by the idea of the happiness he should enjoy in the arms of Camilla.

"The father of the latter (who was my intimate friend) invited me before-hand to the wedding. And although numerous affairs detained him that summer in the city, so that he could not as usual enjoy the pleasures of the country, yet we sometimes went to his pretty villa, situated on the banks of the Brenta; where his daughter's marriage was to be celebrated with all possible splendour.

"A particular circumstance, however, occasioned the ceremony to be deferred for some weeks. The parents of Camilla having been very happy in their own union, were anxious that the same priest who married them, should pronounce the nuptial benediction on their daughter. This priest, who, notwithstanding his great age, had the appearance of vigorous health, was seized with a slow fever which confined him to his bed: however, in time it abated, he became gradually better and better, and the wedding-day was at length fixed. But, as if some secret power was at work to prevent this union, the worthy priest was, on the very day destined for the celebration of their marriage, seized with a feverish shivering of so alarming a nature, that he dared not stir out of the house, and he strongly advised the young couple to select another priest to marry them.

"The parents still persisted in their design of the nuptial benediction being given to their children by the respectable old man who had married *them*.—They would have certainly spared themselves a great deal of grief, if they had never swerved from their determination.—Very grand preparations had been made in honour of the day; and as they could no longer be deferred, it was decided that they should consider it as a ceremony of solemn affiance. At noon the bargemen attired in their splendid garb awaited the company's arrival on the banks of the canal: their joyous song was soon distinguished, while conducting to the villa, now decorated with flowers, the numerous gondolas containing parties of the best company.

"During the dinner, which lasted till evening, the betrothed couple exchanged rings. At the very moment of their so doing, a piercing shriek was heard, which struck terror into the breasts of all the company, and absolutely struck Filippo with horror. Everyone ran to the windows: for although it was becoming dark, each object was visible; but no one was to be seen."

"Stop an instant," said the duke to me, with a fierce smile—His countenance, which had frequently changed colour during the recital, evinced strong marks of the torments of a wicked conscience. "I am also acquainted with that story, of a voice being heard in the air; it is borrowed from the 'Memoirs of Mademoiselle Clairon;" a deceased lover tormented *her* in this completely original manner. The shriek in her case was followed by a clapping of hands: I hope, monsieur le marquis, that you will not omit that particular in your story."

"And why," replied I, "should you imagine that nothing of a similar nature could occur to anyone besides that actress? Your incredulity appears to me so much the more extraordinary, as it seems to rest on facts which may lay claim to belief."

The countess made me a sign to continue; and I pursued my narrative as follows:

"A short time after they had heard this inexplicable shriek, I begged Camilla, facing whom I was sitting, to permit me to look at her ring once more, the exquisite workmanship of which had already been much admired. But it was not on her finger: a general search was made, but not the slightest trace of the ring could be discovered. The company even rose from their seats to look for it, but all in vain.

"Meanwhile, the time for the evening's amusements approached: fireworks were exhibited on the Brenta preceding the ball; the company were masked and got into the gondolas; but nothing was so striking as the silence which reigned during this *fête*; no one seemed inclined to open their mouth; and scarcely was heard a faint exclamation of *Bravo*, at sight of the fireworks.

"The ball was one of the most brilliant I ever witnessed: the precious stones and jewels with which the ladies of the party were covered, reflected the lights in the chandeliers with redoubled lustre. The most splendidly attired of the whole was Camilla. Her father, who was fond of pomp, rejoiced in the idea that no one in the assembly was equal to his daughter in splendour or beauty.

---

* Hippolyte Clairon, a celebrated French actress, published her memoirs in 1798.

"Possibly to satisfy himself of this fact, he made a tour of the room; and returned loudly expressing his surprise, at having perceived on another lady precisely the same jewels which adorned Camilla. He was even weak enough to express a slight degree of chagrin. However, he consoled himself with the idea, that a bouquet of diamonds which was destined for Camilla to wear at supper, would alone in value be greater than all she then had on.

"But as they were on the point of sitting down to table, and the anxious father again threw a look around him, he discovered that the same lady had also a bouquet which appeared to the full as valuable as Camilla's.

"My friend's curiosity could no longer be restrained; he approached, and asked whether it would be too great a liberty to learn the name of the fair mask? But to his great surprise, the lady shook her head, and turned away from him.

"At the same instant the steward came in, to ask whether since dinner there had been any addition to the party, as the covers were not sufficient.

"His master answered, with rather a dissatisfied air, that there were only the same number, and accused his servants of negligence; but the steward still persisted in what he had said.

"An additional cover was placed: the master counted them himself, and discovered that there really was one more in number than he had invited. As he had recently, on account of some inconsiderate expressions, had a dispute with government, he was apprehensive that some spy had contrived to slip in with the company: but as he had no reason to believe, that on such a day as that, anything of a suspicious nature would be uttered, he resolved, in order to be satisfied respecting so indiscreet a procedure as the introduction of such a person in a family *fête*, to beg everyone present to unmask; but in order to avoid the inconvenience likely to arise from such a request, he determined not to propose it till the very last thing.

"Everyone present expressed their surprise at the luxuries and delicacies of the table, for it far surpassed everything of the sort seen in that country, especially with respect to the wines. Still, however, the father of Camilla was not satisfied, and loudly lamented that an accident had happened to his capital red champaigne, which prevented his being able to offer his guests a single glass of it.

"The company seemed anxious to become gay, for the whole of the day nothing like gaiety had been visible among them; but no one around where I sat, partook of this inclination, for curiosity alone appeared to occupy their whole attention. I was sitting near the lady who was so splendidly attired; and I remarked that she neither ate nor drank anything; that she neither addressed nor answered a word to her neighbours, and that she appeared to have her eyes constantly fixed on the affianced couple.

"The rumour of this singularity gradually spread round the room, and again disturbed the mirth which had become pretty general. Each whispered to the other a thousand conjectures on this mysterious personage. But the general opinion was, that some unhappy passion for Filippo was the cause of this extraordinary conduct. Those sitting next the unknown, were the first to rise from table, in order to find more cheerful associates, and their places were filled by others who hoped to discover some acquaintance in this silent lady, and obtain from her a more welcome reception; but their hopes were equally futile.

"At the time the champaigne was handed round, Filippo also brought a chair and sat by the unknown. She then became somewhat more animated, and turned towards Filippo, which was more than she had done to anyone else; and she offered him her glass, as if wishing him to drink out of it.

"A violent trembling seized Filippo, when she looked at him steadfastly.

"'The wine is red!' cried he, holding up the glass; 'I thought there had been no *red* champaigne.'

"'Red!' said the father of Camilla, with an air of extreme surprise, approaching him from curiosity.

"'Look at the lady's glass,' replied Filippo.

"'The wine in it is as white as all the rest,' answered Camilla's father; and he called all present to witness it. They every one unanimously declared that the wine was white.

"Filippo drank it not, but quitted his seat; for a second look from his neighbour had caused him extreme agitation. He took the father of Camilla aside, and whispered something to him. The latter returned to the company, saying,

"'Ladies and gentlemen, I entreat you, for reasons which I will tell you presently, instantly to unmask.'

"As in this request he but expressed in a degree the general wish, everyone's mask was off as quick as thought, and each face uncovered, excepting that of the silent lady, on whom every look was fixed, and whose face they were the most anxious to see.

"'You alone keep on your mask,' said Camilla's father to her, after a short silence: 'May I hope you will also remove yours?'

"She obstinately persisted in her determination of remaining unknown.

"This strange conduct affected the father of Camilla the more sensibly, as he recognised in the others all those whom he had invited to the *fête*, and found beyond doubt that the mute lady was the one exceeding the number invited. He was, however, unwilling to force her to unmask; because the uncommon splendour of her dress did not permit him any longer to harbour the idea that this additional guest was a spy; and thinking her also a person of distinction, he did not wish to be deficient in good manners. He thought possibly she might be some friend of the family, who, not residing at Venice, but finding on her arrival in that city that he was to give this *fête*, had conceived this innocent frolic.

"It was thought right, however, at all events to obtain all the information that could be gained from the servants: but none of them knew anything of this lady; there were no servants of hers there; and those belonging to Camilla's father did not recollect having seen any who appeared to appertain to her.

"What rendered this circumstance doubly strange was, that, as I before mentioned, this lady only put the magnificent bouquet into her bosom the instant previous to her sitting down to supper.

"The whispering, which had generally usurped the place of all conversation, gained each moment more and more ascendancy; when on a sudden the masked lady arose, and walking towards the door, beckoned Filippo to follow her; but Camilla hindered him from obeying her signal, for she had a long time observed with what fixed attention the mysterious lady looked at her intended husband; and she had also remarked, that the latter had quitted the stranger in violent agitation; and from all this she apprehended that love had caused him to be guilty of some folly or other. The master of the house, turning a deaf ear to all his daughter's remonstrances, and a prey to the most terrible fears, followed the unknown (at a distance, it is true); but she was no sooner out of the room than he returned. At this moment, the shriek which they had heard at noon was repeated, but seemed louder from the silence of night, and communicated anew affright to all present. By the time the father of Camilla had returned from the first movement which his fear had occasioned him to make, the unknown was nowhere to be found.

"The servants in waiting outside the house had no knowledge whatever of the masked lady. In every direction around there were crowds of persons; the river was lined with gondolas; and yet not an individual among them had seen the mysterious female.

"All these circumstances had occasioned so much uneasiness to the whole party, that everyone was anxious to return home; and the master of the house was obliged to permit the departure of the gondolas much earlier than he had intended.

"The return home was, as might naturally be expected, very melancholy.

"On the following day the betrothed couple were, however, pretty composed. Filippo had even adopted Camilla's idea of the unknown being someone whom love had deprived of reason; and as for the horrible shriek twice repeated, they were willing to attribute it to some people who were diverting themselves; and they decided, that inattention on the part of the servants was the sole cause of the unknown absenting herself without being perceived; and they even at last persuaded themselves, that the sudden disappearance of the ring, which they had not been able to find, was owing to the malice of some one of the servants who had pilfered it.

"In a word, they banished everything that could tend to weaken these explanations; and only one thing remained to harass them. The old priest, who was to bestow on them the nuptial benediction, had yielded up his last breath; and the friendship which had so intimately subsisted between him and the parents of Camilla, did not permit them in decency to think of marriage and amusements the week following his death.

"The day this venerable priest was buried, Filippo's gaiety received a severe shock; for he learned, in a letter from Clara's mother, the death of that lovely girl. Sinking under the grief occasioned her by the infidelity of the man she had never ceased to love, she died: but to her latest hour she declared she should never rest quietly in her grave, until the perjured man had fulfilled the promise he had made to her.

"This circumstance produced a stronger effect on him than all the imprecations of the unhappy mother; for he recollected that the first shriek (the cause of which they had never been able to ascertain) was heard at the precise moment of Clara's death; which convinced him that the unknown mask could only have been the spirit of Clara.

"This idea deprived him at intervals of his senses.

"He constantly carried this letter about him; and with an air of wandering would sometimes draw it from his pocket, in order to reconsider it attentively: even Camilla's presence did not deter him.

"As it was natural to conclude this letter contained the cause of the extraordinary change which had taken place in Filippo, she one day gladly seized the opportunity of reading it, when in one of his absent fits he let it fall from his hands.

"Filippo, struck by the death-like paleness and faintness which overcame Camilla, as she returned him the letter, knew instantly that she had read it. In the deepest affliction he threw himself at her feet, and conjured her to tell him how he must act.

"'Love *me* with greater constancy than you did her,'—replied Camilla mournfully.

"With transport he promised to do so. But his agitation became greater and greater, and increased to a most extraordinary pitch the morning of the day fixed for the wedding. As he was going to the house of Camilla's father before it became dark, (from whence he was to take his bride at dawn of day to the church, according to the custom of the country,) he fancied he saw Clara's spirit walking constantly at his side.

"Never was seen a couple about to receive the nuptial benediction, with so mournful an aspect. I accompanied the parents of Camilla, who had requested me to be a witness: and the sequel has made an indelible impression on my mind of the events of that dismal morning.

"We were proceeding silently to the church of the Salutation; when Filippo, in our way thither, frequently requested me to remove the stranger from Camilla's side, for she had evil designs against her.

"'What stranger?' I asked him.

"'In God's name, don't speak so loud,' replied he; 'for you cannot but see how anxious she is to force herself between Camilla and me.'

"'Mere chimera, my friend; there are none but yourself and Camilla.'

"'Would to Heaven my eyes did not deceive me!'—'Take care that she does not enter the church,' added he, as we arrived at the door.

"'She will not enter it, rest assured,' said I: and to the great astonishment of Camilla's parents I made a motion as if to drive someone away.

"We found Filippo's father already in the church; and as soon as his son perceived him, he took leave of him as if he was going to die. Camilla sobbed; and Filippo exclaimed:—

"'There's the stranger; she has then got in.'

"The parents of Camilla doubted whether under such circumstances the marriage ceremony ought to be begun.

"But Camilla, entirely devoted to her love, cried:—'These chimeras of fancy render my care and attention the more necessary.'

"They approached the altar. At that moment a sudden gust of wind blew out the wax-tapers. The priest appeared displeased at their not having shut the windows more securely; but Filippo exclaimed: 'The windows! See you not, then, that there is one here who blew out the wax-tapers purposely?'

"Everyone looked astonished: and Filippo cried, as he hastily disengaged his hand from that of Camilla,—'Don't you see, also, that she is tearing me away from my intended bride?'

"Camilla fell fainting into the arms of her parents; and the priest declared, that under such peculiar circumstances it was impossible to proceed with the ceremony.

"The parents of both attributed Filippo's state to mental derangement. They even supposed he had been poisoned; for an instant after, the unfortunate man expired in most violent convulsions. The surgeons who opened his body could not, however, discover any grounds for this suspicion.

"The parents, who as well as myself were informed by Camilla of the subject of these supposed horrors of Filippo, did everything in their power to conceal this adventure: yet, on talking over all the circumstances, they could never satisfactorily explain the apparition of the mysterious mask at the time of the wedding *fête*. And what still appeared very surprising was, that the ring lost at the country villa was found amongst Camilla's other jewels, at the time of their return from church."

"'This is, indeed, a wonderful history!' said the count. His wife uttered a deep sigh: and Ida exclaimed,—

"'It has really made *me* shudder.'

"'That is precisely what every betrothed person ought to feel who listens to such recitals,' answered I, looking steadfastly at the duke, who, while I was talking, had risen and sat down again several times; and who, from his troubled look, plainly shewed that he feared I should counteract his wishes.

"'A word with you!' he whispered me, as we were retiring to rest: and he accompanied me to my room. 'I plainly perceive your generous intentions; this history invented for the occasion—'

"'Hold!' said I to him in an irritated tone of voice: 'I was eye-witness to what you have just heard. How then can you doubt its authenticity, without accusing a man of honour of uttering a falsehood?'

"'We will talk on this subject presently,' replied he in a tone of raillery. 'But tell me truly from whence you learnt the anecdote relative to mixing the blood with wine?—I know the person from whose life you borrowed this idea.'

"'I do assure you that I have taken it from no one's life but Filippo's; and yet there may be similar stories—as of the shriek, for instance. But even this singular manner of irrevocably affiancing themselves may have presented itself to *any* two lovers.'

"'Perhaps so! Yet one could trace in your narration many traits resembling another history.'

"'That is very possible: all love-stories are founded on the same stock, and cannot deny their parentage.'

"'No matter,' replied Marino; 'but I desire that from henceforth you do not permit yourself to make any allusion to my past life; and still less that you relate certain anecdotes to the count. On these conditions, and only on these conditions, do I pardon your former very ingenious fiction.'

"'Conditions!—forgiveness!—And do you dare thus to talk to *me*?— This is rather too much. Now take my answer: To-morrow morning the count shall know that you have been already affianced, and what you now exact.'

"'Marquis, if you dare—'

"Oh! oh!—yes, I dare do it; and I owe it to an old friend. The impostor who dares accuse me of falsehood shall no longer wear his deceitful mask in this house.'

"Passion had, spite of my endeavours, carried me so far, that a duel became inevitable. The duke challenged me. And we agreed, at parting, to meet the following morning in a neighbouring wood with pistols.

"In effect, before day-light we each took our servant and went into the forest. Marino, remarking that I had not given any orders in case of my being killed, undertook to do so for me; and accordingly he told my servant what to do with my body, as if everything was already decided. He again addressed me ere we shook hands;—

"'For,' said he, 'the combat between us must be very unequal. I am young,' added he; 'but in many instances my hand has proved a steady one. I have not, it is true, absolutely killed any man; but I have invariably hit my adversary precisely on the part I intended. In this instance, however, I must, for the first time, *kill* my man, as it is the only effectual method of preventing your annoying me further; unless you will give me your word of honour not to discover any occurrences of my past life to the count, in which case I consent to consider the affair as terminated here.'

"As you may naturally believe, I rejected his proposition.

"'As it must be so,' replied he, 'recommend your soul to God.' We prepared accordingly.

"'It is your first fire,' he said to me.

"'I yield it to you,' answered I.

"He refused to fire first. I then drew the trigger, and caused the pistol to drop from his hand. He appeared surprised: but his astonishment was great indeed, when, after taking up another pistol, he found he had missed me. He pretended to have aimed at my heart; and had not even the possibility of an excuse; for he could not but acknowledge that no sensation of fear on my part had induced me to move, and baulk his aim.

"At his request I fired a second time; and again aimed at his pistol which he held in his left hand: and to his great astonishment it dropped also; but the ball had passed so near his hand, that it was a good deal bruised.

"His second fire having passed me, I told him I would not fire again; but that, as it was possible the extreme agitation of his mind had occasioned him to miss me twice, I proposed adjusting matters.

"Before he had time to refuse my offer, the count, who had suspicions that all was not right, was between us, with his daughter. He complained loudly of such conduct on the part of his guests; and demanded some explanation on the cause of our dispute. I then developed the whole business in presence of Marino, whose evident embarrassment convinced the count and Ida of the truth of the reproaches his conscience made him.

"But the duke soon availed himself of Ida's affection, and created an entire change in the count's mind; who that very evening said to me,—

"'You are right; I certainly ought to take some decided step, and send the duke from my house: but what could win the Apollonia whom he has abandoned, and whom he will never see again? Added to which, he is the only man for whom my daughter has ever felt a sincere attachment. Let us leave the young people to follow their own inclinations: the countess perfectly coincides in this opinion; and adds, that it would hurt her much were this handsome Venetian to be driven from our house. How many little infidelities and indiscretions are committed in the world and excused, owing to particular circumstances?'

"'But it appears to me, that in the case in point, these particular circumstances are wanting,' answered I. However, finding the count persisted in his opinion, I said no more.

"The marriage took place without any interruption: but still there was very little of gaiety at the feast, which usually on these occasions is of so splendid and jocund a nature. The ball in the evening was dull; and Marino alone danced with most extraordinary glee.

"'Fortunately, monsieur le marquis,' said he in my ear, quitting the dance for an instant and laughing aloud, "there are no ghosts or spirits here, as at your Venetian wedding.'

"'Don't,' I answered, putting up my finger to him, 'rejoice too soon: misery is slow in its operations; and often is not perceived by us blind mortals till it treads on our heels.'

"Contrary to my intention, this conversation rendered him quite silent; and what convinced me the more strongly of the effect it had made on him, was, the redoubled vehemence with which the duke again began dancing.

"The countess in vain entreated him to be careful of his health: and all Ida's supplications were able to obtain was, a few minutes' rest to take breath when he could no longer go on.

"A few minutes after, I saw Ida in tears, which did not appear as if occasioned by joy; and she quitted the ball-room. I was standing as close to the door as I am to you at this moment; so that I could not for an instant doubt its being really Ida: but what appeared to me very strange was, that in a few seconds I saw her come in again with a countenance as calm as possible. I followed her, and remarked that she asked the duke to dance; and was so far from moderating his violence, that she partook of and even increased it by her own example. I also remarked, that as soon as the dance was over the duke took leave of the parents of Ida, and with her vanished through a small door leading to the nuptial apartment.

"While I was endeavouring to account in my own mind how it was possible for Ida so suddenly to change her sentiments, a conference in an undertone took place at the door of the room, between the count and his valet.

"The subject was evidently a very important one, as the greatly incensed looks of the count towards his gardener evinced, while *he* confirmed, as it appeared, what the valet had before said.

"I drew near the trio, and heard, that at a particular time the church organ was heard to play, and that the whole edifice had been illuminated within, until twelve o'clock, which had just struck.

"The count was very angry at their troubling him with so silly a tale, and asked why they did not sooner inform him of it. They answered, that everyone was anxious to see how it would end. The gardener added, that the old chaplain had been seen again; and the peasantry who lived near the forest, even pretended that they had seen the summit of the mountain which overhung their valley illuminated, and spirits dance around it.

"'Very well!' exclaimed the count with a gloomy air; 'so all the old idle trash is resumed: the *Death-Bride* is also, I hope, going to play her part.'

"The valet having pushed aside the gardener, that he might not still further enrage the count, I put in my word; and said to the count, 'You might at least listen to what they have to say, and learn what it is they pretend to have seen.'

"'What is said about the *Death-Bride?*' said I to the gardener.

"He shrugged up his shoulders.

"'Was I not right?' cried the count: 'here we are then, and must listen to this ridiculous tale. All these things are treasured in the memory of these people, and constantly afford subjects and phantoms to their imaginations.—Is it permitted to ask under what form?'—

"'Pray pardon me,' replied the gardener; 'but it resembled the deceased mademoiselle Hildegarde. She passed close to me in the garden, and then came into the castle."

"'O!' said the count to him, 'I beg, in future you will be a little more circumspect in your fancies, and leave my daughter to rest quietly in the tomb—'Tis well—'

"He then made a signal to his servants, who went out.

"'Well! my dear marquis!' said he to me.

"'Well?'

"'Your belief in stories will not, surely, carry you so far as to give credence to my Hildegarde's spirit appearing?'

"'At least it may have appeared to the gardener only—Do you recollect the adventure in the Museum at Paris?'

"'You are right: that again was a pretty invention, which to this moment I cannot fathom. Believe me, I should sooner have refused my daughter to the duke for his having been the fabricator of so gross a story, than for his having forsaken his first love.'

"'I see very plainly that we shall not easily accord on this point; for if my ready belief appears strange to you, your doubts seem to me incomprehensible.'

"The company assembled at the castle, retired by degrees; and *I alone* was left with the count and his lady, when Ida came to the room-door, clothed in her ball-dress, and appeared astonished at finding the company had left.

"'What can this mean?' demanded the countess. Her husband could not find words to express his astonishment.

"'Where is Marino?' exclaimed Ida.

"'Do *you* ask us where he is?' replied her mother; 'did we not see you go out with him through that small door?'

"'That could not be;—you mistake.'

"'No, no; my dear child! A very short time since you were dancing with singular vehemence; and then you both went out together.'

"'*Me!* my mother?'

"'Yes, my dear Ida: how is it possible you should have forgotten all this?'

"'I have forgotten nothing, believe me.'

"'Where then have you been all this time?'

"'In my sister's chamber,' said Ida.

"I remarked that at these words the count became somewhat pale; and his fearful eye caught mine: he however said nothing. The countess, fearing that her daughter was deceiving her, said to her in an afflicted tone of voice:—

"'How could so singular a fancy possess you on a day like this?'

"'I cannot account for it; and only know, that all on a sudden I felt an oppression at my heart, and fancied that all I wanted was Hildegarde. At the same time I felt a firm belief that I should find her in her room playing on her guitar; for which reason I crept thither softly.'

"'And did you find her there?'

"'Alas! no: but the eager desire that I felt to see her, added to the fatigue of dancing, so entirely overpowered me, that I seated myself on a chair, where I fell fast asleep.'

"'How long since did you quit the room?'

"'The clock in the tower struck the three-quarters past eleven just as I entered my sister's room.'

"'What does all this mean?' said the countess to her husband in a low voice: 'she talks in a connected manner; and yet I know, that as the clock struck three-quarters past eleven, I entreated Ida on this very spot to dance more moderately.'

"'And Marino?'—asked the count.

"'I thought, as I before said, that I should find him here.'

"'Good God!' exclaimed the mother, 'she raves: but the duke—Where is he then?'

"'What then, my good mother?' said Ida with an air of great disquiet, while leaning on the countess.

"Meanwhile the count took a wax-taper, and made a sign for me to follow him. A horrible spectacle awaited us in the bridal-chamber, whither he conducted me. We there found the duke extended on the floor. There did not appear the slightest signs of life in him; and his features were distorted in the most frightful manner.

"Imagine the extreme affliction Ida endured when she heard this recital, and found that all the resources of the medical attendants were employed in vain.

"The count and his family could not be roused from the deep consternation which threatened to overwhelm them. A short time after this event, some business of importance occasioned me to quit their castle; and certainly I was not sorry for the excuse to get away.

"But ere I left that county, I did not fail to collect in the village every possible information relative to the *Death-Bride;* whose history unfortunately, in passing from one mouth to another, experienced many alterations. It appeared to me, however, upon the whole, that this affianced bride lived in this district, about the fourteenth or fifteenth century. She was a young lady of noble family, and she had conducted herself with so much perfidy and ingratitude towards her lover, that he died of grief; but afterwards, when she was about to marry, he appeared to her the night of her intended wedding, and she died in consequence. And it is said, that since that time, the spirit of this unfortunate creature wanders on earth in every possible shape; particularly in that of lovely females, to render their lovers inconstant.

"As it was not permitted for her to appear in the form of any living being, she always chose amongst the dead those who the most strongly resembled them. It was for this reason she voluntarily frequented the galleries in which were hung family portraits. It is even reported that she has been seen in galleries of pictures open to public inspection. Finally, it is said, that, as a punishment for her perfidy, she will wander till she finds a man whom she will in vain endeavour to make swerve from his engagement; and it appears, they added, that as yet she had not succeeded.

"Having inquired what connection subsisted between this spirit and the old chaplain (of whom also I had heard mention), they informed me, that the fate of the last depended on the young lady, because he had assisted her in her criminal conduct. But no one was able to give me any satisfactory information concerning the voice which had called the duke by his name, nor on the meaning of the church being illuminated at night; and why the grand mass was chanted. No one either knows how to account for the dance on the mountain's top in the forest.

"For the rest," added the marquis, "you will own, that the traditions are admirably adapted to my story, and may, to a certain degree, serve to fill up the gaps; but I am not enabled to give a more satisfactory explanation. I reserve for another time a second history of this same *Death-Bride;* I only heard it a few weeks since: it appears to me interesting; but it is too late to begin to-day, and indeed, even now, I fear that I have intruded too long on the leisure of the company present by my narrative."

He had just finished these words, and some of his auditors (though all thanked him for the trouble he had taken) were expressing their disbelief of the story, when a person of his acquaintance came into the room in a hurried manner, and whispered something in his ear. Nothing could be more striking than the contrast presented by the bustling and uneasy air of the newly arrived person while speaking to the marquis, and the calm air of the latter while listening to him.

"Haste, I pray you," said the first (who appeared quite out of patience at the marquis's *sang-froid):* "In a few moments you will have cause to repent this delay."

"I am obliged to you for your affecting solicitude," replied the marquis; who in taking up his hat, appeared more to do, as all the rest of the party were doing, in preparing to return home, than from any anxiety of hastening away.

"You are lost," said the other, as he saw an officer enter the room at the head of a detachment of military, who inquired for the marquis. The latter instantly made himself known to him.

"You are my prisoner," said the officer. The marquis followed him, after saying Adieu with a smiling air to all the party, and begging they would not feel any anxiety concerning him.

"Not feel anxiety!" replied he whose advice he had neglected. "I must inform you, that they have discovered that the marquis has been detected in a connection with very suspicious characters; and his death-warrant may be considered as signed. I came in pity to warn him of his danger, for possibly he might then have escaped; but from his conduct since, I can scarcely imagine he is in his proper senses."

The party, who were singularly affected by this event, were conjecturing a thousand things, when the officer returned, and again asked for the marquis.

"He just now left the room with you," answered someone of the company.

"But he came in again."

"We have seen no one."

"He has then disappeared," replied the officer, smiling: he searched every corner for the marquis, but in vain. The house was thoroughly examined, but without success; and the following day the officer quitted the baths with his soldiers, without his prisoner, and very much dissatisfied.

The Death-Bride, by Edward Vernon Utterson. (Watercolor illustration painted in homage to the story in *Tales of the Dead*, 1813.)

"The Fated Hour": uncredited illustration of Friedrich Laun's story (as translated by Sarah Elizabeth Utterson) from the magazine *The Penny Story-Teller* (1832).

V.

THE FATED HOUR

BY FRIEDRICH LAUN

(TRANSLATED INTO ENGLISH BY SARAH ELIZABETH UTTERSON)

——"Wan the maiden was,
Of saintly paleness, and there seem'd
to dwell
In the strong beauties of her
countenance
Something that was not earthly."
—SOUTHEY'S JOAN OF ARC.[*]

"The clock has toll'd; and, hark! the
bell
Of death beats slow."
—MASON'S ELEGIES.[†]

A HEAVY rain prevented the three friends from taking the morning's walk they had concerted: notwithstanding which, Amelia and Maria failed not to be at Florentina's house at the appointed hour. The latter had for some time past been silent, pensive, and absorbed in thought; and the anxiety of her friends made them very uneasy at the visible impression left on her mind by the violent tempest of the preceding night.

Florentina met her friends greatly agitated, and embraced them with more than usual tenderness.

---

[*] From the epic poem by Robert Southey, first published in 1796.
[†] From William Mason's "An Elegy, on the Death of a Lady," first published in 1760.

"Fine weather for a walk!" cried Amelia: "how have you passed this dreadful night?"

"Not very well, you may easily imagine. My residence is in too lonely a situation."

"Fortunately," replied Maria, laughing, "it will not long be yours."

"That's true," answered Florentina, sighing deeply. "The count returns from his travels to-morrow, in the hope of soon conducting me to the altar."

"Merely in the hope?" replied Maria: "the mysterious manner in which you uttered these words, leads me to apprehend you mean to frustrate those hopes."

"I?—But how frequently in this life does hope prove only an untimely flower?"

"My dear Florentina," said Maria, embracing her, "for some time past my sister and I have vainly attempted to account for your lost gaiety; and have been tormented with the idea, that possibly family reasons have induced you, contrary to your wishes, to consent to this marriage which is about to take place."

"Family reasons! Am I not then the last of our house; the only remaining one, whom the tombs of my ancestors have not as yet enclosed? And have I not for my Ernest that ardent affection which is natural to my time of life? Or do you think me capable of such duplicity, when I have so recently depicted to you, in the most glowing colours, the man of my heart's choice?"

"What then am I to believe?" inquired Maria. "Is it not a strange contradiction, that a young girl, handsome and witty, rich and of high rank, and who, independently of these advantages, will not by her marriage be estranged from her family, should approach the altar with trembling?"

Florentina, holding out her hand to the two sisters, said to them:

"How kind you are! I ought really to feel quite ashamed in not yet having placed entire confidence in your friendship, even on a subject which is to me, at this moment, incomprehensible. At this moment I am not equal to the task; but in the course of the day I hope to be sufficiently recovered. In the meanwhile let us talk on less interesting subjects."

The violent agitation of Florentina's mind was so evident at this moment, that the two sisters willingly assented to her wishes. Thinking that the present occasion required trifling subjects of conversation, they endeavoured to joke with her on the terrors of the preceding night. However, Maria finished by saying, with rather a serious air,—

"I must confess, that more than once I have been tempted to think something extraordinary occurred. At first it appeared as if someone opened and shut the window of the room in which we slept, and then as if they approached my bed. I distinctly heard footsteps: an icy trembling seized me, and I covered my face over with the clothes."

"Alas!" exclaimed Amelia, "I cannot tell you how frequently I have heard similar noises. But as yet nothing have I seen."

"Most fervently do I hope," replied Florentina in an awful tone of voice, "that neither of you will ever, in this life, be subject to a proof of this nature!"

The deep sigh which accompanied these words, and the uneasy look she cast on the two sisters, produced evident emotions in them both.

"Possibly *you* have experienced such proof?" replied Amelia.

"Not precisely so: but—suspend your curiosity. This evening—if I am still alive—I mean to say—that this evening I shall be better able to communicate all to you."

Maria made a sign to Amelia, who instantly understood her sister; and thinking that Florentina wished to be alone, though evidently disturbed in her mind, they availed themselves of the first opportunity which her silence afforded. Her prayer-book was lying open on the table, which, now perceiving for the first time, confirmed Maria in the idea she had conceived. In looking for her shawl she removed a handkerchief which covered this book, and saw that the part which had most probably occupied Florentina before their arrival was the Canticle on Death. The three friends separated, overcome and almost weeping, as if they were never to meet again.

Amelia and Maria awaited with the greatest impatience the hour of returning to Florentina.—They embraced her with redoubled satisfaction, for she seemed to them more gay than usual.

"My dear girls," said she to them, "pardon, I pray you, my abstraction of this morning. Depressed by having passed so bad a night, I thought myself on the brink of the grave; and fancied it needful to make up my accounts in this world, and prepare for the next. I have made my will, and have placed it in the magistrate's hands: however, since I have taken a little repose this afternoon, I find myself so strong, and in such good spirits, that I feel as if I had escaped the danger which threatened me."

"But, my dear," replied Maria, in a mild yet affectionate tone of reproach, "how could one sleepless night fill your mind with such gloomy thoughts?"

"I agree with you on the folly of permitting it so to do; and had I encouraged sinister thoughts, that dreadful night would not have been the sole cause, for it found me in such a frame of mind that its influence was not at all necessary to add to my horrors. But no more of useless mystery. I will fulfil my promise, and clear up your doubts on many parts of my manner and conduct, which at present must appear to you inexplicable. Prepare yourselves for the strangest and most surprising events.—But the damp and cold evening air has penetrated this room, it will therefore be better to have a fire lighted, that the chill which my recital may produce be not increased by any exterior cause."

While they were lighting the fire, Maria and her sister expressed great joy at seeing such a happy change in Florentina's manner; and the latter could scarcely describe the satisfaction she felt, at having resolved to develop to them the secret which she had so long concealed.

The three friends being alone, Florentina began as follows:—

"You were acquainted with my sister Seraphina, whom I had the misfortune to lose; but I alone can boast of possessing her confidence; which is the cause of my mentioning many things relative to her, before I begin the history I have promised, in which she is the principal personage.

"From her infancy, Seraphina was remarkable for several singularities. She was a year younger than myself; but frequently, while seated by her side I was amusing myself with the playthings common to our age, she would fix her eyes, by the half hour together, as if absorbed in thought: she seldom took any part in our infantine amusements. This disposition greatly chagrined our parents; for they attributed Seraphina's indifference to stupidity; and they were apprehensive this defect would necessarily prove an obstacle in the education requisite for the distinguished rank we held in society, my father being, next the prince, the first person in the country. They had already thought of procuring for her a canonry* from some noble chapel, when things took an entirely different turn.

"Her preceptor, an aged man, to whose care they had confided her at a very early age, assured them, that in his life he had never met with so astonishing an intellect as Seraphina's. My father doubted the assertion: but an examination, which he caused to be made in his presence, convinced him that it was founded in truth.

"Nothing was then neglected to give Seraphina every possible accomplishment:—masters of different languages, of music, and of dancing, every day filled the house.

"But in a short time my father perceived that he was again mistaken: for Seraphina made so little progress in the study of the different languages, that the masters shrugged their shoulders; and the dancing-master pretended,

---

* That is, a person admitted to the priesthood.

that though her feet were extremely pretty, he could do nothing with them, as her head seldom took the trouble to guide them.

"By way of retaliation, she made such wonderful progress in music that she soon excelled her masters. She sang in a manner superior to that of the best opera-singers.

"My father acknowledged that his plans for the education of this extraordinary child were now as much too enlarged, as they were before too circumscribed; and that it would not do to keep too tight a hand over her, but let her follow the impulse of her own wishes.

"This new arrangement afforded Seraphina the opportunity of more particularly studying the science of astronomy; which was one they had never thought of as needful for her. You can, my friends, form but a very indifferent idea of the avidity with which (if so I may express myself) she devoured those books which treated on celestial bodies; or what rapture the globes and telescopes occasioned her, when her father presented them to her on her thirteenth birth-day.

"But the progress made in this science in our days did not long satisfy Seraphina's curiosity. To my father's great grief, she was wrapped up in reveries of astrology;* and more than once she was found in the morning occupied in studying books which treated on the influence of the stars, and which she had begun to peruse the preceding evening.

"My mother, being at the point of death, was anxious, I believe, to remonstrate with Seraphina on this whim; but her death was too sudden. My father thought that at this tender age Seraphina's whimsical fancy would wear off: however, time passed on, and he found that she still remained constant to a study she had cherished from her infancy.

"You cannot forget the general sensation her beauty produced at court: how much the fashionable versifiers of the day sang her graceful figure and beautiful flaxen locks; and how often they failed, when they attempted to describe the particular and indefinable character which distinguished her fine blue eyes. I must say, I have often embraced my sister, whom I loved with the greatest affection, merely to have the pleasure of getting nearer, if possible, to her soft angelic eyes, from which Seraphina's pale countenance borrowed almost all its sublimity.

---

* Astrology historically meant the calculation and prediction of natural phenomena and meteorological events (such as the measurement of time, the times of tides and eclipses) on the basis of astronomical observations, but it appears that Seraphina was delving into the pseudoscience as well as basic astronomy.

"She received many extremely advantageous proposals of marriage, but declined them all. You know her predilection in favour of solitude, and that she never went out but to enjoy my society. She took no pleasure in dress; nay, she even avoided all occasions which required more than ordinary expense. Those who were not acquainted with the singularity of her character might have accused her of affectation.

"But a very extraordinary particularity, which I by chance discovered in her just as she attained her fifteenth year, created an impression of fear on my mind which will never be effaced.

"On my return from making a visit, I found Seraphina in my father's cabinet,* near the window, with her eyes fixed and immoveable. Accustomed from her earliest infancy to see her in this situation, without being perceived by her I pressed her to my bosom, without producing on her the least sensation of my presence. At this moment I looked towards the garden, and I there saw my father walking with this same Seraphina whom I held in my arms.

"In the name of God, my sister—!" exclaimed I, equally cold with the statue before me; who now began to recover.

"At the same time my eye involuntarily returned towards the garden, where I had seen her; and there perceived my father alone, looking with uneasiness, as it appeared to me, for her, who, but an instant before, was with him. I endeavoured to conceal this event from my sister; but in the most affectionate tone she loaded me with questions to learn the cause of my agitation.

"I eluded them as well as I could; and asked her how long she had been in the closet. She answered me, smiling, that I ought to know best; as she came in after me; and that if she was not mistaken, she had before that been walking in the garden with my father.

"This ignorance of the situation in which she was but an instant before, did not astonish me on my sister's account, as she had often shewn proofs of this absence of mind. At that instant my father came in, exclaiming: 'Tell me, my dear Seraphina, how you so suddenly escaped from my sight, and came here? We were, as you know, conversing; and scarcely had you finished speaking, when, looking round, I found myself alone. I naturally thought that you had concealed yourself in the adjacent thicket; but in vain I looked there for you; and on coming into this room, here I find you.'

---

* A small chamber, a boudoir.

"'It is really strange,' replied Seraphina; 'I know not myself how it has happened.'

"From that moment I felt convinced of what I had heard from several persons, but what my father always contradicted; which was, that while Seraphina was in the house, she had been seen elsewhere. I secretly reflected also on what my sister had repeatedly told me, that when a child (she was ignorant whether sleeping or awake), she had been transported to heaven, where she had played with angels; to which incident she attributed her disinclination to all infantine games.

"My father strenuously combated this idea, as well as the event to which I had been witness, of her sudden disappearance from the garden.

"'Do not torment me any longer,' said he, 'with these phænomena, which appear complaisantly renewed every day, in order to gratify your eager imagination. It is true, that your sister's person and habits present many singularities; but all your idle talk will never persuade me that she holds any immediate intercourse with the world of spirits.'

"My father did not then know, that where there is any doubt of the future, the weak mind of man ought not to allow him to profane the word *never*, by uttering it.

"About a year and half afterwards, an event occurred which had power to shake even my father's determined manner of thinking to its very foundation. It was on a Sunday, that Seraphina and I wished at last to pay a visit which we had from time to time deferred: for notwithstanding my sister was very fond of being with me, she avoided even my society whenever she could not enjoy it but in the midst of a large assembly, where constraint destroyed all pleasure.

"To adorn herself for a party, was to her an anticipated torment; for she said, she only submitted to this trouble to please those whose frivolous and dissipated characters greatly offended her. On similar occasions she sometimes met with persons to whom she could not speak without shuddering, and whose presence made her ill for several days.

"The hour of assembling approached; she was anxious that I should go without her: my father doubting her, came into our room, and insisted on her changing her determination.

"'I cannot permit you to infringe every duty.'

"He accordingly desired her to dress as quickly as possible, and accompany me.

"The waiting-maid was just gone out on an errand with which I had commissioned her. My sister took a light to fetch her clothes from a wardrobe in the upper story. She remained much longer absent than was requisite. At length she returned without a light:—I screamed with fright. My father asked her in an agitated manner, what had happened to her. In fact, she had scarcely been absent a quarter of an hour, and yet during that time her face had undergone a complete alteration; her habitual paleness had given place to a death-like hue; her ruby lips were turned blue.

"My arms involuntarily opened to embrace this sister whom I adored. I almost doubted my sight, for I could get no answer from her; but for a long while she leaned against my bosom, mute and inanimate. The look, replete with infinite softness, which she gave my father and me, alone informed us, that during her continuance in this incomprehensible trance, she still belonged to the material world.

"'I was seized with a sudden indisposition,' she at length said in a low voice; 'but I now find myself better.'

"She asked my father whether he still wished her to go into society. He thought, that after an occurrence of this nature her going out might be dangerous: but he would not dispense with my making the visit, although I endeavoured to persuade him that my attention might be needful to Seraphina. I left her with an aching heart.

"I had ordered the carriage to be sent for me at a very early hour: but the extreme anxiety I felt would not allow me to wait its arrival, and I returned home on foot. The servant could scarcely keep pace with me, such was my haste to return to Seraphina.

"On my arrival in her room, my impatience was far from being relieved.

"'Where is she?' I quickly asked.

"'Who mademoiselle?'

"'Why, Seraphina.'

"'Mademoiselle, Seraphina is in your father's closet.'

"'Alone?'

"'No with his excellency.'

"I ran to the boudoir: the door, which was previously shut, at that instant opened, and my father with Seraphina came out: the latter was in tears. I remarked that my father had an air of chagrin and doubt which not even the storms of public life had ever produced in his countenance.

"He made us a sign full of gentleness, and Seraphina followed me into another room: but she first assured my father she would remember the promise he had exacted, and of which I was still ignorant.

"Seraphina appeared to me so tormented by the internal conflicts she endured, that I several times endeavoured, but in vain, to draw from her the mysterious event which had so recently thrown her into so alarming a situation. At last I overcame her scruples, and she answered me as follows:

"'Your curiosity shall be satisfied, in part. I will develop some of the mystery to you; but only on one irrevocable condition.'

"I entreated her instantly to name the condition: and she thus continued:—

"'Swear to me, that you will rest satisfied with what I shall disclose to you, and that you will never urge nor use that power which you possess over my heart, to obtain a knowledge of what I am obliged to conceal from you.'

"I swore it to her.

"'Now, my dear Florentina, forgive me, if, for the first time in my life, I have a secret from you; and also for not being satisfied with your mere word for the promise I have exacted from you. My father, to whom I have confided everything, has imposed these two obligations on me, and his last words were to that effect.'

"I begged her to come to the point.

"'Words are inadequate to describe,' said she, 'the weight I felt my soul oppressed with when I went to get my clothes. I had no sooner closed the door of the room in which you and my father were, than I fancied I was about to be separated from life and all that constituted my happiness; and that I had many dreadful nights to linger through, ere I could arrive at a better and more peaceful abode. The air which I breathed on the staircase was not such as usually circulates around us; it oppressed my breathing, and caused large drops of icy perspiration to fall from my forehead. Certain it is, I was not alone on the staircase; but for a long while I dared not look around me.

"'You know, my dear Florentina, with what earnestness I wished and prayed, but in vain, that my mother would appear to me after her death, if only for once. I fancied that on the stairs I heard my mother's spirit behind me. I was apprehensive it was come to punish me for the vows I had already made.'

"'A strange thought, certainly!'

"'But how could I imagine that a mother, who was goodness itself, could be offended by the natural wishes of a tenderly beloved child, or have imputed them to indiscreet curiosity? It was no less foolish to think that she, who had been so long since enclosed in the tomb, should occupy herself in inflicting chastisement on me, for faults which were nearly obliterated from my recollection. I was so immediately convinced of the weakness of giving way to such ideas, that I summoned courage and turned my head.

"'Although my affrighted survey could discover nothing, I again heard the footsteps following me, but more distinctly than before. At the door of the room I was about to enter, I felt my gown held. Overpowered by terror, I was unable to proceed, and fell on the threshold of the door.

"'I lost no time, however, in reproaching myself for suffering terror so to overcome me; and recollected that there was nothing supernatural in this accident, for my gown had caught on the handle of an old piece of furniture which had been placed in the passage, to be taken out of the house the following day.

"'This discovery inspired me with fresh courage. I approached the wardrobe: but judge my consternation, when, preparing to open it, the two doors unclosed of themselves, without making the slightest noise; the lamp which I held in my hand was extinguished, and—as if I was standing before a looking-glass,—my exact image came out of the wardrobe: the light which it spread, illumined great part of the room.

"'I then heard these words:—Why tremble you at the sight of your own spirit, which appears to give you warning of your approaching dissolution, and to reveal to you the fate of your house?'

"'The phantom then informed me of several future events. But when, after having deeply meditated on its prophetic words, I asked a question relative to you, the room became as dark as before, and the spirit had vanished. This, my dear, is all I am permitted to reveal.'

"'Your approaching death!' cried I:—That thought had in an instant effaced all other.

"Smiling, she made me a sign in the affirmative; and gave me to understand, at the same time, that I ought to press her no further on this subject. 'My father,' added she, 'has promised to make you acquainted, in proper time, with all it concerns you to know.'

"'At a proper time!' repeated I, in a plaintive voice; for it appeared to me, that since I had learned so much, it was high time that I should be made acquainted with the whole.

"The same evening I mentioned my wishes to my father: but he was inexorable. He fancied that possibly what had happened to Seraphina might have arisen from her disordered and overheated imagination. However, three days afterwards, my sister finding herself so ill as to be obliged to keep her bed, my father's doubts began to be shaken; and although the precise day of Seraphina's death had not been named to me, I could not avoid observing by her paleness, and the more than usually affectionate manner of embracing my father and me, that the time of our eternal separation was not far off.

"'Will the clock soon strike nine?' asked Seraphina, while we were sitting near her bed in the evening.

"'Yes, soon,' replied my father.

"'Well then! think of me, dear objects of my affection:—we shall meet again.' She pressed our hands; and the clock no sooner struck, than she fell back in her bed, never to rise more.

"My father has since related to me every particular as it happened; for at that time I was so much overcome that my senses had forsaken me.

"Seraphina's eyes were scarcely closed, when I returned to a life which then appeared to me insupportable. I was apprehensive that the state of stupefaction into which I was thrown by the dread of the loss that threatened me, had appeared to my sister a want of attachment. And from that time I have never thought of the melancholy scene without experiencing a violent shuddering.

"'You must be aware,' said my father to me (it was at the precise hour, and before the same chimney we are at this moment placed)—you must be aware, that the pretended vision should still be kept quite secret.' I was of his opinion; but could not help adding, 'What! still, my father, though one part of the prediction has in so afflicting a manner been verified, you continue to call it a pretended vision?'

"'Yes, my child; you know not what a dangerous enemy to man is his own imagination. Seraphina will not be the last of its victims.'

"We were seated, as I before said, just as we now are; and I was about to name a motive which I had before omitted, when I perceived that his eyes were fixed in a disturbed manner on the door. I was ignorant of the cause, and could discover nothing extraordinary there: notwithstanding, however, an instant afterwards it opened of its own accord."

Here Florentina stopped, as if overcome anew by the remembrance of her terror. At the same moment Amelia rose from her seat uttering a loud scream.

Her sister and her friend inquired what ailed her. For a long while she made them no reply, and would not resume her seat on the chair, the back of which was towards the door. At length, however, she confessed (casting an inquiring and anxious look around her) that a hand, cold as ice, had touched her neck.

"This is truly the effect of imagination," said Maria, reseating herself. "It was my hand: for some time my arm has been resting on your chair; and when mention was made of the door opening of its own accord, I felt a wish to rest on some living object—"

"But *à-propos*,—And the door—?"

"Strange incident! I trembled with fear; and clinging to my father, asked him if he did not see a sort of splendid light, a something brilliant, penetrate the apartment.

"''Tis well!' answered he, in a low and tremulous voice, 'we have lost a being whom we cherished; and consequently, in some degree, our minds are disposed to exalted ideas, and our imaginations may very easily be duped by the same illusions: besides, there is nothing very unnatural in a door opening of its own accord.'

"'It ought to be closely shut now,' replied I; without having the courage to do it.

"''Tis very easy to shut it,' said my father. But he rose in visible apprehension, walked a few paces, and then returned, adding, 'The door may remain open; for the room is too warm.'

"It is impossible for me to describe, even by comparison, the singular light I had perceived: and I do assure you, that if, instead of the light, I had seen my sister's spirit enter, I should have opened my arms to receive it; for it was only the mysterious and vague appearance of this strange vision which caused me so much fear.

"The servants coming in at this instant with supper, put an end to the conversation.

"Time could not efface the remembrance of Seraphina; but it wore off all recollection of the last apparition. My daily intercourse with you, my friends, since the loss of Seraphina, has been for me a fortunate circumstance, and has insensibly become an indispensable habit. I no longer thought deeply of the prediction relative to our house, uttered by the phantom to my sister; and in the arms of friendship gave myself up entirely to the innocent gaiety which youth inspires. The beauties of spring contributed to the restoration of my peace of mind. One evening, just as you had left me, I continued walking in the garden, as if intoxicated with the delicious vapours emitted from the flowers, and the magnificent spectacle which the serenity of the sky presented to my view.

"Absorbed entirely by the enjoyment of my existence, I did not notice that it was later than my usual hour for returning. And I know not why, but that evening no one appeared to think of me; for my father, whose solicitude for everything concerning me was redoubled since my sister's death, and who knew I was in the garden, had not, as was his usual custom, sent me any garment to protect me from the chilling night air.

"While thus reflecting, I was seized with a violent feverish shivering, which I could by no means attribute to the night air. My eyes accidentally fixed on the flowering shrubs; and the same brilliant light which I had seen at the door of the room on the day of Seraphina's burial, appeared to me to rest on these shrubs, and dart its rays towards me. The avenue in which I was happened to have been Seraphina's favourite walk.

"The recollection of this inspired me with courage, and I approached the shrubs in the hope of meeting my sister's shade beneath the trees. But my hopes being frustrated, I returned to the house with trembling steps.

"I there found many extraordinary circumstances: nobody had thought of supper, which I imagined would have been half over. All the servants were running about in confusion, and were hastening to pack up the clothes and furniture.

"'Who is going away?' I demanded.

"'Why surely, mademoiselle!' exclaimed the steward, 'are you not acquainted with his excellency's wish to have us all?'

"'Wherefore then?'

"This very night we are to set out for his excellency's estate."

"'Why so?'

"They shrugged their shoulders. I ran into my father's cabinet, and there found him with his eyes fixed on the ground.

"'Seraphina's second prophecy is also accomplished,' said he to me, 'though precisely the least likely thing possible.—I am in disgrace.'

"'What! did she predict this?'

"'Yes, my child; but I concealed it from you. I resign myself to my fate, and leave others better to fill this perilous post. I am about to retire to my own estates, there to live for you, and to constitute the happiness of my vassals.'

"In spite of the violent emotions which were created by my father's misfortune, and the idea of separating from all the friends I loved, his apparent tranquility produced a salutary effect on my mind. At midnight we set off. My father was so much master of himself under his change of condition, that by the time he arrived at his estate he was calm and serene.

"He found many things to arrange and improve; and his active turn of mind soon led him to find a train of pleasing occupations.

"In a short time, however, he was withdrawn from them, by an illness which the physicians regarded as very serious. My father conformed to all they prescribed: he abstained from all occupation, though he entertained very little hope of any good resulting from it. 'Seraphina,' he said to me (entirely changing his former opinion), 'Seraphina has twice predicted true; and will a third time.'

"This conversation made me very miserable; for I understood from it that my father believed he should shortly die.

"In fact, he visibly declined, and was at length forced to keep his bed. He one evening sent for me; and after having dismissed his attendants, he, in a feeble voice, and with frequent interruptions, thus addressed me:—

"'Experience has cured me of incredulity; When the clock strikes nine, according to Seraphina's prediction, I shall be no more. For this reason, my dear child, I am anxious to address a few words of advice to you. If possible, remain in your present state; never marry. Destiny appears to have conspired against our race.—But no more of this.—To proceed: if ever you seriously think of marrying, do not, I beseech you, neglect to read this paper; but my express desire is, that you do not open it beforehand, as in that case its contents would cause you unnecessary misery.'

"Saying these words, which with sobbing I listened to, he drew from under his pillow a sealed paper, which he gave me. The moment was not favourable for reflecting on the importance of the condition which he imposed on me. The clock, which announced the *fated hour*, at which my father, resting on my shoulder, drew his last gasp, deprived me of my senses.

"The day of his interment was also marked by the brilliant and extraordinary light of which I have before made mention.

"You know, that shortly after this melancholy loss I returned to the capital, in hopes of finding consolation in your beloved society. You also know, that youth seconded your efforts to render existence desirable, and that by degrees I felt a relish for life. Neither are you ignorant that the result of this intercourse was an attachment between the count Ernest and me, which rendered my father's exhortations abortive. The count loved me, and I returned his affection, and nothing more was wanting to make me think that I ought not to lead a life of celibacy: besides, my father had only made this request conditionally.

"My marriage appeared certain; and I did not hesitate to open the mysterious paper. There it is, I will read it to you:—

"'Seraphina has undoubtedly already told you, that when she endeavoured to question the phantom concerning your destiny, it suddenly disappeared. The incomprehensible being seen by your sister had made mention of you, and its afflicting decree was, that three days before that fixed on for your marriage, you would die at the same *ninth* hour which has been so fatal to us. Your sister recovering a little from her first alarm, asked it, if you could not escape this dreadful mandate by remaining single.

"'Unhappily, Seraphina did not receive any answer: but I feel assured, that by marrying you will die. For this reason I entreat you to remain single: I add, however—if it accords with your inclinations; as I do not feel confident that even this will ensure you from the effect of the prediction.

"'In order, my dear child, to save you from all premature uneasiness, I have avoided this communication till the hour of danger: reflect, therefore, seriously on what you ought to do.

"'My spirit, when you read these lines, shall hover over and bless you, whatever way you decide.'"

Florentina folded up the paper again in silence; and, after a pause which her two friends sensibly felt, added:—

"Possibly, my dear friends, this has caused the change in me which you have sometimes condemned. But tell me whether, situated as I am, you would not become troubled, and almost annihilated, by the prediction which announced your death on the very eve of your happiness?

"Here my recital ends. To-morrow the count returns from his travels. The ardour of his affection has induced him to fix on the third day after his arrival for the celebration of our marriage."

"Then 'tis this very day!" exclaimed Amelia and Maria at the same moment; paleness and inquietude depicted on every feature, when their eyes glanced to a clock on the point of striking nine.

"Yes, this is indeed the decisive day," replied Florentina, with a grave yet serene air. "The morning has been to me a frightful one; but at this moment I find myself composed, my health is excellent, and gives me a confidence that death would with difficulty overcome me to-day. Besides, a secret but lively presentiment tells me that this very evening the wish I have so long formed will be accomplished. My beloved sister will appear to me, and will defeat the prediction concerning me.

"Dear Seraphina! you were so suddenly, so cruelly snatched from me! Where are you, that I may return, with tenfold interest, the love that I have not the power of proving towards you?"

The two sisters, transfixed with horror, had their eyes riveted on the clock, which struck the *fated* hour.

"You are welcome!" cried Florentina, seeing the fire in the chimney, to which they had paid no attention, suddenly extinguished. She then rose from her chair; and with open arms walked towards the door which Maria and Amelia anxiously regarded, whilst sighs escaped them both; and at which entered the figure of Seraphina, illumined by the moon's rays. Florentina folded her sister in her arms.—"I am thine forever!"

These words, pronounced in a soft and melancholy tone of voice, struck Amelia and Maria's ears; but they knew not whether they were uttered by Florentina or the phantom, or whether by both the sisters together.

Almost at the same moment the servants came in, alarmed, to learn what had happened. They had heard a noise as if all the glasses and porcelain in the house were breaking. They found their mistress extended at the door, but not the slightest trace of the apparition remained.

Every means of restoring Florentina to life were used, but in vain. The physicians attributed her death to a ruptured blood-vessel. Maria and Amelia will carry the remembrance of this heart-rending scene to their graves.

The Fated Hour, by Edward Vernon Utterson. (Watercolor illustration painted in homage to the story in *Tales of the Dead*, 1813.)

Engraved illustration from *La Lecture Journal de Roman*: "Apparation Dame Blanche au Chevet d'un Mourrant," by Labeauce et Minne (1857).

VI.

THE REVENANT

BY FRIEDRICH LAUN

(TRANSLATED INTO ENGLISH BY ANNA ZIEGELHOF)

HERR Soller's large estate, which included three palatial houses in town, caused Julie*, his only daughter and beneficiary, to have many more admirers than even her flawless figure and appealing face alone might have won her. And so, at the age of seventeen, and knowing she needn't settle for anything less than what her heart entirely wished for, she had already rejected several marriage proposals by offering ambiguous responses and several more by rejecting them outright.

Her father, with whom she had shared that each suitor thus far was not one who could entirely hold her heart, was pleased to have such a prudent daughter.

When one day he was informed of Julie's particular friendliness toward a Doctor Gustav Hess, he responded confidently, "You don't know my Julie! She is content here with me."

Soller believed that his daughter's dreams had not yet outgrown the realm of his calm and comfortable house. But at his age, content with passable health and a quiet life, he'd forgotten that youthful yearnings differed, and that a tranquil, sheltered life might irritate rather than placate certain desires.

Therefore, when a letter addressed to Julie happened to reach him during her absence due to a lamentable error on the part of a messenger, Soller was surprised. The writing on the envelope quite clearly indicated an unknown male's hand, and so he awaited his daughter's return impatiently.

When the moment arrived, he handed her the letter, and watched her startle so visibly at the penmanship that he knew there was an impropriety

---

* Orig. written as "Julien," an archaic manner of expressing the dative, accusative, or genitive case in German language.

afoot. He snatched the letter back from her, opened it, and read aloud the repeated declarations of Doctor Gustav Hess's steadfast love. A grave interrogation followed an even graver prohibition, for Soller learned this letter had not even been the first! Oh, the promises Julie had to quickly make to ease her father's fury!

Later, when Julie's beloved Gustav came to her window inquiring as to the disruption in exchanging letters, she explained with tear-streaked eyes what had occurred, and of her father's opinion of the matter. This caused the uproarious heart of the young doctor to seek an audience with Herr Soller, at which Gustav formally asked for Julie's hand in marriage; he was promptly and equally-formally rejected by her father.

Though perhaps not at a moment of ideal timing, the rejection was a mystery, as Gustav possessed a considerable, independent fortune, a good reputation, pleasant behavior, and in short, everything that would ordinarily support a proposal. Even a small scar on his cheek, attained during a duel in his student days, did not mar his honorable reputation, as it was known that it had not been he who had begun the quarrel.

In vain, Julie hoped that her father, who was usually compassionate, would not be able to withstand forever her cajolery to change his opinion. She and Gustav each tried to persuade him to permit the union which they so dearly desired.

After a number of failed attempts, the girl eventually divined the cause for her father's obstinacy, and thus the hope that her wedding wish would be granted while he was still alive dwindled: since suffering from an affliction that caused him to ultimately retire from his business affairs—and much to his chagrin—Herr Soller was able to see ghosts. He had even developed, *contra* Doctor Jung*, his own theory of the spirit realm, according to which persons, who, while still alive, "made themselves visible" in ghostly form were thus revealed to have a particularly dubious character.

Julie began to suspect that her lover's spirit had appeared to her father, and she did not rest until it was confirmed that this was indeed the case: the night of the letter's interception, Doctor Gustav Hess, dressed in his usual clothing, had passed by Soller's bed in ghostly form.

Only one desperate measure remained to Julie, and even though her sense of modesty rebelled, she attempted it. She approached her father with

---

* Reference to Johann Heinrich Jung-Stilling, a doctor who authored mystical works on the spirit world, *Scenen aus dem Geisterreiche* (1795–1801) [*Scenes From the Spirit Realm*] and *Theorie der Geister-Kunde* (1808) [*Theory of the Study of Ghosts*].

a false confession: driven by his rage and her own tender heart, she had opened the gates that night and allowed the doctor to enter, so that Soller had seen the man himself, not his spirit. Her account was embellished with such detail and such probability—down to her exact method of attaining the keys to house and atrium—that there was no doubt left on her father's mind to believe the falsehood.

Julie had chosen her strategy well. She was reprimanded for her supposed confession, but her father's dislike of Gustav was assuaged, and Julie joyfully told her beloved about her father's change of heart. Gustav repeated his marriage proposal and Soller, to whom it now seemed precarious to shelter a daughter under his roof who was wont to open her chamber door to her lover in the middle of the night, consented.

Unfortunately, eight days before the wedding, Gustav's spirit appeared again to Soller. And this time Soller paid such close attention to the locked doors that Julie could not have used her previous self-accusation successfully again. Soller now insisted on cancelling the wedding. A formal prophecy addressed to his daughter regarding her certain future misfortune began to cause Julie some doubt, but her dear Gustav succeeded in distracting her from such a prophecy of doom. Their engagement had already been made public, and the couple insisted her father keep his previously given word. Soller also knew that everyone would regard the reason for the withdrawal of his marriage consent as a figment of his imagination, and he couldn't find a better reason, so he agreed eventually, but refused obstinately to witness the wedding ceremony.

After the wedding and over time, Soller reestablished the naturally harmonious relationship between father and child, returned the couple's visits, and even confessed to the young woman that he had found his concerns regarding her husband so far unfounded.—

Gustav retired from the practice of medicine, only treating some personal friends *pro bono*. The couple thus had the luxury of engaging in all of love's whims and did so, not seldom to excess. With feverish yearning, they sought to eliminate everything that might change their current circumstances in the least, and when Soller's ghost-seeing was addressed in this context, the lovers discussed their own wish to reunite after death.

The couple began to consider whether Soller's stories about ghosts occasionally visiting him might have a certain substance, even while they maintained that his conclusions and the ghostly taxonomy of his own making were objectionable. Gustav knew a story about two lovers who promised each other never to part, not even in death. The husband indeed kept his word and returned. Julie expressed her hope that this might be the same for them, and Gustav concurred warmly. The couple began collecting strange and archaic books regarding the ghostly realm. Several rare manuscripts completed their studies, which they engaged in studying with fervor.

Soon, the couple progressed from being willing to consider the possibility of ghostly apparitions to a firm belief in their existence. Aided by several rather arbitrary hypotheses, they derived, like Soller, their own theory. According to this theory, an earnestly loving couple would not be separated by death, but rather, the individual first to depart from life would retain the right to hover close to the bereaved one as a guardian angel until the couple reunited.

Unfortunately, the fervor of Julie and Gustav's new obsession was gradually lessened by time and life. Each discovered human weaknesses in the other, which destroyed their ideal of perfection to such an extent that, soon following the birth of their first child, their hopes regarding a return from the realm of shadows were entirely forgotten. Their formerly unwavering love wavered more and more as the months passed. When the baby, who had become the center of his mother's life, passed away, Gustav was unable to fill the void.

Both Julie and Gustav, once so happily united, began to assert their independent existences again and while neither could accuse the other formally of infidelity, both began to doubt the other's steadfastness in this regard.

Three years later, their connection seemed dissolved entirely. Only outward appearances were kept up, and quarrels were never permitted to leave their house. After all, her father's prophecies simply had to be proven wrong, and friends who had not forgotten their extraordinary love on their wedding day, could absolutely not be given a reason to now laugh at them. A certain change in attitude toward each other, however, could not be concealed entirely from closer acquaintances.

Although Gustav had given up his life as a doctor for profit, he still promoted self-care through natural effects, and advocated a tranquil and indulgent life. He had spent the summer months of the first two years of their marriage taking the waters at a spa town with Julie. He'd made plans to visit the spa town also during the third summer, but Julie declined that invitation, given the recent stillbirth of their second child and her resulting lingering sickliness as her reason.

She didn't mind much that her husband understood, as his smile proved, that this was merely an excuse.

Only following his departure did she remember a minor ailment he had complained about a few months prior. She had assumed it had been due to their mutual discontent with each other. But what if it was a real sickness? And what if he were to become seriously ill among strangers?

She was on the verge of calling for a carriage to go meet him—

Merry company, however, soon expelled such worries from her youthful mind. How silly of her to have thought with such concern about a man who was surely recuperating from the boredom of their marital life in another lover's arms.

She found she enjoyed her solitude. She didn't have to worry about carrying on with a fair number of tasks and behaviors her husband would have expected of her. Nothing but personal virtue dictated her life, and she thought of her husband's impending return with dread. Then a letter arrived, postponing the doctor's return by three weeks.

Even though she welcomed this development, she felt a tinge of annoyance that Gustav failed to disclose the reason for his extended absence.

After a week had passed, she received another letter, this from her husband's brother, a government official in a distant country, who had, as Julie learned from his letter, now undertaken the strenuous journey to the spa town in order to meet his only brother, whom he loved dearly, after a long absence. Further, the letter mentioned her husband's serious illness.

Julie was shaken by this news and had barely prepared a hasty departure when a second letter arrived from him, and Julie understood that the first letter had only been in preparation for the second one, lamenting her husband's demise. A sudden stroke had ended his young life prematurely.

Gustav's funeral had already occurred, the letter went on to say, which was both an emotional and festive occasion, since his jovial personality had gained him many friends in the spa town. The brother further reported in the letter that it had truly been his intention to deliver the news to the widow in person, but unfortunately urgent official business had called him away. He did mention, though, once having heard from the deceased that a third of his entire fortune was to be left to Julie in bonds and cash.

Julie was deeply hurt by the sudden death, and this economic diligence seemed only to taint the solemnity of the moment. She developed a pronounced antipathy against the letter's author who had deemed it appropriate to consider the financial situation before the first days of mourning had passed.

The worry she had felt immediately following her husband's departure now seemed nearly to crush her. Every joyous moment of their love suddenly emerged from the twilight of her memory, particularly that long-forgotten, solemn moment in which they had promised each other their reciprocal apparition following their deaths.

Her dwelling became dim and lonely, and she felt a feverish terror.

When she had undressed and her chamber maid was about to leave, she called the girl back, but immediately changed her mind and let the maid go after all. Julie was disinclined to shackle her husband's ghost with the presence of witnesses; even though she trembled so, she was barely able to reach the bed. Still, she desired no protection other than of sleep.

But slumber would not come, as much as she clenched her eyes shut and even though the bed curtains, usually kept open, were drawn. An impossibly strange rushing sound arose there in the solitary bed chamber. And when Julie finally, trembling with terror and prepared for anything, turned to open the bed curtains, lamplight cast a confoundingly asymmetrical shimmer, forming an enigmatic shadow on one side of the chamber, the likes of which she had never seen before.

She glanced at the shadow with fearful suspicion. The longer her eyes attempted to penetrate the twilight, the more of a wavering quality the shadow appeared to gain. The lamp's flame flickered, as if something external had begun to move it.

What perturbed Julie most, however, was the continuous ticking of a clock near the bed, which seemed only to grow louder in her mind. Julie gathered her courage, but just as she sat up to stop the clock, the sound of it striking midnight threw her back as if it were the moan of the phantom itself. Julie's eyes flew wide open at the bright chiming, and she saw how the sickly spirit of her husband emerged from the dreadful shadow and directed its silent steps toward her bed.—

This was the last she saw before succumbing to unconsciousness. The following morning she awoke, struck by a terribly high fever.

Her recovery took several months, but once she had recuperated, her father implored her for information about the ghost, whose appearance she had mentioned during her feverish illness. But Julie temporarily could not remember anything about the night that led to her indisposition and avoided mentioning the subject to him.

Once her health allowed, Julie's foremost thought was to embark immediately on a faithful pilgrimage to her husband's grave. As luck would have it, a close friend had just received doctor's orders to travel to the same spa town, so she accompanied the grieving widow.

Julie was glad to see that her departed loved one was remembered fondly in the town where he had passed his final days. Grateful and moved, she regarded the headstone that friends had placed upon his grave. Her husband, she learned, had passed on while following the call of duty of his medical profession. Full of sympathy, he had taken in a helpless ailing man whose disease Gustav had caught, and which had ultimately caused his demise by way of stroke. At first, nobody told Julie that his death had also been hastened by a fall from his bed, but many people had heard about this circumstance, and eventually Julie heard it, too.

Her husband's grave was the only place in town where the mourning widow found an inkling of solace, and when her traveling companion remarked that the spa town's waters did not seem to improve her condition, Julie was glad to together depart.

She returned home to find more distressing news: her father was bedridden, and doctors informed Julie that death was to be the only cure from his suffering.

She dedicated herself to his care, as knowing the impending loss of another dear person heightened her love. Julie rarely left her father's chamber. If anyone wished to see her, they had to visit the sick man, and therefore, Soller was witness to several visits from young men who were clearly hoping to transform Julie's widowed life into one of new matrimony.

The comely widow's inobtrusive yet attentive care for the dying man, catering even to requests not yet spoken aloud, even deepened visiting witnesses' interest. After all, she denied herself the joys of her youth for months, dedicating herself completely to catering to every need and wish of a hopelessly sick man, who often subjected her to irrational whims—what an asset she would be to a husband! But no matter how plain a suitor made his interest, no matter how many exquisite matches there were for her to choose from, she did not take any, even when, after ten months of sickness, her father passed away and was buried.

Julie began to again socialize following the death of her father, however she did not intend to end widowhood. The memory of the first weeks of her marriage still remained vivid. The couple's mutual love proved too strong to permit her to hope for a future liaison of similar passion; she was reluctant to invite anything less passionate into her life, for any compromise was too high a price for her independence. She made this plain to several suitors, so that her choice to remain a widow led some of them to invent dishonorable quips of her in passing gossip.

A lack of rest and sleep during her father's illness had also caused her beauty and grace to wane slightly, but both were fully restored after his death.

Occasionally she blamed herself for having allowed her husband to travel to the spa town on his own, even though his ghost had not made another appearance. She even began to doubt whether it really was his ghost and began to attribute the event to her guilty conscience and the onset of her nervous fever. She deeply regretted her terrified reaction; if it truly had been his ghost, she told herself, it was more probable that her dear husband had remembered his promise to visit her as a guardian angel, not as a frightening apparition.

Her already tranquil and increasingly withdrawn life became even more solitary when her faithful maid married. This maid had grown up alongside Julie; they'd even received the same education, yet now she deigned to marry a person who was not her equal, neither in education nor in social standing.

Julie permitted the marriage and even hosted the wedding. However, she could no longer associate with the maid as this naturally might have caused Julie to descend into less educated circles herself.

Though she had other personal staff, none compared to that dear maid, and so loneliness grew and Julie escaped into vivid memories of the first days of her courtship. She even began to wish her lover would return in his ghostly form, so that he might see how much joy she achieved from rereading his fiery love letters, or how she pressed his picture or some other souvenir of his to her heart; in short, how her entire life was lived in reference to their past joined one.

She had fallen asleep with this thought in mind, when carriages rattled past outside, returning revelers from a masquerade, another invitation to which Julie had declined.

She returned to sleep for several hours when she was woken again. And there, in a far corner of the adjoining room, she perceived a shadow approaching slowly. The apparition she had longed for, certainly!

But had she disturbed her husband's rest by wishing for his return with such fervor? The thought robbed her of any joy, and she could not bring herself to address the ghost. Fear took her breath away and she closed her eyes when the shadow was still far away in the adjoining room.

Out of fear, she blinked and—there!—the apparition stood close to her bed.

Julie lay still, afraid, for a long time, until the figure finally crept away.

It took Julie half an hour to recover enough from her terror to ring the service bell. She rang three times, but her new maid did not come.

The clock struck two then, and she went to look for the maid. She found an empty bed. Both the cook and the footman were asleep on one of the upper floors, which lacked bells. Julie knew that the maid, who was quite pretty and desirous, led an immoral life. Julie deemed it likely that the shameless girl had snuck out of the house, convinced she would not be missed. At least Julie found the house's door locked behind.

The following morning, the maid's sleep-deprived eyes prophesied what she would later confess to Julie: she had indeed snuck out to attend the masquerade, and not modestly either. Since Julie had prohibited her nocturnal escapades several times before, the maid was dismissed. Julie managed to hire a replacement on the same day, who seemed a much better choice than the three other maids Julie had given a chance since the marriage of her first maid.

Every night now, the widow was haunted by fear as if it were a bad fever. The sound of wind or the rustling of reeds made her whole body shiver. While her eyes refused to identify the apparition of her loved one, her ear heard his movements. She recalled her father's words, and felt no doubt as to ghostly apparitions now. She also did not keep the matter a secret and gladly debated anyone who expressed disbelief that a figure had appeared at her bedside. Nobody, Julie decided, was going to deny her the discerning powers of her eyes and ears. She now also mentioned her previous experience, shortly following her husband's death. She had not previously mentioned it to anybody, because she doubted her own mental state after having been struck by a fever. She challenged her interlocutors by asking whether anyone had noticed any traits of mental weakness in her since then. Rational explanations, which were given often, vexed her. Some people suggested that she could have seen one of her former maid's lovers, who had entered the wrong chamber. Wasn't it likely that Julie had seen one of them, since her so-called ghost was wearing regular, fashionable clothing, and not a ghostly shroud?

Julie countered the first suggestion by saying that those lovers of her frivolous maid, who were familiar enough with the girl to have come into the possession of a key, would surely have been able to find her chamber, located on the other side of the house. And that the outer door was securely locked could hardly be denied by anyone.

The explanation regarding the ghost's clothing was dismissed by Julie, too; a disembodied being wishing to be recognized in the physical realm simply had to take on a recognizable form. Didn't she deserve to be believed, she asked passionately; she was ready to swear under oath that there was no difference between the apparition and her departed husband. Her keen eye had even perceived the scar on his cheek!

Julie retold the incident so persuasively and with such conviction that many people believed her account, and her ghost-seeing ability became a topic of conversation so often that it would have been a miracle if the affair had escaped the attention of newspaper publishers, who were ready to print almost anything sensational.

Although the little news pamphlet put forth by some anonymous author was brimming with errors, nobody asked the heroine of the story for any public corrections; she had certainly told the story often enough, but her name was not disclosed in the piece. Occasional scoffers did not make her belief falter either. Since her new maid now slept in her room with her, Julie had neither seen nor heard any disturbance around the house. When summer arrived and the nights became shorter, she even grew courageous enough to sleep alone again. Yet her belief in the verity of the apparition was never weakened.

Toward the end of summer, Julie attended a party where she encountered a dear friend of her late husband's, whom she had not seen since long before his death. She was happily surprised to see the man, who was pleasant in both personality and appearance, and whose only shortcoming was that he enjoyed an unsteady life and had no intention to marry. Julie's arrival deprived the party of the gentleman's lively wit and graceful conversation; Herr von Rosen began a private conversation with her, which lasted all evening and was continued the following morning in Julie's house.

The topic of their conversation was Julie's encounter with the ghost.

Herr von Rosen was known as a skeptic. Even while her husband was still alive, he had skillfully found natural explanations for stories about ghostly apparitions. He denounced the appearance of his departed friend, and proof and rebuttal were exchanged by both debaters with so much passion that it seemed impossible to bring their dispute to a conclusion.

After Herr von Rosen claimed in vain that Julie was deceived either by her own senses or by other people, he suddenly exclaimed, "But what if everything could be explained in a different way?"

"Differently, perhaps," she countered, "but also truthfully?"

"Who knows. You have not yet disclosed the exact circumstances of your husband's death. He died while visiting a spa town, you were absent, and it happened suddenly."

"You are shaking your head as if you doubt this. Are you trying to convince me that he didn't really die?"

"I only want to attempt to give an explanation. You may dismiss it if you don't like it."

"And I," Julie said, miffed, "would like to ask you not to conduct such explanatory experiments on the ashes of the person I cherished most in this world."

Herr von Rosen insisted that, as a close friend of the deceased, he had a right to learn exactly how he died, and when Julie refused to give any such detail, he rose with some reluctance and looked around for his hat.

"It's true," Julie admitted then, "you have a right to the details of his death, but I maintain that I have the right to ask you not to abuse this knowledge."

The widow shed many tears while recounting the story in all its detail. After concluding and unable to make sense of his serious face, she said, "What do you say now?"

"Nothing you would want to hear."

"Your shrugging insults me, Herr von Rosen. I believe that there cannot be any other explanation, given there were so many witnesses to his death."

"And you yourself forbade me from disrupting your belief."

"Herr von Rosen," she pronounced solemnly, when he indicated his intention to depart again, "I want to hear—no—I *must* hear your explanation now."

"Then please also allow me to mention a previous circumstance."

"Please, mention whatever fact you deem necessary to take into account."

"I am ready: I learned from you personally that the relationship between you and your husband at the time preceding his death was less harmonious than it once had been. Hence, I must conjecture that both of you, perhaps secretly, had considered the possibility of a separation. Some years ago, your husband's dearest wish was to travel. Of course this wish was abandoned when he fell in love with you and won your hand in marriage. When, however, circumstances changed, his longing to travel was reawakened. There were two ways in which he could fulfill his wish, either to travel with you or without you. Now, you could not be burdened with the inconveniences that come with traveling to other countries, particularly at a time during which, truth be told, you didn't exactly enjoy his company. If he traveled without you, however, you would have been subjected to boredom and eternal worry of disruption in your enjoyment of solitude by his return. Neither solution was ideal.

"There were, however, two other methods by which the situation could be remedied—one would have been divorce. But that ugly word upset your husband. It would have subjected you to gossip by those who were annoyed by your former unusual affection. Your own father's reservations against your union would also have made your life difficult. Thus, this solution was also rejected. The last solution may seem strange and adventurous, but it would grant my friend his freedom and you, after a short time as a widow in mourning, the possibility to find a new husband more to your liking."

"Herr von Rosen," the widow interrupted, "you're behaving like an attorney at a bad trial. In order to tire out your opponent, you draw the matter out with futile arguments. I would not protest if only you would please refrain from touching so relentlessly upon those moments in my life I regret most, those feelings which are most painful to me!"

"Dear friend," Herr von Rosen conceded, "I do feel bad for addressing these unpleasant memories. But I simply had to remind you of them as they are the necessary foundation upon which I shall build an argument that is now already half-finished."

"But why even build this house of cards when it will topple the instant I show you the death certificate?"

"A death certificate? As if those are never issued falsely! But since I have already presented the most difficult part of my argument, please allow me to develop my hypothesis further. Your husband travels to the spa town, where he meets his brother to whom he confesses his domestic strife. He tells him that he would be willing to forego a third of his fortune if that would regain him his freedom.—Consider also the following situation: there are several sick and poor people in the spa town, whom your husband treats out of pure human kindness, some of whom are at death's doorstep, and thus supply the means to regain his freedom. One of those ailing people lives in such a dismal apartment that your husband invites this poor soul to stay in his house, inhabited by your husband and his brother. As could have been predicted, the sick man dies, despite excellent care and medicine, and your husband sneaks out at night to leave everything else up to his brother. Are you starting to find my hypothesis more likely now?"

"Not at all. However, please continue your speculation of what happened next."

"If I am not tiring you, I shall do so with pleasure.—Your husband, who has been feigning a slight indisposition for a few weeks at this point, leaves behind his pajamas, which are put on the dead man, whose convalescence was brought up a few days earlier, so that now the claim can be made that he returned home.—Further, it is now claimed that the dead man *is* your husband and he is buried.—Thus, I should think, the enigma is solved."

"Except for some details you are neglecting to consider.—You must admit that a secret does not remain a secret if it is spread among many people. How many people must have been privy to this plot?"

"No one except for your husband's old servant, whose exceptional loyalty, as I recall, was lauded many times in this very room. Perhaps your husband and his brother relied solely on this individual's services while away in the spa town. He would not have jeopardized the secret."

Julie said, "I have an objection that should satisfy once and for all your improbable and faulty reasoning, for you are forgetting several other aspects, Herr von Rosen. My dearly departed husband had many friends in the spa town and would certainly have received many visitors upon his death. Friends always wish to see the beloved remains one last time and surely they would have noticed a lack of familiar features in a randomly substituted corpse."

"True, dear friend. I, too, am convinced that your husband's brother received visitors and had to recount the incident many times. The latter seems to me a tricky endeavor, but your brother-in-law is an experienced man of the world and as such would have been successful. It is certain, too, that many saw the corpse, except, that is, for the face, which was so disfigured by the alleged fall from the bed, that it was probably covered."

"And how about the corpse washer, Herr von Rosen? Or do you suppose there isn't anyone practicing that profession in a famous spa town, or aren't they obligated to ascertain a person's death by natural causes there?"

"Obviously such professions and obligations exist there. But who would have suspected a respected and law-abiding man such as your brother-in-law of an attack upon the life of his own brother? A gold coin could have convinced the corpse washer not to disturb the wound on the dead man's face. The poor dead man might really have fallen from the bed and suffered a disfiguring injury, or his face could have been made unrecognizable by violent means following his death."

"My dear Rosen, what have you achieved by giving this long and labored explanation or, rather, contortion of the event?"

"Perhaps your consideration of the possibility that your husband might still be alive?"

"Only the certainty of this would console me, yet your strange explanation does not do so. Are you going to conclude that it wasn't an apparition I saw in my chamber, but my husband in the flesh, wrongly assumed dead?"

"If it wasn't due to your own nervous imagination or due to a trick from someone else, certainly."

"Your urge to appear clever is leading you astray again, dear Rosen! The man who—according to your explanation—sought to buy his freedom from me by sacrificing one third of his fortune—the same man, supposedly snuck back into my apartment to expose himself once again to the dangers of my demands? I admit, my poor reasoning skills are not quite sufficient to grasp this circumstance."

"It's not that far-fetched. Let's assume that your husband fulfilled his urgent wish to live in another country. For a while he felt quite satisfied. There was no space for any other thoughts in his soul. Let's assume that remorse only struck him after he had fulfilled his wish.—But remorse did come, and he felt deeply for you once again. He realizes now how much he hurt you and that there is no way to tell which consequences his supposed death would have, given the past disagreements with you. Once this thought strikes him, your image in his mind rejuvenates and takes on the glory of past times. His longing for you brings him back. He comes here and wishes nothing more than to convince himself of your well-being. He finds a way to enter your house and is taken for a ghost by you."

"By God," exclaimed the widow, "if only you were speaking the truth. Alas, this explanation is even more improbable than the explanation of his death. Let's assume everything happened as you said it did, up to and including his return: why would he have to resort to paying me such a bizarre visit at night?"

"Why? Because he had no idea how you felt and, as a person believed dead, he could not allow himself to be seen by day in a town where every child knows him."

"And how do you explain his entering and exiting through a locked door?"

"Quite easily, since you told me that your pretty maid was away at a masquerade on the night in question. Couldn't he have arrived on that very night and gone to the masquerade, perhaps hoping to see you there or at least to gain some information about you while in disguise?—Isn't it possible that he may have encountered your pretty maid there coincidentally and couldn't he, during this time of freedom imparted upon him by wearing a disguise, have learned about your maid's lifestyle and impure circumstances? He might have given the maid a few glasses of wine too many, then, when she was inebriated, secretly took her keys, and used them to gain entry. Since he knows every corner of this house, he would have found your bed easily, even in the dark."

"You've really gone to extraordinary lengths, Herr von Rosen," Julie responded, "only to conclude with a scene befitting low comedy. I am convinced that my dearly departed husband would be too proud to pursue base adventures such as chasing after a servant. I am offended that you even suggest he might have behaved in such a way."

"But dear friend," countered Herr von Rosen, "you misunderstand. By outlining that possibility I merely wanted to show one of many ways in which he may have gained possession of the key, since you insist upon the importance of this aspect. I admit, in my rush to give you an explanation, I invented a scenario that did not match your husband's character. It is much more likely that the good doctor had a co-conspirator who would have partaken in such adventures at a masquerade more eagerly. While your husband was asking around about you, this co-conspirator could have encountered the maid, found out that she worked for you, alerted the doctor to this fact, somehow gotten him the keys, secretly returned the keys to the girl, semi-conscious after drinking, without her noticing anything at all."

"Let's end this, Herr von Rosen. You have reminded me quite painfully of how guilty I feel for my behavior in the time leading up to my husband's death, but in vain. In vain, you have found a way to demonstrate your skill in finding reasonable explanations for ghostly apparitions. I must assume that this was the point of your endeavor, otherwise your trouble was entirely futile. I cannot be convinced that the figure I saw was my husband in his physical form. Its gait, its ethereal aura shook me so that I am convinced I saw a being from a higher plane of existence."

"It was your fear, dear friend, which imbued the figure with an ethereal aura."

Julie protested steadfastly: the apparition did not have the distinct outline of a human figure.

"Well," Herr von Rosen continued, "then somebody doubtlessly played a trick on you."

"I will not have it!" Julie countered. "A trick could never be this convincing!"

"You don't know such trickery well enough," said Herr von Rosen. "I, on the other hand, know the methods of tricksters trying to conjure up ghostly apparitions."

Julie vehemently rejected his proposal to demonstrate such methods. But he seemed to want to cure her of her belief in supernatural phenomena with an almost violent passion and became more importunate every moment. In order to rid herself of him, the widow finally relented and allowed him a demonstration, under the condition that he would never again attempt to convince her to reject her belief in ghosts.

She hid her annoyance when he requested the use of one of her rooms for eight days of preparations. The room had a separate entry and he even had locks installed. The whole undertaking was displeasing, but she told herself that she was permitting this demonstration not on a whim, but to remove any doubt.

On the night of the demonstration she was beset by a wave of emotions when Herr von Rosen made his appearance with an extraordinarily solemn air and clad entirely in ominous black clothing.

"You do realize," he said, "that even though you know I have prepared a show for you, the atmosphere must seem already very strange. Perhaps the ghost, which I will conjure shortly, might wear the same ethereal guise that your senses attributed to the previous apparition? But let me challenge this; I want to destroy a part of the illusion right away and assure you again that we are dealing with an explicable deception. I will show you, ahead of time, the clothes in which the apparition is going to approach you."

Julie was surprised when he showed her a miniature painting of her husband wearing the very coat in which he had last approached her bed, which she had never mentioned to anybody.

"What would you say, dear friend," Herr von Rosen said, "if instead of the promised illusion, the truth would emerge from this room—your husband himself? What if I were to tell you that the trap which I tried to set—in vain, according to you—was indeed the true story, except for some embellishments about what happened at the masquerade?"

Julie's astonishment gave way to delight when she heard Herr von Rosen's confident tone. He slowly approached the door and opened it to present the final proof for the truth of the matter.

The lovers sank into a silent embrace.

Herr von Rosen himself was the co-conspirator at the masquerade and then the person sent to test the steadfastness of the supposed widow's convictions. Gustav would not have plotted the adventure if he had not chanced upon the news pamphlet in which the ghost story was reported and if he had not recognized in its anonymous protagonist his wife and her loyalty and longing for him after his supposed death.

For obvious reasons, the story of Gustav's return was never made public in the town in which it happened. Julie sold her estate and moved away, without telling anyone where. Romandy,* where the doctor's then-ailing brother was recuperating, became the couple's home. There they lived under the name which Gustav had used since his supposed death, and if anyone were to see the happy couple and learned about their story, they might wish many a marriage burdened by too high expectations to be rescued by a similar risky leap of faith.

—-—-

A FRIEND brought to my attention that a similar event really happened after they read my story, which had previously been published under the title "Journey to Pyrmont." Even though some aspects are coincidentally similar in the previous story, I thought it worth reworking. Accept this as my apology if I was wrong.

—F.L. (Friedrich Laun)[†]

---

* The French-speaking region of Switzerland.

[†] Postscript, by author Friedrich Laun, is from the original German text and not included in the French translation by Jean-Baptiste Benoît Eyriès.

Interior engraving for *Démoniana, ou, Nouveau Choix* by Gabrielle de Paban (1820).

VII.

THE GREY CHAMBER,

A TRUE STORY

BY HEINRICH CLAUREN

(TRANSLATED INTO ENGLISH BY MARJORIE BOWEN)

YOUNG Blendau was travelling to Italy in the suite of a German princess to whom he acted as secretary. Arrived in the town in the north of Germany where the princess had decided to remain several days, he obtained permission to visit a certain M. Rebmann, who then held the office of chancellor to an adjacent royal estate. This gentleman lived several miles from the town where the princess and her train had halted.

Blendau had been educated with him and had not seen him since he was fourteen years old, that is to say, for about seven years. He thought, therefore, that he would make this visit a surprise to this friend and his family, and as he knew the country perfectly well he hired a horse and set out alone across the forests although it was the middle of winter.

The weather was very fine in the morning, but in the afternoon he perceived that the sky became covered over, and towards evening a heavy snow began to fall. This caused a considerable delay to Blendau: the path became heavy, large snowflakes blew into his eyes and blinded him so that he could not guide his horse properly; he mistook his way several times, and though he calculated on reaching M. Rebmann's early in the afternoon, it was not till nine o'clock at night that he at last arrived, cold and exhausted, at this friend's, having made a detour of twenty miles.

M. Rebmann hardly recognised him, so much had he changed since he had last seen him. When, however, he discovered who was this late guest he received him with great pleasure and only regretted that his wife and children had gone to the neighbouring town on the occasion of the marriage of a relative and would not return for several days.

He ordered a good meal for his friend and some of the best wine in his cellar, and after Blendau had drunk three bottles of Meersteiner* and gossiped over all that had happened to him during the last seven years he felt the fatigue and vexation of his long cold ride pass. Nevertheless, an extreme lassitude overcame his spirits and he was forced at last to break off the hilarious conversation and demand permission to retire to bed.

M. Rebmann admitted with a laugh that this put him in a difficulty. His lady was away and all the chambers save those occupied by the family were dismantled, while the prudent housewife had taken with her the key to the coffers which held the sheets, the coverlets, and the mattresses. On calling the old servant, Bridget, and putting to her his difficulty, she replied: "There is a bed already made in the Grey Chamber—you know, sir, the guest chamber. M. Blendau can sleep there if he pleases."

"No," replied M. Rebmann. "My friend Blendau would not wish to pass the night in the Grey Chamber, of that I am sure."

"And why not, sir?" asked the old woman.

"What, in the Grey Chamber! Have you already forgotten the Lady Gertrude?" M. Rebmann turned slyly to his guest.

"Bah! That's such a long time ago that I thought no more of it," cried Blendau. "What, do you think I am still troubled by such childish follies? Go along with you! Let me pass the night in this famous chamber. I am no longer afraid of ghosts or evil spirits, and if the beautiful Gertrude should come to keep me company I am so tired that I don't think she'll prevent me from sleeping."

M. Rebmann gave the young man a doubtful glance.

"Well, my friend, you've certainly singularly changed. Seven years ago nothing in the world would have made you consent to sleep in the Grey Chamber, even if you'd had two people to keep you company. Where did you find so much courage?"

"Seven years ago is seven years ago," laughed Blendau. "I have grown up since then. For five years I have lived in the capital, remember. Believe me, I now know too much to give any credit to old legends."

"Very well, my friend, I've no more objection to make. May Heaven watch upon your rest. Bridget, take the light and conduct M. Blendau into the Grey Chamber."

Blendau said good night to his old friend, then he followed Bridget to the famous Grey Chamber, situated at the second stage of the extremity of one of the wings of the castle.

---

* This is likely a typographical error for Niersteiner, a wine of the Rheinheissen, central western district of Germany.

Bridget put her two candles on a dressing-table on either side of a mirror of oval form surrounded by an interlaced antique border. The old woman seemed ill at ease in this vast chamber; she made a slight curtsey to Blendau and hurried away.

The young traveller stood for a moment considering the apartment which had once been familiar enough to him and had always, in the days of his youth, filled him with terror. It was still in the same state as it had been when he had seen it last. The enormous iron stove bore the date of 1616; a little beyond this, in the corner, was a narrow door the upper part of which was composed of squares of ancient glass, heavily leaded. This led to a long, sombre passage which wound round the tower to the subterranean dungeons.

The furniture consisted of six ormolu chairs, two tables in heavy brasswork supported by finely carved stag's feet, and a great bed with a baldaquin* which was hung with curtains of heavy grey silk embroidered in tarnished gold. Nothing in the room had been changed for perhaps more than a hundred years, for the chancellorship of this royal domain had been confided from time immemorial to the family Rebmann.

The *châtelaine*† Gertrude was of an even greater antiquity. How often had not Blendau heard her horrible story! According to this old legend, which he had heard whispered fearfully by his nurse in his boyhood, Gertrude had from an early age vowed to God her youth and beauty, and had been about to enclose herself forever in a convent when the splendours of her youthful loveliness had aroused the base desires of a certain Graf Hugues, who one night broke into her room, this very Grey Chamber, and despoiled her by force of her honour.

Gertrude swore on the crucifix that she had called for help, but in this lonely part of the castle, so far from the other apartments, who could hear the cries of agony and innocence? The wickedness of Hugues did not entail any consequences that could reveal it, but the unhappy Gertrude avowed the crime to her confessor, who refused her permission to enter the convent and closed to her the door of the sanctuary of the virgins of the Lord. And as she had intended to tempt God by concealing her fault and taking the veil, he told her that in expiation she must suffer the torments of purgatory during three hundred years.

The wretched girl, a prey to despair, poisoned herself and expired in

---

* A canopy.
† Governess of a castle or large house.

the Grey Chamber at the age of nineteen years. Her rigorous penitence was still lasting and would not be terminated for another forty years, that is to say in 1850, and until the expiration of the fatal term, Gertrude would continue to appear every night in the Grey Chamber.

Blendau had frequently heard this tale and he had even met several people who were ready to swear that they had seen Gertrude in the Grey Chamber. All these tales agreed that the phantom had a dagger in one hand, probably to pierce the heart of the perfidious lover, and a crucifix in the other, destined without doubt to reconcile the criminal with Heaven in offering him the image of the Saviour who died to expiate the sins of mankind.

The ghostly apparition only showed itself in the Grey Chamber, and for this reason this apartment had long remained uninhabited. But when M. Rebmann inherited the castle and the post of chancellor, he had turned the haunted room into a guest-chamber as a proof of his complete disbelief in phantom or legend.

Blendau looked steadily round the room. Although he had boasted of not believing any longer in ghosts, he was not too much at ease. He locked the door by which he had entered and the glass door which gave on to the long, obscure passage. He put out one of the candles, placed the other near the bed, undressed, and slipped beneath the sheets and under the warm coverlet, recommending his soul to God, then extinguished the other candle, sunk his head upon the pillow, and at once fell into a profound sleep.

But about two hours afterwards he woke and heard a clock in the neighbouring tower strike midnight. He opened his eyes and saw that there was a faint light in the chamber. He raised himself on his elbow—extreme terror caused him to become immediately wide awake. The curtains at the end of the bed were half-pulled and his glance fell on the mirror on the dressing-table directly in front of him. In this he could see the reflection of the spectre of Gertrude wrapped in a shroud, a crucifix in the left hand and a dagger in the right.

Blendau's blood froze in his veins: this that he saw before him was not a dream, a vision, but a frightful reality, it was not a skeleton or a shade, it was Gertrude herself, the face discoloured with the livid tint of death. A garland of ivy and rosemary was interlaced among her dry, colourless locks, and as she moved Blendau heard the rustle of the leaves of this dead chaplet and the sound of the hem of the shroud dragging on the floor. He saw in the mirror by the light of the two candles, both of which were now brightly burning, the fixed brilliancy of the eyes of Gertrude, the pallor of her lips.

He tried to leap from his bed and to run to the door by which he had entered, but the fright had paralysed him—he found that he could not move.

Gertrude kissed the crucifix. She seemed to be praying under her breath; Blendau distinguished the movement of her lips which still carried the marks of the burning poison. He saw the eyes of the unfortunate wretch turned towards heaven; she raised her dagger and advanced towards the bed with a terrible glance.

Blendau was about to lose consciousness as she opened the curtains of the bed. Horror was painted in her fixed and inanimate eyes as she perceived a man crouching on the pillows, and she pressed her little dagger on the bosom of him whom she took for her false lover. As she did so a cold drop of poison fell from her garland on to Blendau's pallid face. At this he gave a piercing cry, flung himself from the bed, and rushed to the window to cry for help.

But Gertrude prevented him. When he reached the window she was there with one hand on the catch so that he could not open it. With the other she caught him round the waist and he gave a piercing cry, for he felt through his nightshirt the glacial impression of the cold sweat of death coming from her clasp.

He observed that she had now neither crucifix nor dagger, and that she seemed no longer to wish for the life of the unhappy Blendau, but, what was more horrible, that she appeared to offer and to expect the embraces of love.

As the icy spectre folded him in her arms Blendau dragged himself away with long shudders of terror and hurled himself towards the little glass door.

As he opened this (it was not locked, though he had turned the key himself the night before) he found himself face to face with a skeleton that blocked the long passage—that of Graf Hugues, without doubt. His ghastly face, on which still clung a remnant of skin and muscle, was distorted in a frightful grimace. He entered the chamber, letting the door fall behind him with a sound that echoed like thunder throughout the tower.

Blendau, between the two phantoms, that of Gertrude and that of the skeleton, sank to the ground unconscious into darkness.

When he recovered, the cold wintry dawn was showing through the unshuttered windows. Blendau, stiff and chilled, his shirt still bathed with sweat, rose from the floor and with trembling hands searched for his clothes. Though unutterably weary and shaken by nausea, nothing would have persuaded him to endeavour to obtain any repose in that apartment.

At first he endeavoured to persuade himself he had been the victim of some frightful dream, but such an idea was no longer plausible when he perceived, on the dressing-table in front of the mirror, the second candle that he had placed near his bed and put out after he had got between the sheets. He remarked that these candles were half burnt down, although they had only just been lit for a second the night before. He also discovered that the two doors which he had locked the night before were again fastened as he had left them.

Blendau had not the courage to relate his adventure to anyone. He did not wish to be laughed at for a susceptible fool and made the subject of the pleasantries of the family of Rebmann. On the other hand, if he was able to persuade his host of the reality of his vision, who would dare to continue to inhabit the castle where Gertrude and the hideous skeleton of her lover had a rendezvous every evening?

Then, again, if he was silent, he would be asked to spend another night in the Grey Chamber and that he felt he had not the strength to do.

He therefore dressed himself in haste, crept through the castle while everyone was still asleep, went to the stable, mounted his horse, and without taking leave of anyone rode away through the snowy forest towards the city.

—·—

Blendau, a conscientious and reliable man, vouched for the truth of each word in this story with his honour and with his life.[*][†]

---

[*] This last sentence as a testament to the "veracity" of the story was omitted from Marjorie Bowen's English translation, but added back in here, as it appeared in both Heinrich Clauren's original German tale as well as Jean-Baptiste Benoît Eyriès's French translation.

[†] Author Heinrich Clauren published "The Grey Chamber" as a standalone piece in *Der Freimüthige* in April, 1810, and then published a continuation to the story (picking up after the original ending) in May, 1810. Clauren's own story collections continued to keep the two separated: *Erzählungen*, Volume 1 (1818) includes the original story, while a later collection, *Erzählungen*, Volume 3 (1819) includes the second part. Jean-Baptiste Benoît Eyriès however chose to embed the second part of "The Grey Chamber" inside the story "The Black Chamber" (written by Johann August Apel as a parody reaction to "The Grey Chamber"). The continuation to this story is thus structured in the same manner as by Eyriès, beginning on pg. 175 within "The Black Chamber."

Portrait of author Heinrich Clauren by German artist and copperplate engraver Friedrich Fleischmann (ca. 1830).

Cut-out from the bookplate of Charles P. Searle,
engraved by Sidney Lawton Smith (1904).

VIII.

THE BLACK CHAMBER,

AN ANECDOTE

BY JOHANN AUGUST APEL

(TRANSLATED INTO ENGLISH BY ANNA ZIEGELHOF)

OUR literary society included only three members. Investigator Wermuth discussed the scholarly papers, town physician Baermann the opinion pieces, and I whatever was neither scholarly nor opinion, or both. Despite the small size of our group, our meetings and dinners were as good as those of any other learned society, perhaps even better, since we convened and dined every day, as soon as the investigator was done dealing with his suspects and the doctor with his patients. We gathered at my house and, over a pipe and a beer, we read the latest journals and discussed them.

One day Wermuth took longer than usual to arrive. We grumbled for fifteen minutes, then decided to begin our review of the day's newspapers without him. *The Daily Gazette* was already on the table, and the gray envelope containing *The Candid Review* had just been delivered by mail. There was no time to waste. I took the *Gazette*, which belonged in my realm, and read. The first page contained a scathing accusation against *The Candid Review* regarding its publication of the article "The Grey Chamber." I read it with secret glee, since Doctor Baermann and I had debated the case of the Grey Chamber before, and I was hoping that the article run by the *Gazette* would aid me in delivering a final argumentative blow to the good doctor and his unyielding belief in ghosts.

"I have been wondering," I said. "*The Candid Review* is usually known for being quite rational. I mean, based in Berlin they are practically direct witnesses to the Enlightenment. Yet they still ran this story of the Grey Chamber. It all but transforms the paper into manipulative propaganda. I am certainly interested in how they are going to reason their way out of this one."

"Why, of course by staying silent on the matter," the doctor replied. "Their critics do not deserve a response!"

He sat back into his chair and took a great drag so that pipe and mouth fumed like two volcanic craters.

"But let me ask you," I said, "who is supposed to believe fancies about roaming skeletons and 'Ghostly Gertrude,' who is actually quite tangible and able to light candles like any corporeal chamber maid?"

"Let me ask *you*," countered he, somewhat flushed, "who is supposed to believe that you enlightened intellectuals have all the answers and know exactly what nature is or is not capable of? You ramble and ramble, and the less you understand a matter, the louder becomes your chatter."

While speaking, he stuffed his finger into his pipe with such vehemence that the bowl broke off and smoldering ashes dropped onto his chair.

"My apologies," he said, brushing the ashes away. "So sorry, don't they always use inferior clay for pipe bowls nowadays? Well, what I was going to say, my dear friend, is that you, as a school administrator, don't have much opportunity for becoming as acquainted with nature and its powers as us physicians. Believe me, we know so little about what nature can and cannot do that . . . that . . . "

" . . . that it's quite incredible you should be able to cure the sniffles," I suggested.

"Well, why do *you* believe that we can?" he cut in. "Why do you send for us physicians, have us travel for miles and miles, and seek our advice, and obey our directions, and open your purses for us? There you are! You believe whatever you want to believe and whatever causes you the least inconvenience. That's how you approach matters of ethics, politics, absolutely everything. Don't tell me that people have not been arrested only because they claimed the enemy won a battle. But the enemy still entered your country nonetheless and just like that, ghosts enter your house, even though you want the 'propaganda manipulators,' as you call them, to go to Hell."

"I'm curious," I said, shaking my head. "It almost sounds like you're about to tell me *you* have seen a ghost before."

"Well," he replied, "I wouldn't claim to be a *ghost-seer*, but Blendheim's tale about the Grey Chamber—something similar did happen to me and curiously enough, my accommodation was called the *Black Chamber*."

After this revelation, the doctor simply *had* to tell his tale about the Black Chamber. He gave pause, but then prepared a fresh pipe, took on a solemn air, and began:

"After concluding my university studies, I worked alongside Doctor Wendeborn for several years. He was a well-known physician and I wanted to familiarize myself with the profession. He was getting older and since I was known to be a good horseman, he let me attend to his patients who lived a little farther away. One of these journeys took me to a neighboring castle—that of Lieutenant Colonel von Silberstein, whose daughter was suffering from a severe fever. There wasn't much I could do except prescribe medicine and diet, and so I prepared to leave. But the girl's parents wouldn't let me go even though I gave them my instructions in writing and thus errors in treating the sick girl would be unlikely. Still, they were adamant; I had to stay. The lady of the house quickly had a bed chamber prepared for me, and since the sick girl was resting quietly, I excused myself at nightfall and retired.

"The whole castle was a rather dark place and my little chamber was far from the brightest in it. The heavy, old-fashioned doors were painted black, as were the wood-paneled ceiling and the panels lining the walls, from about the height of the windowsills to the floor. Nothing in that chamber gave me a homely feeling, except for the bed pushed against the wall, which was covered in snow-white sheets and surrounded by heavy curtains of green silk.

"I decided to compose a detailed report to Doctor Wendeborn about the girl's condition, yawning at every comma. But then came a sudden and great rap on my door! I must admit being startled, although I pulled myself together quickly and called as brusquely as I could: 'Come in!'

"The interruption, ultimately, was nothing remarkable. Only the Lieutenant Colonel's gamekeeper inquiring if I needed anything else. Bear with me now: I am mentioning every little detail because it's important to be exact in such matters, almost pedantic, as when called upon to present medical evidence in court. The gamekeeper was a young, courteous man, and we chatted about this and that. Among other matters he asked if I didn't feel too isolated in that chamber and he offered to keep me company. I laughed because he seemed to be a little frightened in that grim room. Warily his eyes surveyed the chamber at each slightest noise. Eventually he told me that the little room was called the Black Chamber and that there were all kinds of stories about it, which had to be kept from the lord and lady of the house, lest their tenancy be spoiled. He recounted several anecdotes about hauntings and offered once again to stay with me or to share his own room, which was much nicer. I was intent not to agree to any offer which might place doubt upon my courage, and when he realized that I couldn't be convinced to share either my or his room, he finally left, though not without repeating a warning against disbelief, which had brought ruinous consequences upon many others.

"And so I was left alone in the infamous Black Chamber. In those days my attitude towards ghosts was rather dismissive, and just like certain 'enlightened individuals,' I hoped to have chanced upon a situation in which I could finally rip the disguise off a so-called ghost and emerge the hero. As such, I was looking forward to the stroke of midnight.

"Before the time came, I examined my room thoroughly. I locked both doors and even used bolts to bar them from the inside. I locked the windows in a similar way. And just to be completely certain, I swiped my rapier under the bed and under all the tables and armoires. Satisfied that neither human nor animal would be able to pay me a nocturnal visit, I undressed. I placed the nightlight into the cast iron stove so that the room lay in complete darkness. You see, dim illumination fuels my fear rather than alleviates it.

"Having completed these preparations I lay down and was so tired that I fell soon asleep. I had only just drifted off however, when I perceived the faintest whispering of my name. I startled and listened closely and heard it again: 'August!' The sound seemed to emanate from the bedcurtains. I opened my eyes wide yet saw nothing but pure darkness all around. I must admit that the whispering of my own name had made me shudder. But I closed my eyes again and began to drift back off to sleep, when suddenly a rushing of the bedcurtains woke me and I perceived my name being called more distinctly than before: 'August!' I opened my eyes partway, and the room appeared as if abruptly transformed, now laced with a mysterious light. All at once, an icy hand tapped me, and there I saw next to me in bed a shrouded figure of deadly pallor, reaching for me with a cold arm! I shrieked and scrambled away, then came the sound of a loud thud, and the figure was gone, and I saw nothing around me but that previous darkness. I pulled my blanket over my head in fright, and the clock chimed. I counted its strokes—it was midnight.

"I chastised myself, and gathered my courage, and jumped out of bed to ascertain that I hadn't dreamed the occurrence. I lit two lamps and examined the room as before. Everything was exactly as I had left it: the door bolts were in place, the windows still closed. I was about to attribute the apparition to a dream or to the fact that the gamekeeper had stirred my imagination with his spooky stories, even though I had seen the events so clearly. But then I shone my light on the bed, and there I found a long dark lock of hair on my pillow. Now this could certainly not have been delivered by dream or by deceit. I picked it up and was about to write an account of the occurrences of the night when I heard a new noise. Something serious was occurring as I listened to hastening footsteps and slamming doors. The sounds approached my room and there was an urgent rapping at my door.

"'Who's there?' I called.

"'Rise quickly, Herr Baermann,' was the response from outside, 'the young lady is dying.'

"I dressed hastily and ran to the sick girl's room, but I was too late. The girl had died just before midnight, they said. She'd awakened, gasping for air, and then passed away very shortly after that. Her parents were devastated and in need of my care themselves, especially the mother, who refused to leave the dead body, so that we had to remove her from the room by near-forceful means. She finally relented but I had to permit her to keep a strand of her deceased daughter's hair as a memento. Imagine my shudder when I recognized the long dark ringlets cascading from the corpse's head as the same I had found on my pillow. The next day I fell ill myself and—take heed! —it was the same illness that struck down my young patient."

"So what do you say now?" Baermann asked. "This story really happened, and I'd swear an oath on it!"

"Very strange indeed," I responded. "If you didn't seem so serious and if you hadn't assured me that you'd examined the entire room most carefully, I might have a few doubts."

"As I said," emphasized the doctor, "deception would have been impossible. I was fully awake when I saw and heard the things I did, and the lock of hair completely eliminates all doubt."

"I must confess," I replied, "the hair actually seems suspicious to me. If your apparition was not a deception, then it must have been a ghostly intervention or however you want to call it, but if it was that, then how does a tangible, physical lock of hair fit in? A ghost who leaves bodily remnants seems very suspect to me, almost like an actor who breaks character."

The doctor fidgeted in his chair. "That's what I get for sharing my story!" he exclaimed. "First you claim not to believe in ghosts at all, and nothing could be further from your beliefs, yet now you suddenly have a whole theoretical paradigm of ghosts and are ready to critique their appearance!"

At this point, our friend Wermuth, the investigator, entered, wiping his brow.

"Been to the theater again, have you?" we exclaimed and extended to him the penalty box.⸱

"I wish," he replied. "You try dealing with cheats, crooks, and that sort of people, sunrise to sunset, all day, every day. Yesterday they arrested a couple that nearly cost me my last nerve today."

"Please," the doctor cried out, "spare me your stories about tricksters and crooks today! We've been quarreling about the Grey Chamber for the past hour and have yet to read the *Gazette* and *The Candid Review*."

"Ah, the Grey Chamber? Speaking of which, I may have just the tale for you," the investigator stated. "You can submit it to *The Candid Review* if you wish, but title it 'The Black Chamber'."

"The Black Chamber?" the doctor and I exclaimed at the same time but each in a different tone.

"Yes, yes!" confirmed the investigator. "And just listen; it's a story about both a ghost and a brilliant trickster."

"Now I'm curious," mumbled the doctor, drumming his fingers on the table.

"You must know Tippel, the attorney?" began the investigator. "That little buffoon, always trying to charm the ladies? You must know him!"

"Yes, yes," we both cried. "Will you get to the point?"

"Well," he proceeded, "Tippel had a case at the court in Rabenau, on the von Silberstein estate. Other cases before his ran late, so it's nighttime before Tippel's case is heard. And, you know, he is not the bravest soul to begin with and especially that he's heard all those stories about highwaymen and robbers and whatnot, so he absolutely refuses to travel at night. The von Silbersteins are nice people and they see how afraid he is, so they invite him to spend the night at their castle. Tippel accepts, thanks them profusely, and apologizes in advance for possibly making some noise in the early morning as he would have to depart at daybreak. Morning comes but Tippel is nowhere to be seen. Hour after hour passes, and staff knock on his door, shouting for him, but there is no reply. Finally the von Silbersteins get worried and they force open the door. And there's Tippel—pale as ice, unconscious on the bed, looking close to death. Eventually they get him to wake up, and he tells them about these terrifying events he experienced during the night. As he'd said, he went to bed early in order to depart at first light. Shortly after going to sleep however, he's awakened by a rapping at the

---

⸱ From German: *Strafbüchse*, meaning a box or pail into which one would pay small fines for minor infractions such as tardiness; similar in America to a "Swear Jar."

door. Tippel being Tippel, immediately thinks of the most horrific stories, scoots close to the wall, and hides under his blanket. He manages to fall back asleep when he's awakened again, this time by a rushing sound of the bedcurtains. He looks out from under the blanket and sees a pale figure standing near an armoire he hasn't noticed in the chamber before, and from inside that armoire emanates a glow as if from gold and silver and jewels. The ghost stands there, jingling coins and gems as if assessing its riches, then it closes the armoire and approaches the bed. Tippel sees the sunken pallid face of a corpse, wearing an old-fashioned headband upon black hair. An icy cold breeze chills him and the ghost seems about to remove its musty shroud in order to lay in bed next to Tippel. Stricken by deadly terror, Tippel turns, screws shut his eyes, and pulls away as far as he can. But then there's a shrill scream and a loud thud! He thereupon lost consciousness and lay there until the late hours of morning when he was found in bed, half-dead from fright.

"You can imagine that the matter caused quite a commotion in the castle. The Silberstein family, prone to visions anyway, told the story of an old aunt supposedly haunting the place and another story about treasures in the walls, which some dowser* allegedly divined for the previous owner. Tippel was ready to swear a thousand oaths that every word of his account was true. He did in fact make a report at court but the judge, a skeptic, insisted on personally visiting the chamber where Tippel had spent the night. Initially old Lieutenant Colonel von Silberstein did not agree to the visit, saying he didn't want to upset any ghosts residing in his house. He didn't need the Black Chamber anyway, and would be happy to leave it undisturbed if that meant the ghost would stay confined to only that room, but the judge was insistent. The Black Chamber was opened. Tippel found it difficult to state where the armoire with the treasure had been; opposite the bed were windows and no place where a such a piece of furniture could be placed, visibly or invisibly. The entire small chamber was searched but not even the faintest trace of anything uncanny or suspicious was discovered. The judge and those witnessing agreed it was therefore proven that something supernatural had taken place. Tippel asked for a notarized copy of the report and his statement, so that he could write to all the newspapers and have them report that he was truly and honestly an officially confirmed ghost-seer; but then the judge had the idea to examine the bed in which such ghost-seer had slept. The judge shook, pushed, knocked, and rummaged around it when suddenly the wall panel behind the bed rose,

---

* A person who uses a divining rod to find things, usually water.

sliding up along two grooves, and revealed an opening into a second bed on the other side of the wall, and beyond the curtains of that second bed, there was the neatest, daintiest room."

"By Jove!" Doctor Baermann exclaimed with a jolly kind of anger and slapped his hand against his forehead. The investigator didn't quite understand the reason for his exclamation and continued:

"That's exactly what Tippel said when the panel suddenly slid open. The entire group now climbed through both beds into the adjacent room. Tippel recognized his ghost's armoire, and the lord of the house recognized the sleeping quarters of the chamber maid. They opened the armoire. It didn't quite glimmer with jewels and gold and silver, as Tippel claimed, but it did contain a fair amount of silver, jewelry, and bank notes. Now the pretty inhabitant of the little room was sought so that she might enlighten the group as to the treasure and the nocturnal apparitions, but alas, she had become quite invisible as had the estate's gamekeeper."

"The gamekeeper?" repeated the doctor.

"Yes, the estate's gamekeeper, August Leisegang."

"The trickster's name was August?" the doctor interrupted once more. "Are you quite certain?"

"Why wouldn't I be?" the investigator countered, a little miffed. "I interrogated him and the pretty maid right before I joined you tonight. Why does the name strike you?"

"We share a first name," the doctor mumbled casually and fiddled with his collar. "Go on, continue your story."

"You can probably guess the rest," he said. "The moveable wall may have served the purposes of some previous tenant of the castle, but it had been forgotten and then rediscovered and put to use by our trickster couple. Tippel disturbed the mechanism in his sleep and raised the panel. That was the rushing sound that awakened him. The chamber maid screamed when she saw some stranger in her bed instead of the gamekeeper, and she let the panel drop again. That was the thudding noise he heard. Everything was explained completely and rationally. The couple were put on the constable's wanted list and yesterday they were arrested. And so I've been sitting there since this morning, interrogating them. The most entertaining aspect was that Tippel had to appear and nearly burst with anger when he saw the pretty pink-cheeked girl with black hair whom he had mistaken for a pallid phantom and had caused him to hide away during the night. 'Damned if I let that happen to me again,' Tippel said, and leaned in to steal a quick kiss, but the little dark-eyed trickster turned away so quickly that Tippel's lips made contact with the red nose of a legal clerk.

"'Be careful,' she said, 'April Fool's Day comes around every year and its traditions will be kept.'"

"Oh, blast it!" murmured Doctor Baermann who now had to recount his own tale a second time.

"However," the doctor concluded after the investigator and I finished laughing, "even though I must now admit that my Black Chamber was a trick, you are not going to convince me that the Grey Chamber was one. So now: let's read the papers!"

He took *The Candid Review*. "The story, 'The Grey Chamber'!" he exclaimed. "But that's an old piece from last month!"

We looked at it. The date was current. The doctor began reading...

—

THE CANDID REVIEW

Journal intended for the amusement of educated and unprejudiced readers.

Berlin, Thursday, May 3, 1810.

THE GREY CHAMBER.*
(by Heinrich Clauren†)

Blendau continued his journey to Italy and came through the town where I live. We were old friends, so he paid me a visit. We spent the winter evening drinking punch and chatting. He told me about his terrible night in the Grey Chamber. At first, I laughed heartily; I had heard the tale of *châtelaine* Gertrude before but of course I didn't believe it. However, when he insisted that not a single syllable of his story was made up, I became curious and decided to get personally acquainted with Gertrude. This was easily accomplished: I knew the chancellor, M. Rebmann, and had some business near his estate anyway.

It was spring when I set out on my short journey. Upon arrival, M.

---

* A continuation of the story "The Grey Chamber" from pgs 159–164.

† No author attribution was assigned in the original French translation by Jean-Baptiste Benoît Eyriès.

Rebmann and his family received me with gracious hospitality. They remembered me from many years ago and when they heard that I had business in the area, they offered me a place to stay in their castle and to conduct my affairs from there. I accepted their offer with gratitude. After lunch, the castle's administrator reported that a great dam had suffered a breach causing the nearby river to flood the pastures. M. Rebmann and his sons Fritz and Karl set out by horse to investigate, and Rebmann's wife and their daughter Charlotte led me up several flights of stairs so that we might observe the spectacle from a window. Charlotte opened a door and we entered a large room: coincidentally it was the Grey Chamber. Blendau's description had been extremely accurate. Even the two wax candles, burned down halfway during his terrible night, were still on the table below the mirror!

I half-considered abandoning my idea of spending the night in the chamber, but that would have been embarrassing, even to myself. Even in daylight the room had something repulsive about it, and how much eerier would it be at night! God knows what purpose it had once served! Why build a large, vaulted chamber three stories up that connected to the dungeon tower? But I had set out to confront "Ghostly Gertrude," hadn't I? So I steered our conversation toward the topic of the chamber.

"This must be your guest room," I commented while glancing at the bed.

"Only when we have so many visitors that we run out of space on the ground floor," responded Mrs. Rebmann. "Usually our guests stay down there with us."

"Oh, then might I be permitted to stay up here? I adore chambers large enough to walk around in."

"You won't enjoy staying up here," said pretty Charlotte while giving her mother a knowing glance.

"Why is that, mademoiselle? The view is ravishing; smoking my morning pipe, right here by the window, I can't imagine anything more pleasurable."

"What my daughter is trying to say," interrupted the chancellor's wife while giving the sweet girl a strict frown, "is that you won't enjoy staying here because the chamber is difficult to heat and sometimes the wind pushes smoke in through the chimney. You're right, though—the view is quite nice. On a clear day you can see as far as four miles. If you really wish to stay here I can have your things brought up."

I agreed emphatically but the glances exchanged between mother and daughter definitely carried meaning. I admit, I was then getting scared of the night for something was going on. Blendau had not dreamed it.

Our conversation turned to the broken dam. The river had widened and created a large lake, at least one square mile wide. The evening sun reflected off the new lake, which looked calm—certainly calmer than I would feel trying to sleep in that huge bed with its baldaquin.

M. Rebmann and his sons returned. We drank coffee, chatted, played games, and thus passed the evening.

I drank a few glasses of wine and sensed a subtle tremor begin within me at thought of soon sleeping in that room. I tried to warm my insides but I shivered helplessly and nothing seemed to be able to change that. Please do not laugh at me, dear readers! If you had visited that hidden, grey vault all alone . . . you may deny it, but you would rather spend the night in a welcoming room near other people than up there, in that god-forsaken chamber, in that huge cold bed, possibly the very bed in which Gertrude suffered her death throes, convulsing from self-administered poison.

The Rebmanns and I sat together for another hour after dinner, then retired. The chancellor and his sons all exclaimed an astonished "Aha?" when they heard that I had asked to spend the night in the Grey Chamber. This fatal "Aha?" coming from a wise chancellor and two strong young men nearly made me falter. I was close to requesting an explanation of their "Aha?" and to tell the whole family about the terrifying visions Blendau experienced in that cursed Grey Chamber. But the same reasons that had caused Blendau to stay silent on the matter made me bite my tongue as well.

Yet I had not even seen anything with my own eyes, had not heard anything with my own ears. Nothing had occurred thus far that would have corroborated Blendau's tale, and I was not about to tell his story and make my friend Blendau look like a fool in front of the Rebmann family. Now, if the family *did* believe in ghostly apparitions, then I might also have exacerbated their fear of Gertrude and might even have caused the family, who seemed to live in their castle quite contentedly, to have to move to another residence. So I stayed silent. I should also note that I had taken care not to mention my friendship with Blendau. What would I have said if they had learned that I had spoken to him recently, and what if they had asked me why he had ridden off without saying goodbye? So I carried on as if there wasn't a Blendau in the world.

The old servant Bridget accompanied me with a lamp. When I bid the family good night, they all exchanged glances. Only Mrs. Rebmann returned their suspicious looks with one that implied a wordless warning.

Jokingly, I asked Bridget to keep me company, telling her that perhaps I'd feel a little lonely up there after all.

"Keep you company here, in the Grey Chamber?" asked the maid while she used the lamp to light the very same wax candles Blendau had described. "Absolutely not! You couldn't get me to spend the night up here if you gave me a thousand gold coins!"

"What's the matter with this chamber? It seems to me that it isn't much different from any other room."

"If you really want company, you may yet get it without even having to ask. Good night, dear sir." And thus, the maid left the room. I could tell she was afraid.

And then I was alone in the cursed chamber. At this point, I was still fairly calm. After all, I had a newly sharpened rapier and several pistols. I made sure the latter were equipped with gunpowder, then placed all my weaponry on a chair near the bed. I prepared another pipe but I suddenly didn't like the taste of my tobacco; I was getting frazzled by the distant rushing of the river and the eternal steady grinding sound of the clockwork in the nearby tower. The river's rushing sounded so wild, so destructive, and the clock's grinding like the rasp of a giant death worm.

I took a lamp and one of my pistols and searched the entire room: I looked for hidden doorways, trapdoors in the floor boards; I examined the bed and the space under it. The table below the mirror was covered with a tablecloth whose folds touched the floor. I lifted it; with my hand I felt around for any springs or locks or hidden hinges. I found nothing suspicious whatsoever. My bed was covered in white sheets. I locked the windows carefully, barred both doors— first the small wooden door through which Bridget and I had entered, then the large door with glass insets. While I was locking the latter, I happened to glance through the glass into the long passage that led to the dungeon tower—*Lord in Heaven!* There in the passage stood a gruesome skeleton, none other than the wicked Graf Hugues, imposing and fearsome, holding a sword in his bony hand.

My hair stood on end. Driven more by fright than courage I gathered my wits, unlocked the door, jumped out, and yelled like one possessed, "Graf Hugues! A final bout against me!"

I drew my pistol and pulled the trigger. But no shot was fired! The skeleton lifted its sword, skull grinning, and I fled. I dropped my failing pistol, hastened back into the Grey Chamber, barred the door behind me, and jumped into bed.

There I was, hiding in the same bed in which Gertrude died, she who had suffered terrible seizures after ingesting her poison; the same bed in which no human being could rest quietly, and in which my poor friend Tobias Blendau suffered the biggest fright of his life.

The candles slowly burned. I considered the second pistol on the chair near the bed, fully loaded.

Instead, I only laid there, still and breathless, for a long while. An involuntary shudder overcame me, and then—*what was that?* A slow dragging sound, as of large feet on thinly spread sand. I listened. Again, I tried to gather my senses. I grasped my rapier as I couldn't rely on the cursed pistols, and I held it clenched tight in both hands, prepared for the worst.

A hellish cackle sounded through the passage. A man's and a woman's voice . . . Hugues and Gertrude!

Just like Blendau, I hid under the blanket, my rapier next to me, and commended my soul to the highest power. I remained like that for some hours before I dozed off.

When I woke, it was morning. My candles had burned down; I had overslept. I vowed never to enter that chamber again.

I dressed hastily and hurried into the family's living room where I found them all at breakfast.

I absolutely had to learn whether the family knew more about Graf Hugues and Gertrude, the cursed couple. I told them both mine and Blendau's story. The three children nearly burst with laughter.

Charlotte, that impish little trickster, had come up with the whole production. Originally she had invented the prank for poor Tobias Blendau, but then I had graciously been offered an encore.

In his youth, Tobias Blendau had always borne the brunt of practical jokes the children of the family played on each other. When they were all children, they had teased Blendau relentlessly when he stayed with them, and he had always been particularly scared of the Grey Chamber. One might have offered him a million coins and he would not have entered it. But then he'd returned, seven years older, bragging about how his intellect had been sharpened; how he had progressed in this time of Enlightenment and so on. As it were, M. Rebmann had told his family all this the evening Tobias arrived for his visit, and confirmed that little Toby Blendau was indeed all grown up, a different person.

That was when Charlotte had the idea to put Tobias's supposed "rational mind" to the test.

Her two brothers were recruited to assist the new Ghostly Gertrude. Obviously, the parents were not privy to their plan. The tricksters knew from their childhood how sound Tobias's sleep was; whenever cousin Tobias had been physically active during the day, one might as well fire off a canon next to him, as he would sleep right through any ruckus. Now, at the time in question, he had been traveling by horse all day, so he was sure to sleep soundly. They snuck up to the large door with the glass insets. Indeed, Tobias was snoring like a steam engine. One of the round glass panes in the door was broken, so Charlotte reached through and opened the door from the inside. They all entered in socks and also opened the smaller door. They brought a skeleton, which their teacher had once used to teach them human anatomy, and placed it near the small door, leaving it slightly ajar. They lit the two wax candles using a lantern they had brought and positioned themselves in such a way that Fritz was outside the small door, Karl was crouching under the table hidden by the draping tablecloth, and Charlotte—dressed in a hastily stitched-together shroud, a garland of ivy and rosemary on her head, and her face and neck powdered white— positioned herself right in front of the mirror when the clock struck twelve. She held a crucifix in her left hand and a large icicle in her right. Now they all started making noise until Blendau woke up.

The drop of poison that fell from Gertrude's hand upon Blendau's face was only water from the melting icicle Charlotte held. The deathly cold of her arm with which Charlotte embraced Blendau was completely natural; her hand was cold and wet from holding the icicle, which Charlotte had then slipped under Blendau's pillow.

The skeleton did not pull the door shut behind it—Fritz did, and he'd done so with all his strength, which explained the terrible crash and why Blendau thought the skeleton was lunging for him.

Charlotte snuffed out the light while she sank to the floor. While Blendau crossed toward the small door, Carl left his hiding place under the table and blew out the other light on the table after Charlotte had extinguished hers.

Blendau had hastened back into the bed, where the large icicle was melting. At its touch, he'd then rolled away to the floor, shivering. All three tricksters remained still until they heard Tobias having fallen asleep in such a way and snoring again some time later. They took the skeleton away, put everything back where it belonged, barred the small door, left via the glass door, and locked this one again too, by reaching through the broken pane. The three bottles of wine Blendau had imbibed earlier that evening may of course also have helped with their illusion.

Incidentally, Blendau had mentioned to the chancellor that he was about to visit me. The family were aware of Blendau's chattiness; they deemed it quite likely that he would tell me, an old friend, of the events he'd witnessed during that night in the Grey Chamber. And when I arrived and didn't even mention Blendau, yet asked to spend the night in the Grey Chamber, the little trickster Charlotte saw right through my plan. Charlotte felt like giving an encore, this time with me as the victim. Though when she saw me bring pistols and a rapier to my room, she hesitated after all. However, before she noticed my ghost-defying weaponry, she had already taken the damned skeleton into the passageway so it would be ready for their show.

Bridget was in on the plot, too. My pistol failed because Carl had poured water on it. They all denied that the skeleton lifted its arm with the sword; that was due to my shaken-up imagination. The three siblings dragged their feet on a thin layer of sand in the passageway; they snuck up to the glass door; and when they perceived me sitting up in bed holding on to my rapier in fright, they all had burst into laughter. That was the hellish cackle I'd heard. They hadn't taken the joke any further that night because their parents had already scolded them for tricking Blendau into fleeing without even saying goodbye.

Charlotte's rosy lips had to pay the price for her trickery: I kissed our charming Gertrude until she promised never to play another trick on anyone spending the night in the Grey Chamber.

—·—·-

Before Doctor Baermann had finished the conclusion of "The Grey Chamber," he threw the newspaper onto the table, incensed, for what should it contain but a different version of the original tale, with a logical and crystal-clear resolution of the notorious supernatural wonders of the Grey Chamber.

"Good heavens," he exclaimed, "we are living in awful times! Every good thing is doomed, and not even an honest ghost can survive. Don't ever bother me with another ghost story!"

"Watch out though," we countered. "Just when you think nobody believes in ghosts anymore, the era for stories about them dawns anew. Both stories and histories are written in the wake of reality after all, and readers may thus, if they are lucky, awaken to the truth."

THE END.

Engraved illustration by Théodore Galle, from the book *Duodecim Specula Deum Aliquando Videre Desideranti Concinnata* by Joannne (Jan) David (1610).

EDITOR'S NOTE II

FOLLOWING this page are the additional contents of *Tales of the Dead* by editor and English-translator Sarah Elizabeth Utterson. Without having to reprint the same stories from each edition, we have listed here the order that Utterson chose to arrange the stories in her anthology, and leave it to the reader to go back and enjoy in such sequence as they choose.

Of note, Utterson omitted three stories that had appeared in *Fantasmagoriana* ("The Revenant," "The Grey Chamber," and "The Black Chamber") and added in one of her own ("The Storm"), as well as an introduction ("Advertisement") and rearranged the contents as such:

Tales of the Dead (1813)

i. "Advertisement" (Preface) by Sarah Elizabeth Utterson
1. "The Family Portraits" by Johann August Apel
2. "The Fated Hour" by Friedrich Laun
3. "The Death's Head" by Friedrich Laun
4. "The Death-Bride" by Friedrich Laun
5. "The Storm" by Sarah Elizabeth Utterson
6. "The Spectre-Barber" by Johann Karl August Musäus

For comparison, *Fantasmagoriana* is arranged as such:

Fantasmagoriana (1812)

i. "Preface of the Translator" by Jean-Baptiste Benoît Eyriès
1. "The Spectre-Barber" by Johann Karl August Musäus
2. "The Family Portraits" by Johann August Apel
3. "The Death's Head" by Friedrich Laun
4. "The Death-Bride" by Friedrich Laun
5. "The Fated Hour" by Friedrich Laun
6. "The Revenant" by Friedrich Laun
7. "The Grey Chamber" by Heinrich Clauren
8. "The Black Chamber" by Johann August Apel (including the second part to "The Grey Chamber" by Heinrich Clauren)

The material original to *Tales of the Dead* commences . . .

TALES OF THE DEAD

LONDON:

PRINTED FOR WHITE, COCHRANE,
AND CO., FLEET-STREET.

Printed by S. Hamilton, Weybridge.

1813.

"Graves, at my command,
Have waked their sleepers; oped, and
let them forth
By my so potent art."

—SHAKSPEARE.[*]

---

* *The Tempest* (1610-11), Act V, Scene 1.

Illustration by Thomas Nast for the novella "The Ghost. A Christmas Story" by William Douglas O'Connor (1867).

ADVERTISEMENT
(or, PREFACE OF THE ENGLISH TRANSLATOR)

ALTHOUGH the passion for books of amusement founded on the marvellous relative to ghosts and spirits may be considered as having very much subsided; yet I cannot but think that the tales which form the bulk of this little volume, may still afford gratification in the perusal. From the period when the late Lord Orford* first published *The Castle of Otranto*, till the production of Mrs. Ratcliffe's romances,† the appetite for the species of reading in question gradually increased; and perhaps it would not have been now surfeited, but for the multitude of contemptible imitations which the popularity of the latter writer called forth, and which continually issued from the press, until the want of readers at length checked the inundation.

The Northern nations have generally discovered more of imagination in this description of writing than their neighbours in the South or West; and in proportion as they have been more the victims of credulity with respect to spirits, they have indulged in the wanderings of fancy on subjects of this kind, and have eagerly employed their invention in forming narrations founded on the supposed communication between the spiritual world and mankind. The productions of Schiller, and others of the modern German literati, of this nature, are well known in England.

The first four tales in this collection, and the last, are imitated from a small French work, which professes to be translated from the German‡. It contains several other stories of a similar cast; but which did not appear equally interesting, and they have therefore been omitted. The last tale has been considerably curtailed, as it contained much matter relative to the

---

* Horace Walpole, the fourth Earl of Orford.

† Ann Radcliffe (1764–1823), one of the first great writers of Gothic fiction.

‡ [Author's note:] *Fantasmagoriana; ou Recueil d'Histoires d'Apparitions, de Spectres, Revenans, Fantômes, &c. Traduit de l'Allemand, par un Amateur.* Paris, 1812. 2 tom[es]. 12mo.

loves of the hero and heroine, which in a compilation of this kind appeared rather misplaced. The fifth tale, (or rather fragment,) is founded on an incident similar in its features, which was some years since communicated to me, by a female friend of very deserved literary celebrity, as having actually occurred in this country; and I have therefore no other claim in respect to it, than that of having a little amplified the detail. The termination is abrupt, and necessarily so, as I must candidly confess a want of imagination to fulfil the expectations which may have been excited by the early part of the tale.

The translation was the amusement of an idle hour; and if it afford an equal portion of gratification to the reader, the time has not been altogether misemployed.

—SARAH ELIZABETH UTTERSON.
1813.

Portrait of author and translator Sarah Elizabeth Utterson. (Mezzotint by Samuel William Reynolds, based on a portrait by Alfred Edward Chalon painted around 1803–1807.)

Life and Death Contrasted, by Valentine Green (ca. 1770).

IX.

THE STORM

BY SARAH ELIZABETH UTTERSON[*]

——"Of shapes that walk
At dead of night, and clank their
chains, and wave
The torch of hell around the
murderer's bed."——
——PLEASURES OF IMAGINATION.[†]

ON the evening of the 12th of June 17—, a joyous party was assembled at Monsieur de Montbrun's *château* to celebrate the marriage of his nephew, who had, in the morn of that day, led to the altar the long-sought object of his fond attachment. The mansion, which was on this occasion the scene of merriment, was situated in the province of Gascony, at no very great distance from the town of——.

It was a venerable building, erected during the war of the League,[†] and consequently discovered in its exterior some traces of that species of architecture which endeavoured to unite strength and massiveness with domestic comfort. Situated in a romantic, but thinly peopled district, the family of Monsieur de Montbrun was compelled principally to rely on itself for amusement and society. This family consisted of the chevalier, an old soldier of blunt but hospitable manners; his nephew the bridegroom,

---

[*] Utterson (1781–1851) translated most of the stories in this book from the French; this one, however, was added by her.

[†] From a poem by the English physician/poet Mark Akenside, first published in 1808.

[†] Likely a reference to the "War of the Grand Alliance," also called "War of the League of Augsburg," which took place from 1689–97. In this war, the expansionist plans of the French king Louis XIV were stymied by a "league" of England, the Netherlands, and the Hapsburgs of Austria.

whom (having no male children) he had adopted as his son, and
Mademoiselle Emily, his only daughter: the latter was amiable, frank, and
generous; warm in her attachments, but rather romantic in forming them.
Employed in rural sports and occupations, and particularly attached to
botany, for which the country around afforded an inexhaustible field, the
chevalier and his inmates had not much cultivated the intimacy of the few
families which disgust to the world or other motives had planted in this
retired spot. Occasional visits exchanged with the nearest of their
neighbours sometimes enlivened their small circle; with the greater part of
those who lived at a distance, they were scarcely acquainted even by name.

The approaching nuptials, however, of Theodore (which was the
name of Monsieur de Montbrun's adopted son) excited considerable
conversation in the adjacent district: and the wedding of her cousin, it was
determined by Emily, should not pass off unaccompanied by every
festivity which the nature of their situation and the joyfulness of the event
would allow. On this occasion, therefore, inquiries were made as to all the
neighbouring gentry within a considerable distance around; and there
were none of the least note neglected in the invitations, which were
scattered in all directions. Many persons were consequently present, with
whose persons and character the host and his family were unacquainted:
some also accepted the summons, who were strangers to them even in
name.

Emily was attentive and courteous to all; but to one lady in particular
she attached herself during the entertainment with most sedulous regard.
Madame de Nunez, the immediate object of Emily's care, had lately settled
in the neighbourhood, and had hitherto studied to shun society. It was
supposed that she was the widow of a Spanish officer of the Walloon
guards,* to whom she had been fondly attached; indeed so much so, that,
notwithstanding he had been dead several years, the lady never appeared but
in the garb of mourning. She had only lately settled in Gascony; but her
motives for retiring from Spain and fixing on the French side of the Pyrenees
were not known, and but slightly conjectured. Isabella de Nunez was about
twenty-eight years of age, tall and well-formed: her countenance was
striking, nay even handsome; but a nice physiognomist would have traced in
her features evidence of the stronger passions of human nature. He would
have seen pride softened by distress; and would have fancied, at times, that

---

* An elite infantry corps of the Spanish army, primarily recruited from the area now
forming part of Belgium—known for their blue uniforms.

the effects of some concealed crime were still evident in her knit brow and retiring eye, when she became the object of marked scrutiny.

She had never before entered the *château* de Montbrun, and her person had hitherto been unnoticed by Emily; but who, having now seen her, devoted herself with ardour to her new friend. The lady received the attentions of her amiable hostess with grateful but dignified reserve.

The morning had been extremely sultry, and an oppressive sensation in the air, which disordered respiration, threw, as the day closed, an air of gloom over the company, ill suited to the occasion of their meeting. Madame de Nunez appeared more than anyone else to feel the effects of the lurid atmosphere; the occasional sparks of gaiety which she had discovered, gradually disappeared; and before the day had entirely shut in, she seemed at times perfectly abstracted, at other times to start with causeless apprehension. In order to divert or dispel this increasing uneasiness, which threatened to destroy all the pleasure of the festival, dancing was proposed; and the enlivening sounds of the music in a short time dissipated the temporary gloom. The dancing had not however long continued, ere the expected storm burst in all its fury on the *château:* the thunder, with its continued roar, reverberated by the adjoining mountains, caused the utmost alarm in the bosom of the fair visitors; the torrents of rain which fell, might almost be said to swell the waters of the neighbouring Garonne, whilst sheets of lightning, reflected on its broad waves, gave a deeper horror to the pitchy darkness which succeeded. The continuance of the storm gradually wound up the apprehensions of the greater part of the females to horror; and they took refuge in the arched vaults, and long subterranean passages which branched beneath the *château*, from the vivid glare of the lightning; although unable to shut their ears to the reiterated claps of thunder which threatened to shake the building to its foundations. In this general scene of horror, Isabella alone appeared unappalled. The alternate abstraction and alarm, which before seemed to harass her mind, had now vanished, and had given place to a character of resignation which might almost be considered as bordering on apathy. While the younger females yielded without resistance to the increasing horrors of the tempest, and by frequent shrieks and exclamations of dread bore testimony to the terror excited in their bosoms by the aggravated circumstances of the scene, she suffered no symptom of apprehension to be visible in her now unvarying features. Agitation had yielded to quiet: she sat ostensibly placid; but her apparent inattention was evidently not the effect of tranquility, but the result of persevering exertion.

The hour was approaching towards midnight; and the storm, instead of blowing over, having increased in violence, the hospitable owner of the mansion proposed to his guests, that they should abandon the idea of returning home through the torrents of rain, which had already deluged the country, and rendered the roads in the vicinity impassable; but should accommodate themselves, with as little difficulty as possible, to the only plan now to be devised,—of making themselves easy during the remainder of this dismal night. Although his mansion was not extensive, yet he proposed (with the aid of temporary couches, and putting the ladies to the inconvenience of sleeping two in each room) to render the party as comfortable as his means would allow; and which would, at all events, be more agreeable than braving abroad the horrors of the tempest.

Reasonable as such a plan was in itself, it was still more strongly recommended by the circumstance, that the carriages which were expected to convey the parties to their respective abodes had not arrived; and from the state of the roads, and the continuance of the still pitiless storm, it seemed visionary to expect them.

The party, therefore, yielded without regret to the offered arrangement, save with one dissenting voice. The fair Spaniard alone positively declined the offered accommodation. Argument in vain was used for a considerable space of time to detain her; she positively insisted on returning home: and would alone in the dark have faced the storm, had not an obstacle which appeared invincible, militated against her resolve; this was too imperious to be resisted—her carriage and servants were not arrived; and from the representation of Monsieur de Montbrun's domestics (some of whom had been detached to examine the condition of the neighbouring roads), it was perfectly clear, that with that part of the district in which she resided, no communication could for several hours take place. Madame de Nunez, therefore, at length yielded to necessity; although the pertinacity of her resistance had already excited much surprise, and called forth innumerable conjectures.

The arrangements between the respective parties were soon made, and the greater part of the ladies gladly retired to seek repose from the harassing events of the day. Emily, who had not relaxed in her marked attention to her interesting friend, warmly pressed her to share her own room, in which a sopha* had been prepared as a couch, and to which she herself insisted on retiring, while madame de Nunez should take

---

* Archaic for sofa.

possession of the bed. The latter, however, again strenuously objected to this plan, asserting, that she should prefer remaining all night in one of the sitting-rooms, with no other companion than a book. She appeared obstinately to adhere to this resolution, until Emily politely, yet positively, declared, that were such the intention of her new friend, she would also join her in the saloon, and pass the time in conversation until the day should break, or until Madame's servants should arrive. This proposition, or rather determination, was received by the frowning Isabella with an air of visible chagrin and disappointment, not altogether polite. She expressed her unwillingness that Mademoiselle should be inconvenienced, with some peevishness; but which, however, soon gave place to her former air of good-breeding.

She now appeared anxious to hurry to her room; and the rest of the party having sometime retired, she was escorted thither by the ever-attentive Emily. No sooner had they reached the chamber, than Isabella sunk into a chair; and after struggling for some time in evident emotion for utterance, at length exclaimed:—

"Why, dearest Emily, would you insist on sharing with me the horrors of this night? To me the punishment is a merited one: but to you—"

"What, my dearest madam, do you say?" replied Emily affectionately— "The terrors of the night are over, the thunder appears retiring, and the lightning is less vivid; and see in the west (added she, as she went to the window) there are still some remains of the summer twilight. Do not any longer, then, suffer the apprehension of the storm which has passed over us, to disturb the repose which you will, I hope, so shortly enjoy."

"Talk you of repose!" said Madame de Nunez, in a voice almost choked with agitation—"Know you not, then, that on the anniversary of this horrid night?—but what am I saying!—to you, at present, all this is mystery; too soon your own feelings will add conviction to the terrible experience which six revolving years have afforded me, and which, even now but to think on, harrows up my soul.—But no more—."

Then darting suddenly towards the door, which had hitherto remained ajar, she closed it with violence; and locking it, withdrew the key, which she placed in her own pocket.—Emily had scarcely time to express her surprise at this action and the apparent distraction which accompanied it, ere Madame de Nunez seized both her hands with more than female strength, and with a maddened voice and eye straining on vacancy, exclaimed:—

"Bear witness, ye powers of terror! that I imposed not this dreadful scene on the female whose oath must now secure her silence."

Then staring wildly on Mademoiselle de Montbrun, she continued:—

"Why, foolish girl, wouldst thou insist on my partaking thy bed? The viper might have coiled in thy bosom; the midnight assassin might have aimed his dagger at thy breast—but the poison of the one would have been less fatal, and the apprehension of instant annihilation from the other would have been less oppressive, than the harrowing scene which thou art doomed this night to witness—Doomed, I say; for all the powers of hell, whose orgies you must behold, cannot release you from the spectacle which you have voluntarily sought."

"To *what* am I doomed!" cried Emily, whose fears for herself were lessened in the dread she felt for her friend's intellects, which she supposed were suddenly become affected by illness, or from the incidents of the past day.

Isabella, after a silence of several minutes, during which she endeavoured to recover some degree of composure, in a softened but determined voice, said:—

"Think not, my friend, (if I may use that endearing expression to one whose early prospects and happier days I am unwillingly condemned to blast,) that disorder has produced the agitation which, spite of myself, you have witnessed.—Alas! great as have been my sorrows, and heavy as my crime weighs on me, my reason has still preserved its throne: to seek oblivion in idiocy; to bury the remembrance of my fatal error in temporary derangement; would, I might almost say, be happiness to me. But fate has forbidden such an alleviation, and my impending destiny is not to be guarded against by precaution, cannot be avoided by repentance."

"Nay," said Emily, "exaggerated as your self-condemnation makes the fault to which you allude appear, in religion you may find a solace which could efface crimes of much deeper dye than any with which you can possibly charge yourself."

"Ah! no," replied the fair Spaniard.—"Religion, it is true, holds out her benignant hand to receive the wandering sinner;—she offers to the stranger a home; she welcomes to her bosom the repentant though blood-stained criminal;—but for crimes like mine, what penitence can atone?—But we waste time," added she; "the midnight hour approaches; and ere the clock in the turret first announces that dreaded period, much must be done."

Thus saying, she went into the adjoining oratory, and finding on the little altar at which Emily offered her daily oraisons,* an ivory crucifix, she

---

* Prayers.

returned with it in her hand; and again seizing and forcibly grasping the hand of her now really alarmed hostess, she exclaimed in a hollow, yet determined voice:—

"Swear, that whatsoever you may this night, this eventful night, be a witness to, not all the apprehensions of hell, not all your hopes of heaven, shall tempt you to reveal, until I am committed to the silent tomb—Swear!"

Emily for a moment hesitated to adopt an oath imposed under circumstances of such an extraordinary nature: but whilst she was debating, Madame de Nunez, more violently grasping her hand, exclaimed, in a voice harsh from agitation:—

"Swear; or dread the event!"

"Swear!" Emily fancied she heard echoed from the oratory. Almost sinking with horror, she faintly repeated the solemn oath, which the frantic female, whose character appeared so perfectly changed, thus dictated to her.

She had no sooner thus solemnly bound herself to silence, than Madame de Nunez's agitation appeared to subside; she replaced the crucifix on the altar, and sinking on her knees before the chair in which Emily, almost void of animation, was seated, she feebly exclaimed:—

"Pardon, dearest Emily, the madness of my conduct; necessity has dictated it towards you; and your wayward fate, and not your suffering friend, is answerable for it. For six long years have I confined to my own bosom the horrors which we this night must jointly witness. On the anniversary of this day—But I dare not yet communicate the dreadful event; some hours hence I *may* recover composure to relate it: but remember your oath. While I live, the secret is buried in your bosom. You must have remarked my unwillingness to remain in your dwelling; you could not have been inattentive to my repugnance to share your room—too soon you will have a dreadful explanation of the cause. Be not angry with me—I must endeavour to conceal the circumstances which appal my soul: I must still preserve the respect of society, although I have forever forfeited my own— hence the oath I have imposed on you. But—"

Here further conversation was interrupted by the sound of the turret clock, which began to strike the hour of midnight. It had scarcely finished, ere the slow rolling of a carriage was heard in the paved court-yard; at the noise of which, Madame de Nunez started from the posture in which she had continued at the feet of Emily, and rushed towards the door, which she had previously locked. Emily now heard heavy footsteps ascending the oaken stair-case; and before she could recall her recollection, which so singular a circumstance had bewildered, the door of the room in which they were sitting, spite of its fastening, slowly moved on its hinges; and in the next minute—Emily sunk on the earth in a state of stupefaction.

It is well for the human frame, that when assailed by circumstances too powerful to support, it seeks shelter in oblivion. The mind recoils from the horrors which it cannot meet, and is driven into insensibility.

At an early hour of the ensuing morning Madame de Nunez quitted Monsieur de Montbrun's *château*, accompanied by her servants, whom the retiring torrents had permitted to await their mistress's commands. She took a hasty farewell of the master of the mansion, and without making any inquiries as to the rest of the party, departed.

At the usual hour of breakfast, Emily did not appear; and her father at length went to her room door, and receiving no answer to his inquiries, went in. Judge his horror, when he discovered his daughter lying on the bed in the clothes she had worn the preceding day, but in a state of apparent insensibility. Immediate medical assistance was procured, and she at length discovered symptoms of returning life; but no sooner had she recovered her recollection, than, looking with horror and affright around her, she again relapsed into a state of inanimation. Repeated cordials being administered, she was again restored to life; but only to become the victim of a brain-fever, which in a few days put a period to her existence. In a short interval of recollection, in the early part of her illness, she confided what we have here related to her father; but conscientiously kept from his knowledge what she was bound by her oath to conceal. The very remembrance of what she had witnessed on that fatal night, hurried her into delirium, and she fell a victim to the force of recollection.

Madame de Nunez did not long survive her; but expired under circumstances of unexampled horror.

THE END.

The Storm, by Edward Vernon Utterson. (Watercolor illustration painted in homage to the story in *Tales of the Dead*, 1813.)

Gespensterbuch.

Herausgegeben

von

A. Apel und F. Laun.

Schnor v. K. del.   Schenk sculp. Braunschweig

Erstes Bändchen.

Leipzig, bei G. J. Göschen. 1810.

Original frontispiece for *Gespensterbuch* (trans: *Ghost Book*), vol. 1 by
Johann August Apel and Friedrich Laun: G. J. Göschen, 1810.
(Illustration by Julius Schnorr von Carolsfeld.)

A BRIEF PUBLICATION
ACCOUNT FOR EACH STORY

THE SPECTRE-BARBER (AKA: MUTE LOVE)

Published first in German as:
"Stumme Liebe" by Johann Karl August Musäus, in: *Volksmärchen der Deutschen* (trans: *Folktales of the Germans*), *vol. 4*: C. W. Ettinger, 1786.

Translated and published in French as:
"L'Amour Muet" by Jean-Baptiste Benoît Eyriès, in: *Fantasmagoriana*: Chez. F. Schoell, 1812.

Translated and published in English as:
"The Spectre-Barber" by Sarah Elizabeth Utterson, in: *Tales of the Dead*: White, Cochrane and Co., 1813.

THE FAMILY PORTRAITS

Published first in German as:
"Die Bilder der Ahnen" by Johann August Apel, in: *Cicaden* (trans: *Cicadas* <a collection>), *vol. 1*: Im Kunst und Industrie Comptoir, 1810.

Translated and published in French as:
"Portraits de Famille" by Jean-Baptiste Benoît Eyriès, in: *Fantasmagoriana*: Chez. F. Schoell, 1812.

Translated and published in English as:
"The Family Portraits" by Sarah Elizabeth Utterson, in: *Tales of the Dead*: White, Cochrane and Co., 1813.

THE DEATH'S HEAD

Published first in German as:
"Der Todtenkopf" by Friedrich Laun, in: *Gespensterbuch* (trans: *Ghost Book*), *vol. 2*: G. J. Göschen, 1811.

Translated and published in French as:
"La Tête de Mort" by Jean-Baptiste Benoît Eyriès, in: *Fantasmagoriana*: Chez. F. Schoell, 1812.

Translated and published in English as:
"The Death's Head" by Sarah Elizabeth Utterson, in: *Tales of the Dead*: White, Cochrane and Co., 1813.

THE DEATH-BRIDE

Published first in German as:
"Die Todtenbraut" by Friedrich Laun, in: *Gespensterbuch* (trans: *Ghost Book*), *vol. 2*: G. J. Göschen, 1811.

Translated and published in French as:
"La Morte Fiancée" by Jean-Baptiste Benoît Eyriès, in: *Fantasmagoriana*: Chez. F. Schoell, 1812.

Translated and published in English as:
"The Death-Bride" by Sarah Elizabeth Utterson, in: *Tales of the Dead*: White, Cochrane and Co., 1813.

THE FATED HOUR

Published first in German as:
"Die Verwandtschaft mit der Geisterwelt" by Friedrich Laun, in: *Gespensterbuch* (trans: *Ghost Book*), *vol. 1*: G. J. Göschen, 1810.

Translated and published in French as:
"L'Heure Fatale" by Jean-Baptiste Benoît Eyriès, in: *Fantasmagoriana*: Chez. F. Schoell, 1812.

Translated and published in English as:
"The Fated Hour" by Sarah Elizabeth Utterson, in: *Tales of the Dead*: White, Cochrane and Co., 1813.

THE REVENANT (AKA: THE GHOST OF THE DEPARTED)

Published first in German as:
"Der Geist des Verstorbenen" by Friedrich Laun, in: *Gespensterbuch* (trans: *Ghost Book*), *vol. 1*: G. J. Göschen, 1810.

Translated and published in French as:
"Le Revenant" by Jean-Baptiste Benoît Eyriès, in: *Fantasmagoriana*: Chez. F. Schoell, 1812.

Translated and published in English as:
"The Revenant" by Anna Ziegelhof, in: *Fantasmagoriana Deluxe: A Combined Edition of Fantasmagoriana and Tales of the Dead*: Dark Moon Books, 2023.

THE GREY CHAMBER (AKA: THE GREY ROOM), A TRUE STORY

Published first in German as:
"Die Graue Stube (Eine Buchstäblich Wahre Geschichte)" by Heinrich Clauren (AKA: Carl Gottlieb Samuel Heun), in: *Der Freimüthige* (trans: *The Outspoken*), entertainment newspaper (published in two parts), issue 71 & 72: Kunst und Industrie Comptoir, April and May, 1810.

Translated and published in French as:
"La Chambre Grise" by Jean-Baptiste Benoît Eyriès, in: *Fantasmagoriana*: Chez. F. Schoell, 1812.

*First part translated and published in English as:
"The Grey Chamber" by Marjorie Bowen, in: *Great Tales of Horror*: The Bodley Head, 1933.

*Second part translated and published in English as:
"The Grey Chamber" (at end of "The Black Chamber") by Anna Ziegelhof, in: *Fantasmagoriana Deluxe: A Combined Edition of Fantasmagoriana and Tales of the Dead*: Dark Moon Books, 2023.

THE BLACK CHAMBER (AKA: THE BLACK ROOM), AN ANECDOTE

Published first in German as:
"Die Schwarze Kammer. Anekdote" by Johann August Apel, in: *Gespensterbuch* (trans: *Ghost Book*), vol. 2: G. J. Göschen, 1811.

Translated and published in French as:
"La Chambre Noire" by Jean-Baptiste Benoît Eyriès, in: *Fantasmagoriana*: Chez. F. Schoell, 1812.

Translated and published in English as:
"The Black Chamber" by Anna Ziegelhof, in: *Fantasmagoriana Deluxe: A Combined Edition of Fantasmagoriana and Tales of the Dead*: Dark Moon Books, 2023.

THE STORM

Published first in English as:
"The Storm" by Sarah Elizabeth Utterson, in: *Tales of the Dead*: White, Cochrane and Co., 1813.

ABOUT THE GERMAN-TO-FRENCH TRANSLATOR, JEAN-BAPTISTE BENOÎT EYRIÈS (EDITOR OF *FANTASMAGORIANA*)

JEAN-BAPTISTE BENOÎT EYRIÈS (Jun. 1767–Jun. 1846) was born in Marseille, France to a Catholic military family. His father was a high-ranking officer who would go onto to become Commander of the French navy.

In his early years, Jean-Baptiste travelled and studied widely across much of western Europe, becoming a scientist in multiple disciplines, notably geography, botany, and mineralogy. He spoke nine languages and also began work in the armament trade. Due to his military background, intelligence, and reputation for discretion, he was given a mission in 1804–1805 by Napoleon Bonaparte to travel to Germany and there "rally the French emigrants" to Napoleon's cause. While in Germany, Jean-Baptiste took the opportunity to also collect German stories and books, a pastime he continued all his life, and which led him to become a translator. He translated countless articles and books from German, English, and Scandinavian languages into French, mostly on travel and geography, but including what he became most famous for, translating the prominent anthology of ghost stories *Fantasmagoriana*, which he published anonymously in 1812; it was read in June, 1816 by the collective of young authors Mary Shelley, Percy Bysshe Shelley, Lord Byron, John William Polidori, and Claire Clairmont, and led to the writing of both Mary Shelley's *Frankenstein; or, The Modern Prometheus* (1818) and John Polidori's "The Vampyre" (1819; viewed as a progenitor to the fantasy vampire genre).

Jean-Baptiste additionally had a distinguished academic career as a geographer and was one of the founding members and, later, named Honorary President of the Geographical Society (*Société de Géographie*), the oldest geographical society in the world.

He passed away in the French coastal city of Le Havre at the age of 78, leaving behind a library of over 20,000 volumes collected throughout his life, as well as maps, historic documents, and manuscripts, many of which had otherwise been thought lost to time.

ABOUT THE FRENCH-TO-ENGLISH TRANSLATOR, SARAH ELIZABETH UTTERSON (EDITOR OF *TALES OF THE DEAD*

SARAH ELIZABETH UTTERSON (née BROWN) (1781–Sep. 1851) was born in Middlesex, England to a wealthy and heavily political family. Her father was English banker and radical Timothy Brown (1743–1820) who was an adherent to social liberalism reform.

Sarah married in 1803 to Edward Vernon Utterson, a lawyer, literary antiquary, and editor, who was also an equally politically-charged partisan (becoming one of England's original Six Clerks in Chancery).

In 1812, Sarah read the French translation of a recently-published anthology of German-language ghost stories, *Fantasmagoriana* by Jean-Baptiste Benoît Eyriès. (Of literary note, this book was also later read and responsible for inspiring the minds of young authors Mary Shelley, Percy Bysshe Shelley, Lord Byron, et. al. to create such notable works as *Frankenstein* and "The Vampyre.")

Sarah decided to translate *Fantasmagoriana* into English herself for, as she referred to it, "the amusement of an idle hour." She removed three of the eight original stories however, deeming them "not fitting," and then included one additional story that she herself authored ("The Storm"). This English-language version was published in 1813 under the title *Tales of the Dead*.

Afterward, it does not appear that Sarah wrote or published any other fiction. She bore several children and died in 1851 at the age of 69. She is buried with her husband at St. Thomas Churchyard, Ryde, Isle of Wight, England.

ABOUT ADDITIONAL TRANSLATORS, MARJORIE BOWEN AND ANNA ZIEGELHOF

MARJORIE BOWEN (MARGARET GABRIELLE VERE LONG née BROWN, 1885–1952) was a British author who wrote historical romances, supernatural horror stories, popular (non-fiction) history, and biographies. She began writing at age 16, published her first novel at age 21, and continued to write until her death, ultimately completing over 150 volumes of work, under several pseudonyms. Author Graham Greene wrote for the *Paris Review* that Bowen's books "influence one considerably." The Australian newspaper *The Courier-Mail* described Bowen as "one of the best of our modern novelists." Several of her books have since been adapted to film.

——-

ANNA ZIEGELHOF is a short fiction writer originally from Germany, now based in the San Francisco Bay Area. She is particularly drawn to stories about darker aspects of the human (or alien) experience. Her short fiction can be found, among others, in *The Future Fire, Silver Blade Magazine, Solarpunk*, Flametree Press' *Footsteps in the Dark* anthology, and Short Édition's short story dispensers. Online she can be found at www.annaziegelhof.com and on Instagram as @annawithaz.

The Practice of the Arts, by Cornelis Cort (1578).

SUGGESTED FURTHER
READING OF RELATED FICTION

For readers who have enjoyed *Fantasmagoriana Deluxe*, the following is a small selection of excellent and commensurable books that are of similar voice, theme, or literary style.

———

100 Ghastly Little Ghost Stories (an anthology) edited by Stefan Dziemianowicz, Robert Weinberg, and Martin H. Greenberg (1985): An anthology of one hundred short ghost stories spanning centuries-old classics to contemporary works.

Alone with the Horrors: The Great Short Fiction of Ramsey Campbell by Ramsey Campbell (2005): A collection of thirty-nine of the most popular eerie short stories by Ramsey Campbell ("Britain's most respected living horror writer"—*The Oxford Companion to English Literature*), covering 1961–1991.

The Bell in the Fog & Other Stories by Gertrude Atherton (1905): A collection of five tales of Gothic mystery and the supernatural, written in the vein of Henry James.

The Best of Weird Tales (an anthology) edited by John Betancourt (1995): A selection of twenty-seven of the best stories published between 1988–1993 in the eminent *Weird Tales* magazine.

The Black Spider (German: *Die Schwarze Spinne*) by Jeremias Gotthelf (1842): In this Gothic horror tale, a woman makes pact with the devil in order to save a town from the tyranny of their ruling feudal lord, only to learn a crueler fate when she tries to forego the devil his due.

The Bloody Chamber: and Other Stories by Angela Carter (1979): A collection of ten short stories revisiting classic fairy tales and legends with Gothic twists.

Carmilla by Sheridan Le Fanu (1872): In one of the earliest works of vampire fiction, a young woman falls under the spells of a seductive female vampire.

The Castle of Otranto by Horace Walpole (1764): Generally regarded as the first Gothic novel, an evil lord seeks to avert an ancient foretelling by marrying his dead son's fiancée Isabella in order to attempt birthing another male heir.

The Collected Supernatural and Weird Fiction of Amelia B. Edwards collected by Leonaur Publisher (2009): A collection of twenty otherworldly and Victorian Gothic tales, most notably including the classic, "The Phantom Coach."

Collected works of E.T.A. Hoffmann: Works of the author, a major influencer of 19th-century Gothic horror Romanticism, and a pioneer of the fantasy genre, include novels, short stories, and musical compositions. Of note are the novella "The Nutcracker and the Mouse King" (1816) (of which the famous ballet *The Nutcracker* is based off), and stories "The Sandman" (1816) and "Automata" (1814).

The Collected Works of Edgar Allan Poe (Volumes 1–3) edited by Thomas O. Mabbott (publ. 1969–1978): A definitive annotated scholarly collection of Poe's canon of poetry, stories, and sketches.

The Complete Ghost Stories of Charles Dickens collected by Peter Haining (1982): A collection of twenty humorous and ghostly 19th-century short stories by the author of *Oliver Twist* and *A Christmas Carol*.

Dark Tales by Shirley Jackson (2017) (posthumous collection): A collection of revered author Shirley Jackson's seventeen "scariest" stories, noteworthy for their twists of suspense and subtle terror.

Dracula by Bram Stoker (1897): The most legendary of vampire creatures, Count Dracula, attempts to extend his reach to England from his homeland of Transylvania, but is met by a stalwart band determined to stop him at any cost.

A Dreamer's Tales by Lord Dunsany (1910): A collection of fantasy short stories exploring fables and legends, dreams and doomed cities, realms of wonder, and other illusory topics.

Faust (German: *Urfaust*) by Johann Wolfgang Von Goethe (2 parts: 1772–1775): A retelling of the Faustian legend, in which a doctor seeking knowledge of the divine trades his soul to the devil; this version has an ultimately more benevolent ending.

Frankenstein; or, The Modern Prometheus by Mary Shelley (1818): One of the world's most iconic science fiction and horror novels, in which a young scientist, Victor Frankenstein, creates a hideous sapient creature in an unorthodox scientific experiment, and then abandons him... much to his later regret.

Ghost Stories: Classic Tales of Horror and Suspense (an anthology) edited by Lisa Morton and Leslie S. Klinger (2019): An annotated selection of eighteen lesser-known classic ghost stories from the 1700s through the early 1900s.

Ghost Stories of an Antiquary by M.R. James (1904): A collection of the earliest short stories of M.R. James, these eerie tales of apparitions and other supernatural horrors are now considered classics widely heralded as influential upon later authors of the strange.

The Ghost Stories of Edith Wharton collected by William R. Tyler (1973): A collection of eleven spine-tingling tales of spirits beyond the grave and other supernatural phenomena, by the first woman to ever win the Pulitzer Prize in literature.

Ghostly Tales by Wilhelmina FitzClarence (1896): A collection of eleven short stories "written in a manner similar to accounts of true haunting," and which fall into the supernatural and/or Gothic vein. The inclusions cover a wide span of "weird" or uncanny phenomena, from religious visions and animal telepathy to the narrator's unsettling encounter with a mentally disturbed young man.

Haunted Tales: Classic Stories of Ghosts and the Supernatural (an anthology) edited by Lisa Morton and Leslie S. Klinger (2022): A selection of twenty laudable classic ghost stories.

Hauntings (an anthology) edited by Ellen Datlow (2013): An assemblage of twenty-four contemporary short ghost stories by one of the horror genre's most acclaimed editors.

The Hound of Death and Other Stories by Agatha Christie (1933): A departure from the author's renowned detective stories, this collection of twelve tales are of terror, fate, and the supernatural.

In a Lonely Place by Karl Edward Wagner (1983) (particularly, "The River of Night's Dreaming"): A collection of non-themed short stories revolving around weird horror and dark (bloody) fantasy, from author Karl Edward Wagner, (of *Conan the Barbarian* fame).

In the Shadow of Edgar Allan Poe: Classic Tales of Horror, 1816-1914 (an anthology) edited by Leslie S. Klinger (2015): A collection of tales written in the vein of Poe by overlooked writers of the period (1816-1914).

Lois the Witch and Other Tales by Elizabeth Gaskell (1861): A collection of five stories by a long-standing and anthologized forerunner of female authors of Victorian-era macabre.

Masterpieces of Terror and the Supernatural (an anthology) edited by Marvin Kaye (1985): A selection of fifty-three short stories and poems from the 1770s to the 1980s that are of terror and the "cosmic fear of the unknown."

The Monkey's Paw and Other Tales of Mystery and the Macabre by W.W. Jacobs (Compiled by Gary Hoppenstand) (2005): A collection of eighteen short horror stories by English author W.W. Jacobs, most famous for the popular classic, "The Monkey's Paw."

More Ghost Stories by M. R. James (1911): A follow-up collection to *Ghost Stories of an Antiquary*, this volume contains seven more supernatural short stories by the master author of thoughtful and "quiet" terrors.

The Mysteries of Udolpho by Ann Radcliffe (1794): Cited as a quintessential Gothic romance novel, a young woman suffers the death of her parents, supernatural terrors in a gloomy castle, and the intrigues of a contemptuous Italian nobleman.

The Mysterious Warning, a German Tale by Eliza Parsons (1796): A classic of Gothic tropes, including dark family secrets, incest, seduction, and ghostly apparitions, in which a dead count's youngest son flees his older brother after a ghostly voice warns him his life is in peril over stake in an inheritance.

Nine Ghosts by R. H. Malden (1942): A slim collection of quiet, thoughtful ghost stories in the tradition of (and written as tribute to) M.R. James.

Tales of Horror & the Supernatural (collected works) of Arthur Machen (1983): A collection of reprinted short stories (1895–1936) covering strange happenings, ancient horrors, and portentous myth.

Tales of Terror and Mystery by Arthur Conan Doyle (1922): A collection of some of the stories from *Round the Fire Stories* and a few others.

Tales of Twilight and the Unseen by Arthur Conan Doyle (1923): Another collection of stories, collected from a variety of sources.

The Turn of the Screw by Henry James (1898): A classic novella telling of a deceased English governess's found manuscript detailing her claims of haunting ghosts while she tries to care for two young children.

Twelve Stories and a Dream by H.G. Wells (1903): This influential author of science fiction and horror (*The Time Machine, The Invisible Man,* etc.) was also an established writer of scary Victorian ghost stories as found in this collection of thirteen short stories, notably "The Inexperienced Ghost" and "The Stolen Body."

"The Vampyre" by John Polidori (1819): A short story credited with founding the fantasy vampire genre, in which a young man befriends a suave nobleman, only to learn the nobleman is a vampire, responsible for numerous blood-sucking deaths and able to return from death himself.

Allegory of the Transience of Life, by Master I. A. M. of Zwolle (ca. 1490).

EDITOR'S REQUEST

DEAR reader, fan, or supporter,

It's a dreadful commentary that the worth of indie publications is measured by online 5-star reviews, but such is the state of current commerce.

Should you have enjoyed this book, gratitude is most appreciated by posting a brief and honest online review at Amazon.com, Goodreads.com, and/or a highly-visible blog.

With sincerest thanks,

Eric J. Guignard, co-editor
*Fantasmagoriana Deluxe: A Combined Edition of
Fantasmagoriana and Tales of the Dead*

ALSO FROM ERIC J. GUIGNARD AND DARK MOON BOOKS:

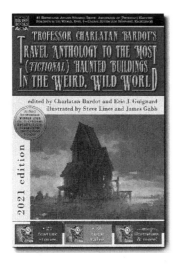

PROFESSOR CHARLATAN BARDOT'S TRAVEL ANTHOLOGY TO THE MOST (*FICTIONAL*) HAUNTED BUILDINGS IN THE WEIRD, WILD WORLD (*2021 EDITION*)

For nearly forty years, renowned paranormal investigator Professor Charlatan Bardot has examined, documented, and acquired stories of haunted buildings around the world. Partnered with leading anthologist Eric J. Guignard, and gifted artists Steve Lines and James Gabb, the greatest of Charlatan's discoveries are made available now in this comprehensive travel anthology of all-new tales!

27 feature stories and 36 tiny tales are included of haunted temples, diners, hotels, shops, hospitals, outposts, theaters, and other building types, along with maps, travel notes, illustrations, and more, all designed to provide an immersive experience for veteran travelers and armchair ghost hunters alike!

Enter *Professor Charlatan Bardot's Travel Anthology to the Most (Fictional) Haunted Buildings in the Weird, Wild World* and explore the strange and curious locales of the globe and of your imagination.

"An ambitious and beautifully constructed anthology that fans of the genre won't want to miss."

—*Library Journal* (starred review)

"High-concept and brilliant . . . A who's-who of supernatural fiction."

—*Publishers Weekly*

"Eric J. Guignard has outdone himself with this imaginative, eerily realistic, and fun anthology."

—*Booklist*

Order your copy at www.darkmoonbooks.com or www.amazon.com
ISBN-13: 978-1-949491-50-0

ALSO FROM ERIC J. GUIGNARD AND DARK MOON BOOKS:

POP THE CLUTCH: THRILLING TALES OF ROCKABILLY, MONSTERS, AND HOT ROD HORROR

Welcome to the cool side of the 1950s, where the fast cars and revved-up movie monsters peel out in the night. Where outlaw vixens and jukebox tramps square off with razorblades and lead pipes. Where rockers rock, cool cats strut, and hot rods roar. Where you howl to the moon as the tiki drums pound and the electric guitar shrieks and that spit-and-holler jamboree ain't gonna stop for a long, long time . . . maybe never.

This is the '50s where ghost shows still travel the back roads of the south, and rockabilly has a hold on the nation's youth; where lucky hearts tell the tale, and maybe that fella in the Shriners' fez ain't so square after all. Where exist noir detectives of the supernatural, tattoo artists of another kind, Hollywood fix-it men, and a punk kid with grasshopper arms under his chain-studded jacket and an icy stare on his face.

This is the '50s of *Pop the Clutch: Thrilling Tales of Rockabilly, Monsters, and Hot Rod Horror*. This is your ticket to the dark side of American kitsch . . . the fun and frightful side!

"A fitting tribute to the 1950s with this 18-story compendium of hot rods, rock 'n' roll, and creature features come to life."

—*Publishers Weekly*

Order your copy at www.darkmoonbooks.com or www.amazon.com
ISBN-13: 978-0-9834335-9-0

ALSO FROM ERIC J. GUIGNARD AND DARK MOON BOOKS:

THE FIVE SENSES OF HORROR

Hearing, sight, touch, smell, and taste: Our impressions of the world are formed by our five senses, and so too are our fears, our imaginations, and our captivation in reading fiction stories that embrace these senses.

Whether hearing the song of infernal caverns, tasting the erotic kiss of treachery, or smelling the lush fragrance of a fiend, enclosed within this anthology are fifteen horror and dark fantasy tales that will quicken the beat of fear, sweeten the flavor of wonder, sharpen the spike of thrills, and otherwise brighten the marvel of storytelling that is found resonant!

Editor Eric J. Guignard and psychologist Jessica Bayliss, PhD also include companion discourse throughout, offering academic and literary insight as well as psychological commentary examining the physiology of our senses, why each of our senses are engaged by dark fiction stories, and how it all inspires writers to continually churn out ideas in uncommon and invigorating ways.

Featuring stunning interior illustrations by Nils Bross, and including fiction short stories by such world-renowned authors as John Farris, Ramsey Campbell, Poppy Z. Brite, Darrell Schweitzer, Lisa Morton, and Richard Christian Matheson, amongst others.

Intended for readers, writers, and students alike, explore *The Five Senses of Horror*!

Order your copy at www.darkmoonbooks.com or www.amazon.com
ISBN-13: 978-0-9988275-0-6

ALSO FROM ERIC J. GUIGNARD AND DARK MOON BOOKS:

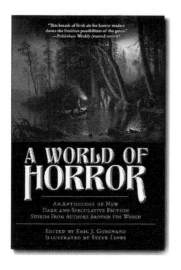

A WORLD OF HORROR

Every nation of the globe has unique tales to tell, whispers that settle in through the land, creatures or superstitions that enliven the night, but rarely do readers get to experience such a diversity of these voices in one place as in *A World of Horror*, the latest anthology book created by award-winning editor Eric J. Guignard, and beautifully illustrated by artist Steve Lines.

Enclosed within its pages are twenty-two all-new dark and speculative fiction stories written by authors from around the world that explore the myths and monsters, fables and fears of their homelands.

Encounter the haunting things that stalk those radioactive forests outside Chernobyl in Ukraine; sample the curious dishes one may eat in Canada; beware the veldt monster that mirrors yourself in Uganda; or simply battle mountain trolls alongside Alfred Nobel in Sweden. These stories and more are found within *A World of Horror*: Enter and discover, truly, there's no place on the planet devoid of frights, thrills, and wondrous imagination.

"This breath of fresh air for horror readers shows the limitless possibilities of the genre."
—*Publishers Weekly* (starred review)

"This is the book we need right now!"
—*Becky Spratford; librarian, reviewer,* RA for All: Horror

"A fresh collection of horror authors exploring monsters and myths from their homelands."

—*Library Journal*

Order your copy at www.darkmoonbooks.com or www.amazon.com
ISBN-13: 978-0-9989383-1-8

FROM WESTON OCHSE AND DARK MOON BOOKS:

SIR GAWAIN AND THE GREEN KNIGHT: A 21ST CENTURY MODERNIZATION

Sir Gawain and the Green Knight stands as one of the earliest literary memories of Medieval England, King Arthur and his Round Table, the mythical Camelot, and those knights who called it home. In this classic tale of chivalry and adventure, a mysterious figure interrupts a New Year's Eve celebration. Dressed all in green, he challenges King Arthur to a dangerous duel, but it is Gawain, the least of them, who is brave enough to accept the challenge on Arthur's behalf. What follows is the young knight's journey into the heart of darkness as he tries to survive the impossible.

Intended for students, academics, and fans of the Knights of the Round Table mythos, no treatment or contemporary retelling of *Sir Gawain and the Green Knight* is as complete and thrilling as this Dark Moon Books edition by Weston Ochse (award-winning and *USA Today* bestselling author, and named as "One of the major horror authors of the 21st Century" by the American Library Association).

Included in this comprehensive edition are:

- The original 1348 tale of *Sir Gawain and the Green Knight* in Middle English verse
- Jessie L. Weston's 1898 poetic translation of the original Middle English version
- Acclaimed author Weston Ochse's 2021 modernized narrative of the story (and supporting preface)
- Afterword by Unconventional Warfare Scholar, Jason S. Ridler, PhD
- Interior Illustrations by Yvonne Navarro

Order your copy at www.darkmoonbooks.com or www.amazon.com
ISBN-13: 978-1-949491-42-5

ALSO FROM ERIC J. GUIGNARD AND DARK MOON BOOKS:

Death. Who has not considered their own mortality and wondered at what awaits, once our frail human shell expires? What occurs after the heart stops beating, after the last breath is drawn, after life as we know it terminates?

Does our spirit remain on Earth while the body rots? Do the remnants of our soul transcend to a celestial Heaven or sink to Hell's torment? Can we choose our own afterlife? Can we die again in the hereafter? Are we given the opportunity to reincarnate and do it all over? Is life merely a cosmic joke or is it an experiment for something greater? Enclosed in this Bram Stoker-award winning anthology are thirty-four all-new dark and speculative fiction stories exploring the possibilities *AFTER DEATH* . . .

Illustrated by Audra Phillips and including stories by: Steve Rasnic Tem, Bentley Little, John Langan, Lisa Morton, and exceptional others.

"Though the majority of the pieces come from the darker side of the genre, a solid minority are playful, clever, or full of wonder. This strong anthology is sure to make readers contemplative even while it creates nightmares."
—*Publishers Weekly*

"In Eric J. Guignard's latest anthology he gathers some of the biggest and most talented authors on the planet to give us their take on this entertaining and perplexing subject matter . . . highly recommended."
—*Famous Monsters of Filmland*

"An excellent collection of imaginative tales of what waits beyond the veil."
—*Amazing Stories Magazine*

Order your copy at www.darkmoonbooks.com or www.amazon.com
ISBN-13: 978-0-9885569-2-8

ALSO FROM ERIC J. GUIGNARD AND DARK MOON BOOKS:

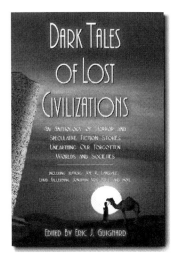

Darkness exists everywhere, and in no place greater than those where spirits and curses still reside. In *DARK TALES OF LOST CIVILIZATIONS*, you will unearth an anthology of twenty-five previously unpublished horror and speculative fiction stories, relating to aspects of civilizations that are crumbling, forgotten, rediscovered, or perhaps merely spoken about in great and fearful whispers.

What is it that lures explorers to distant lands where none have returned? Where is Genghis Khan buried? What happened to Atlantis? Who will displace mankind on Earth? What laments have the Witches of Oz? Answers to these mysteries and other tales are presented within this critically acclaimed anthology.

Including stories by: Joe R. Lansdale, David Tallerman, Jonathan Vos Post, Jamie Lackey, Aaron J. French, and twenty exceptional others.

"The stories range from mildly disturbing to downright terrifying... Most are written in a conservative, suggestive style, relying on the reader's own imagination to take the plunge from speculation to horror."

—*Monster Librarian Reviews*

"Several of these stories made it on to my best of the year shortlist, and the book itself is now on the best anthologies of the year shortlist."

—*British Fantasy Society*

"Almost any story in this anthology is worth the price of purchase. The entire collection is a delight."

—*Black Gate Magazine*

Order your copy at www.darkmoonbooks.com or www.amazon.com
ISBN-13: 978-0-9834335-9-0

THE CRIME FILES OF KATY GREEN by GENE O'NEILL:

Discover why readers have been applauding this stark, fast-paced noir series by multiple-award-winning author, Gene O'Neill, and follow the dark murder mysteries of Sacramento homicide detectives Katy Green and Johnny Cato, dubbed by the press as Sacramento's "Green Hornet and Cato"!

Book #1: DOUBLE JACK (a novella)

400-pound serial killer Jack Malenko has discovered the perfect cover: He dresses as a CalTrans worker and preys on female motorists in distress in full sight of passing traffic. How fast can Katy Green and Johnny Cato track him down before he strikes again?

ISBN-13: 978-0-9988275-6-8

Book #2: SHADOW OF THE DARK ANGEL

Bullied misfit, Samuel Kubiak, is visited by a dark guardian angel who helps Samuel gain just vengeance. There hasn't been a case yet Katy and Johnny haven't solved, but now how can they track a psychopathic suspect that comes and goes in the shadows?

ISBN-13: 978-0-9988275-8-2

Book #3: DEATHFLASH

Billy Williams can see the soul as it departs the body, and is "commanded to do the Lord's work," which he does fanatically, slaying drug addicts in San Francisco…Katy and Johnny investigate the case as junkies die all around, for Billy has his own addiction: the rush of viewing the *Deathflash*.

ISBN-13: 978-0-9988275-9-9

Order your copy at www.darkmoonbooks.com or www.amazon.com

ALSO FROM GENE O'NEILL AND DARK MOON BOOKS:

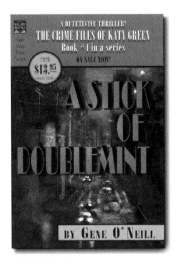

A STICK OF DOUBLEMINT

—Book #4 in the series,
THE CRIME FILES OF KATY GREEN

On a warm San Francisco night, an innocent young woman is gunned down in a gang-related drive-by shooting. The overworked police department have no leads and no suspects, and seemingly little interest in pursuing yet another case involving ongoing gang violence. Then those involved in the shooting start turning up dead, with a stick of Doublemint gum in hand. What does it mean, and who's responsible?

A new detective is assigned to the case, and he quickly realizes he's going to need help to solve it, so turns to old friends, Katy Green and Johnny Cato, now part of a successful private investigation firm!

So begins a race against the clock to stop further murders and to discover the perpetrator. Can the investigating duo, dubbed by newspapers as "Green Hornet and Cato" solve this latest case of the vigilante killings, or will the culprit continue to bloody the city?

Read *A Stick of Doublemint* and then continue the shocking case files of Sacramento's "Green Hornet and Cato" with volumes 1–3 (*Double Jack*; *Shadow of the Dark Angel*; and *Deathflash*).

Order your copy at www.darkmoonbooks.com or www.amazon.com
ISBN-13: 978-1-949491-18-0

ALSO FROM DARK MOON BOOKS:

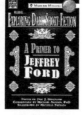

EXPLORING DARK SHORT FICTION
PRIMER SERIES

An exploration of modern masters of literary short fiction, where horror is celebrated as literary, beautiful, and emotionally-resonant.

Cited as "visionary," this series of Primers include short stories, along with their light analysis, of progressive and outstanding authors who deserve wider recognition amongst readers.

<u>Volumes in this series include:</u>

#1: A Primer to Steve Rasnic Tem (2017)

#2: A Primer to Kaaron Warren (2018)

#3: A Primer to Nisi Shawl (2018)

#4: A Primer to Jeffrey Ford (2019)

#5: A Primer to Han Song (2020)

#6: A Primer to Ramsey Campbell (2021)

#7: A Primer to Gemma Files (2022)

. . . and more coming!

In a world of fast-changing tastes and values, there is one constant: Extraordinary writing carries on.

"A fascinating study for fans seeking new reads and for librarians developing wide-ranging collections." —*Library Journal*

"Refreshing and much-needed . . . Addresses significant themes and figures within the horror field." —*Locus Magazine*

"Dark and exquisite . . . Wonderful exposition about authors and selections of their stories." —*The Big Thrill Magazine*

Order your copy at www.darkmoonbooks.com or www.amazon.com

ALSO FROM DARK MOON BOOKS:

+HORROR LIBRARY+
ANTHOLOGY SERIES

Since 2006, the +Horror Library+ series of anthologies has been internationally praised as a groundbreaking source of contemporary horror short fiction stories—relevant to the moment and stunning in impact—from leading authors of the macabre and darkly imaginative.

Filled with Fears and Fantasy. Death and Dark Dreams. Monsters and Mayhem. Literary Vision and Wonder. Managed by award-winning author Eric J. Guignard, each volume of the +Horror Library+ series is packed with heart-pounding thrills and creepy contemplations as to what truly lurks among the shadows of the world(s) we live in.

Read each volume, and watch for more forthcoming.

Shamble no longer through the banal humdrum of normalcy, but ENTER THE HORROR LIBRARY!

"Excellent stories of the highest caliber." —*Dread Central*

"Uniformly well-crafted and original." —*Rue Morgue Magazine*

"A mixture of surprising treats: Stark, livid, engaging." —*SFRreader.com*

"Impactful tales that throw the rules of both reality and genre fiction out the window." —*Fearnet* (*Chiller TV*)

Order your copy at www.darkmoonbooks.com or www.amazon.com

ABOUT THIS BOOK'S EDITORS

Eric J. Guignard has twice won the Bram Stoker Award®, won the Shirley Jackson Award, and been a finalist for the World Fantasy Award and International Thriller Writers Award for his works of dark and speculative fiction. He has over one hundred stories and non-fiction credits appearing in publications around the world, has edited multiple anthologies, and created an ongoing series of primers exploring modern masters of literary short fiction, titled: *Exploring Dark Short Fiction*. His latest books are *Last Case at a Baggage Auction*; *Doorways To The Deadeye*; and short story collection *That Which Grows Wild: 16 Tales of Dark Fiction*. His second collection, *A Graveside Gallery: Tales of Ghosts and Dark Matters*, will be out November, 2024 (Cemetery Dance). For more, visit: www.ericjguignard.com or connect on Twitter at @ericjguignard.

—·—

Leslie S. Klinger is the *New York Times*-best-selling editor of the Edgar®-winning *New Annotated Sherlock Holmes* and the Edgar®-winning *Classic American Crime Fiction of the 1920s* as well as numerous other annotated books, anthologies, and articles on Holmes, Dracula, Lovecraft, Frankenstein, mysteries, horror, and the Victorian age. Twice nominated for the Bram Stoker Award® for Best Nonfiction, his work includes the acclaimed *New Annotated Dracula* and *New Annotated H. P. Lovecraft* as well as the World Fantasy Award-nominated *New Annotated Frankenstein* and five anthologies of classic vampire and horror fiction, three of them with Lisa Morton. His latest books are *New Annotated H. P. Lovecraft: Beyond Arkham*, also nominated for a World Fantasy award, *Annotated American Gods* with Neil Gaiman, and *The New Annotated Strange Case of Dr. Jekyll and Mr. Hyde*.

L'ÉVOCATION DES ESPRITS

Illustration "The Evocation of the Spirits" by Émile Bayard
from *Histoire de la Magie* by Paul Christian (1870).

Made in the USA
Las Vegas, NV
18 November 2024